A Troubling Suggestion

Troubles of the Heart - Book Two

Betty Woods

Scrivenings PRESS
Quench your thirst for story.
www.ScriveningsPress.com

Published by Scrivenings Press LLC
15 Lucky Lane
Morrilton, Arkansas 72110
https://ScriveningsPress.com

Printed in the United States of America

Paperback ISBN 978-1-64917-468-0

eBook ISBN 978-1-64917-469-7

Editors: Elena Hill and Linda Fulkerson

Cover by Linda Fulkerson www.bookmarketinggraphics.com

All scriptures are taken from the KING JAMES VERSION (KJV): KING JAMES VERSION, public domain.

All characters are fictional, and any resemblance to real people, either factual or historical, is purely coincidental.

To my wonderful husband, Craig, who happily eats so many convenience meals and overlooks all the dust bunnies so I can write and live my dream.

To my daughter, Cherish, who always supports me and never gives up on me.

Chapter One

1833

Outside Murfreesboro, Tennessee

Clarisse Matthews squirmed in her spot on the tapestry couch. She checked the clock on the marble fireplace mantel. Again. The Williams' butler had ushered her and her brother into the parlor ten minutes ago. Why was Luke taking so long to greet them? She'd soon have the pattern of the dark blue and gold carpet memorized. If Luke were as angry as she'd heard, would he even see her or Titus this afternoon?

"Can't you sit still? You're worse than a child." Titus whispered as he shifted to look at her from his place beside her.

"I'm sorry." She released her grip on the note she'd come to deliver.

She should have never agreed to bring Eugenia's letter of apology to Luke. But she'd already put off fulfilling this promise for over a month. Eugenia probably hadn't intended for Clarisse to wait until mid-April. She glanced down and

1

smoothed the folds of her skirt for the fourth or fifth time, maybe the sixth. Wearing her favorite dress with the embroidered red roses around the neckline, sleeves, and hem should have given her confidence, but it didn't.

Clarisse had been the one to suggest her friend write the letter explaining why she'd chosen the wheelwright Paul Stuart over Luke, the son of a well-to-do planter. Clarisse hoped and prayed she wouldn't regret the entire idea.

"Good afternoon." Luke gave her a terse nod as he strode into the parlor.

Clarisse started and stared up at him. "Good afternoon to you." His sky-blue eyes were as cold as frost on barren trees in January. Perhaps it would have been better if he'd been out checking the fields with his overseer. *Lord, help me.*

Titus rose and extended his hand to Luke. "We've come as a favor to Eugenia."

Luke jerked back as if her brother had slapped him. His disdainful expression hardened at the mere mention of her dear friend's name. "I owe no favors to Eugenia Hampton, and I'll accept none on her behalf."

"Stuart," Clarisse blurted out the word without thinking. "She's Eugenia Stuart now."

Pain washed over Luke's features before he covered it with another scowl. How she wished she'd kept quiet. Luke, of all people, wouldn't want to be reminded of Eugenia's recent marriage.

Luke spun on his heel, looking ready to bolt from the room.

"Please, Luke." Clarisse jumped up and placed her fingers on his sleeve. Heat rushed to her face. She yanked her hand back.

His frown intensified. "The woman played me for a fool."

"She felt terrible about hurting you." Clarisse thrust the

note at him. "Please. Her words have to be much better than any explanation I could make."

"Yes, I'm sure they are, considering the woman's talent for embellishment." His lip curled as his gaze landed on the letter still in Clarisse's hand.

She squared her shoulders. "How dare you insinuate my best friend is a liar?"

"What else do you call a woman who accepts two gentleman callers while secretly meeting with a third man who is nothing more than a common laborer?"

His glare sent shivers through her. She might as well be looking at a stranger instead of the gentle friend she'd known since childhood. "Did Eugenia ever so much as hint she loved you?"

His face paled. He averted his eyes.

"She told me she tried repeatedly to tell you your hope for her love was in vain." Clarisse worked to keep her tone as kind as possible. This poor man had to be hurting more than he wanted anyone to guess, and she hated to be so blunt with him.

"You have every right to be furious with Eugenia." Titus rose and placed his hand on Luke's shoulder. "But we'd appreciate it if you'd do us the favor of allowing our friend to explain for herself. Please."

Luke stared at the two of them for a few moments before reaching for the letter. His hand trembled as he turned the note over and broke the seal. "Please be seated. I'll read this in your presence so you'll know I saw it, then burn it tonight."

Clarisse and Titus returned to the blue tapestry couch. Luke perched in a cushioned chair across from them, his body as rigid as a statue. She wondered if the letter would already be reduced to ashes if the day wasn't too warm to light a fire.

A welcome breeze teased the lace panels at the open

window. Birds chirping outside mingled with the incessant ticking of the clock. Still, Luke sat staring at the letter. How could a one-page note take so long to read?

"No!" Luke leaped to his feet.

Clarisse jumped.

His eyes burning with rage, Luke waved the paper in the air with one hand and pointed a shaking finger straight at her. "How dare you?"

"What?" She pressed against her brother's shoulder.

"Don't tell me you have no idea what that woman wrote." He spoke through gritted teeth.

"Only her intention to apologize. I never read what she penned." Clarisse gripped Titus's arm.

Luke shook his head. His eyes narrowed as he continued to study her. "I find such a denial coming from Eugenia's coconspirator hard to believe."

Titus shot to his feet. "Eugenia sealed the letter with her personal seal. *You* broke that seal."

"Your sister has known her friend's secrets since childhood. I find it preposterous she doesn't know every word in this letter." Luke clenched his jaw so tightly that Clarisse wondered if he wouldn't soon be in pain.

"My sister is not a liar. A true gentleman never doubts a lady's word." Titus pulled her to her feet. "We'll see ourselves out."

Her brother wasted no time assisting Clarisse out the door and then to their enclosed carriage parked in the circular driveway. She settled onto the cushioned upholstered seat and clasped her trembling hands in her lap. What would she have done if she'd had to face Luke alone? She smiled at her brother sitting across from her. "Thank you for defending me."

"I could do no less."

She sighed. "Perhaps this was one promise I shouldn't have kept."

Titus shook his head. "Luke's outrageous reaction to a well-intentioned apology isn't your fault. If he'd listened to what Eugenia tried to tell him, he'd have never pinned his hopes for love on her."

"No, but I do hope this is the last angry person we have to deal with over Eugenia and Paul."

Her brother stretched out his long legs and leaned back against the seat. "Today wasn't as bad as Mr. Hampton's visit."

She shuddered. Eugenia's father had charged into their house, waving his daughter's farewell note to him and raging like a madman. He'd demanded they tell him everything about Eugenia eloping with the son of his overseer. She doubted Mr. Hampton nor anyone else in Rutherford County would ever believe she nor her brother were aware of Paul and Eugenia's exact destination. Even Paul wasn't sure where they'd settle in Illinois.

"I don't regret helping Eugenia and Paul get away." She never would.

Titus grinned. "Neither do I. We suspected there would be consequences, but we did the right thing."

"Yes, we did." She grinned.

His brown eyes twinkled. "I suppose I can rule out Luke as a future brother-in-law."

Clarisse gasped. "I wouldn't marry that cad if he were the last eligible man in the entire country."

Rather than continue any discussion of a future wedding, she glanced down and smoothed an imaginary wrinkle in her skirt. She couldn't think of marrying any man after losing her dear fiancé. She'd die a spinster before she'd betray Garland's memory or the secrets he'd entrusted only to her.

* * *

LUKE CRUMPLED the offensive page in his hand while staring at Titus and Clarisse's retreating backs. He'd burn the entire thing as soon as he could get a candle. Waiting until he retired to his room for the night was out of the question.

"Are you all right?" Mother rushed into the parlor, almost out of breath. "I heard you shouting from upstairs."

He ducked his head. "I'm sorry."

"Your father is somehow still napping. What has you so upset?"

"Titus and Clarisse just left. I'll be happy to explain myself."

Mother shook her head. "You shrieked like a wild man at our friends and neighbors?"

"Clarisse insisted on delivering an apology from Eugenia." Bile rose in his throat when he uttered the detested name. Until today, he hadn't spoken the name of the woman who wronged him since he'd learned she'd eloped. His fist closed tighter around the crumpled letter.

Mother's silver-flecked eyebrows formed perfect arches. "An apology caused you to raise your voice so?"

"No." He smoothed the page, then shoved it toward his mother. "Read the last paragraph of this preposterous letter, and you'll understand my anger."

Mother seated herself on the couch with her usual easy graceful motion. Luke paced. Sitting still was impossible. She took enough time scanning the note that Luke was sure she was reading the entire thing. She placed the page on her lap and smoothed out a fold line before rereading the letter. "I'm glad to see a reason for Eugenia's peculiar behavior toward you."

"Peculiar behavior?" He fought for self-control lest he yell at his mother. "She admits deliberately misleading me, and then she has the gall to suggest I should call on Clarisse because we might be well suited for each other. The woman is nothing more than a liar trying to make excuses for her deception."

His mother sighed as she smoothed another crease from the letter. She had yet to look up from the paper in her lap. "Yes, Eugenia lied to you. But I can't help wishing my dear sister had had Eugenia's courage and defied our father over her arranged marriage."

"You mean Aunt Elaine?"

Mother nodded. Her brown eyes misted with tears when she peered back at him. "Jacques was not the man Papa believed him to be. We had no loyal friend to caution us the way you warned Eugenia about Alton Parker's flaws, so Papa allowed Jacques to take Elaine to his native New Orleans."

Luke closed his eyes as he halted in front of his mother. His aunt's brief and unhappy life was a sad tale of betrayal, but Mother's sympathy for a lying woman irked him. As did the way she chose to ignore Clarisse's involvement with the letter she'd delivered. The woman had to know the letter's contents. Shouldn't his mother side with her son's battered emotions? This so-called letter of apology ripped open his unhealed wounds.

"Look at me, dear."

He obeyed.

She patted the spot next to her. "Come, sit with me."

Again, he did as she asked.

Placing her hand on his sleeve, she stared into his eyes. "Let go of your anger. Do as God commands. Forgive your friend for the wrong she did to you. She was desperate."

His friend? He clamped his open mouth shut. How could

his mother defend the woman who had wronged her own son? "Does desperation excuse deception?"

"Not completely, but laying the blame solely on Eugenia isn't fair." Her grip tightened on his arm.

"Who else should I blame?" Luke struggled to keep his voice calm. What was Mother implying?

"Yourself." Mother poked him in the chest with her slender finger.

He jerked away from her. "Me? That's outrageous."

"How many times did your father and I warn you that Eugenia might hurt you instead of learning to love you as you wanted?" Mother's voice softened.

Luke swallowed hard. Despite the warm love so evident in his mother's compassionate eyes, chills radiated down his spine. His parents had cautioned him against hoping the woman would love him someday more times than he cared to remember. He'd assumed they didn't want her for a daughter-in-law, but his mother's sympathy for the woman belied that supposition.

"I should check on your father." Mother rose. Luke stood.

She patted his arm. "I pray you'll learn from this painful episode." Her eyes shone with a mischievous glint as she placed the letter in his hand. "Don't ignore Eugenia's suggestion about calling on Clarisse. Eugenia could be speaking more truth than she realized."

Luke stared at his mother's back as she left the room. The only truth that female had taught him was how women said one thing and did the opposite. He had no intention of forgetting that fact.

The conniving woman who had to have known the entire contents of the note she'd handed him was another perfect example of why he'd never again entangle himself romantically with any female.

Chapter Two

Women's voices from the parlor greeted Clarisse as soon as Titus opened the front door. He rolled his eyes upward. She'd hoped to slip into the house without Mother noticing they'd been gone. But they would have to walk past the ladies to get to the other part of the house or the stairs.

"We'd be delighted to come to your ball." Mama's voice drifted into the entryway.

Not another ball. Clarisse longed to declare her true feelings about attending parties of any kind. But Mama hadn't understood her at all when she'd tried to explain she'd never forget Garland. She'd never find another man like him.

The giggle following Mama's announcement had to belong to Marissa Parker. "I'm so glad you'll be there."

Titus brushed every speck of dust from his hat before placing it on the hall tree. Clarisse took her time untying her bonnet. If only Mama understood how much her children dreaded attending any function at the Parkers' house now. They all preferred to spend as little time as possible with people who had so little regard for their dear friends, Eugenia and Paul.

"I hope Clarisse will be home soon. I'd so like to see her."

Marissa's lilting voice assaulted Clarisse's ears. No one in the Parker family would ever set foot in this house again if they had any idea the three younger Matthews had been the ones to help Eugenia escape a forced marriage to Marissa's brother.

"We might as well make our appearance," Titus whispered.

She took one last wishful look at the front door before squaring her shoulders and walking down the hall to the parlor.

"There you are. Jenette said you'd gone for a short drive and should be back soon." The direct look Mama shot their direction said she'd want a good explanation for the carriage ride after their guest departed.

"My dear wife knows me well." Titus gave Jenette an adoring gaze before making a slight bow toward Marissa, who occupied the couch with their mother. "If you'll excuse me, ladies. I need to look at some papers in my office."

Coward. If only she could escape so easily. Clarisse seated herself in the chair next to Jenette while deliberately avoiding her mother's stare. "We couldn't resist a drive on such a lovely day."

"The very reason I couldn't resist riding over to see you." Marissa grinned in Clarisse's direction.

Clarisse forced a smile in return. Marissa's words and blue riding habit dredged up bittersweet memories of Eugenia riding over to call on Clarisse. How she missed her dear friend.

Another giggle interrupted Clarisse's thoughts. "The weather has nothing to do with the real reason I wanted to deliver my invitation in person." She leaned toward Clarisse and Jenette's chairs. "Jonah Browning and I are to be married soon. I couldn't wait to tell you my good news."

"How wonderful." Mama beamed at Marissa before turning to give her daughter a wishful glance.

"Thank you." Marissa looked from one woman to the other. "I must ask you not to tell anyone else. Papa will make the announcement at the ball."

"We'll be happy to keep your wonderful secret." Jenette fanned herself. "Thank you for sharing with us first."

Marissa clapped her hands together like a delighted child. "I had to. Jonah and I met at your Christmas party last year."

"I wish you and Jonah every happiness together." Clarisse hoped her words didn't sound as stiff as her pretend smile felt.

She wished them happiness but not for the reasons everyone else in the room might think. How wonderful another eligible man was no longer on Mama's list of marriage prospects for Clarisse. If those remaining bachelors would propose to other women, she would be left in peace with her memories of Garland and the secrets he'd entrusted only to her.

"I'm sure we'll be very happy." Another giggle accompanied Marissa's words.

Their guest droned on for the next hour about Jonah's good fortune in Nashville and the house he'd started building. Clarisse couldn't help but grin at how Eugenia would have rejoiced with her that both Marissa and Jonah would soon be an entire day's drive away from here. Thankfully, Marissa was none the wiser as to why Clarisse smiled as their guest continued jabbering.

The instant the oak door closed behind Marissa, Mama glared at her and Jenette before either could escape the entry hall. "Now, dear daughters, the real reason for the short drive no one told me about. Just before our friend arrived, I sent for the carriage only to have the butler tell me my carriage was in use."

Jenette clasped and unclasped her hands. "Telling you the truth in front of our caller would have distressed her. Shall we return to the parlor?"

"Shall I soon have an explanation?" Mama's tone matched her stern expression. She whirled and marched across the polished wood floor toward the parlor. She claimed the beige upholstered chair across from the couch and watched Clarisse and Jenette as they settled there beside each other.

Clarisse sat up straight, returning her mother's piercing gaze. Being treated like a child needing to confess some misdeed was totally uncalled for. She and Titus had attempted to do the right thing. "You wouldn't have been happy with us if we'd told you what we were doing."

"And why is that?" Mama tapped her fingers on the armrest.

"While I was reading this morning I found a letter Eugenia had somehow slipped inside my Bible. It was an apology she wanted delivered to Luke. I felt I should honor her wish. Titus came with me since I couldn't call on Luke alone." Clarisse hoped her shaded version of the truth would be acceptable. She *had* kept the letter hidden in her Bible until today.

Mama's eyes widened. "I'm glad Eugenia had the decency to apologize. How is Luke?"

"He's still angry—furious, actually. The note wasn't well received." Clarisse gripped the arm of the couch. Thoughts of Luke's fierce countenance and loud voice still disturbed her.

"Can you blame him? I'll never understand why Eugenia eloped with a common wheelwright instead of marrying a good planter like Luke Williams or Alton Parker."

For love. Clarisse longed to blurt out the words, but challenging her mother would be useless. She doubted Mama's sympathy for Eugenia's father or Luke and Alton would ever change.

Mama rose and fixed them with a serious almost glare. "In the future, you will inform me about any such foolish errands beforehand. Even adult children shouldn't keep secrets from a parent. Your dear father would be quite displeased."

"Yes, Mama." Clarisse and Jenette answered in unison. Whenever Mama brought their late father into the conversation, she was beyond displeased.

"Good. I need to speak with Jasmine about supper preparations." She spun on her heel and marched out of the parlor.

"I'm sorry," Jenette whispered after Mama disappeared. "I couldn't think of anything to tell her."

Clarisse squeezed her sister-in-law's hand. "She'll be fine."

Jenette's blue-gray eyes held doubt. "I hope you're right. I don't ever want her to suspect Paul and Eugenia were married in our barn with our help while she slept."

"The only other people who can reveal that secret should be settled somewhere in Illinois by now." Clarisse gazed down and smoothed her skirt.

No one in her family had any idea how many secrets she held in her heart. She missed her fiancé as much now as she had when he'd died almost two years ago. The more everyone insisted Clarisse should set aside her love for Garland, the tighter she gripped her memories and their secrets.

Chapter Three

Luke walked inside, tossed his hat onto the hall tree then wiped the perspiration from his brow. They needed rain for the recently planted cotton, and he needed a cool glass of water straight from the well. This particular Tuesday was much too warm for late April.

"My apologies to you both." A strange man's voice drifted from the parlor. "The letter I sent before we departed must not have arrived."

"Of course, she's welcome to stay, but I wish someone had given us notice first." Luke couldn't mistake his father's irritated tone.

Father wasn't in good enough health to be perplexed by anyone or anything. Luke marched into the parlor. He halted just inside the doorway. A well-dressed older man sat on the gold chair closest to the couch where his mother sat. A young woman clothed in black perched next to Mother.

"Oh, Luke." Mother smiled through tears as she gestured toward the stranger sitting beside her. "This young lady is your cousin, Angelique."

"My cousin?" He'd never heard of any relative by such a

15

name. Who were these people who agitated his father and made his mother cry?

"Yes, the only child of my dear sister, Elaine. She's come to us from New Orleans, along with the DuBois family attorney, Mr. Chirac." Mother's face glowed as she stared at Angelique.

"I see." But he didn't see. How could Mother know who these strangers really were? What proof had they offered to their identity? He'd discover the answers soon. Before leaving college, he'd read enough law to know he needed to proceed carefully.

Mother scowled at him as if she'd guessed his thoughts.

"Forgive my poor manners. I wasn't expecting a visit from my long-lost cousin. Welcome to Oakridge." Luke forced a smile as he made a slight bow toward Angelique, or whoever she was. No one on either side of their family had flaming red hair like hers.

"Thank you." Angelique peered up at him with brown eyes almost identical to his mother's. "I've longed to meet my Tennessee family since I discovered you."

"I wish I'd known about you sooner." Mother's voice quivered. She dabbed at her misty eyes with her handkerchief. "Your father wrote me of my sister's death during childbirth but never mentioned you survived."

Luke's "cousin" bit her trembling lip. Was her emotion real or pretend?

The clock on the fireplace mantel struck three times. Mother jumped. "Oh, dear. Where are my manners? I'm sure both of you would like to rest and change into clothes not choked with road dust. Angelique, dear, I'll show you upstairs, then send our daughters' former maid up to help you. You're welcome to choose either of our daughters' old rooms."

Mother rose to usher Angelique into the hall. She gaped at the attorney as if she'd forgotten him. "Mr. Chirac, I assume you'll spend the night before returning to New Orleans. I'd be happy to show you to a room."

"Yes, thank you, *Madame* Williams." Mr. Chirac pulled his cane toward him and leaned on the ornate gold handle to rise from his chair.

Mother took Angelique's arm and guided her into the hall, leaving Mr. Chirac to follow behind.

"Do you need to rest?" Luke studied his father's pale features. He looked more like sixty instead of almost fifty. If this incident caused Father's heart more problems, Luke would see this "cousin" found another place to stay. Soon.

"I assume you'd like an explanation for all of this first." Father's sky-blue eyes twinkled. "I well know that look of confusion you're wearing."

"Yes, sir." Luke took the chair closest to his father.

"I'm certain Angelique is your cousin." Father picked up a framed miniature and a packet of old letters from the end table next to his chair.

Luke reached to take the painting his father held out. He didn't need to study the two smiling young women standing with their brothers. The identical full-size portrait of his mother and her siblings hung in the hall by the stairs.

"Angelique brought this and your mother's letters to Elaine with her. She discovered them after her father's death." Father thrust the yellowed pages toward Luke.

He recognized Mother's flowing handwriting as soon as he scanned the outside of the first folded letter. "Why is she here now?"

Father mopped his damp forehead with his handkerchief. "She literally has nowhere else to go. Quite unfortunate circumstances for a girl of almost eighteen."

"I'd like to know those circumstances before you decide for sure to allow her to stay." Hard-hearted or not, his parents' well-being came first. Luke wished for even a slight breeze to ease the heat, but the lace window curtains hung limp and still.

A look of consternation washed over his father's face. "Must you always be the practical attorney?"

Yes, he'd very much like to be an attorney today—and the rest of his life. Luke shifted in his chair. But he couldn't voice such thoughts to the ailing father who had never understood his son's yearnings. "I'd feel better if I had the facts, please."

"Mr. Chirac spoke to me in my office out of the ladies' hearing while your mother got to know Angelique."

He waited for his father to settle against the back of his chair and get comfortable. Father didn't look up to this long talk, no matter how necessary it was.

"Your cousin's father was killed by a jealous husband in a scandalous duel. The attorney says Jacques so mismanaged the DuBois fortune that Angelique is almost penniless. As the only legitimate heir, she'll barely have enough for a small dowry and a meager allowance if Mr. Chirac can manage to sell the family home and a few other assets for enough to settle debts."

"Legitimate heir? What do you mean?" Luke cringed at the possibility of other unknown people of questionable character showing up at their door, claiming who knew what, especially if any money might be left over after the debts were paid.

Father pointed a thin finger at him. "Exactly what you think I mean. Jacques didn't marry again after Elaine's death, but he never lacked for female companionship."

"Oh."

"Yes. *Oh*. Mr. Chirac has been the DuBois family attorney since Jacques was a boy. He brought Angelique here to give her a new start away from the scandal her father created in New Orleans."

"So, you and Mother are willing to take in Angelique."

"Of course."

"But what of your fragile health?" Luke leaned toward his father and peered into his eyes.

Father worked to take a deep breath. "The girl has no one and nowhere else to turn."

"A seventeen-year-old is no girl. Have you forgotten how chaotic our house could be when Rachel and Beth were still home? How frenzied our lives were with Beth's wedding only a little over a year ago?"

"Luke Andrew, what has happened to your heart?" Father shook his gray head.

Everything. God, who was supposed to be love, hadn't answered a single prayer for Luke in months. Because of love for his parents, he'd given up his dream of being an attorney and returned home from college to run the family's plantation he little cared about. The woman he'd loved had spurned him and chosen a common laborer instead. The cost of love had destroyed his heart.

"My heart is fine. I only want to be sure you and Mother are able to manage another young lady coming of age."

Father's wry smile lit up his haggard face. "We learned from your sisters and should do even better this time."

Luke shrugged. His parents could do as they pleased in their own home.

"Since I've satisfied your curiosity, I'll go upstairs and try to nap in this heat."

"And I should get out of these dusty clothes." Luke matched Father's slow pace as he walked upstairs with him.

He took his time changing into clean clothes then enjoyed the quiet and solitude while everyone else rested. After living with two sisters, such tranquil times would be rare unless Angelique was more reserved than any seventeen-year-old female he'd ever met. He could almost hear and see the endless parade of people coming to their house once his cousin was no longer in mourning. So much for avoiding social functions when his parents could be the hosts sooner than he'd like.

Rather than dwell on things he couldn't wish away, Luke spent the rest of the afternoon in the library reading a law book his father wouldn't understand. He had no idea when he'd have another quiet afternoon to himself. Voices in the hallway urged him to slide open the pocket door.

His parents and Mr. Chirac walked toward the dining room. Father appeared to be rested and refreshed. How long would that last with his cousin in the house now?

Mother smiled. "I told Angelique we eat at five. She should be down soon."

Father took Mother's elbow and escorted her to her chair. The clock in the parlor struck five as Luke and Mr. Chirac seated themselves. The servants finished bringing in the food and setting the dishes on the sideboard.

"We should wait for Angelique." Mother unfolded her napkin and placed it in her lap. Her thin smile didn't completely disguise the agitation Luke could see in her eyes. Angelique had no idea how much his mother valued promptness. She'd soon learn to appease her aunt, if she valued any kind of peace.

"I do wish the weather wasn't so warm today." Mother ran her hand over her silverware as she glanced toward the dining room door.

Mr. Chirac smiled at her. "Anyone from New Orleans is accustomed to heat. Today is fine."

The day wouldn't be fine much longer if Angelique didn't make her appearance soon. Luke lost count of how many times Mother glanced at the door while trying to make polite conversation with their guest.

Footsteps sounded on the wood floor in the hall. Angelique

breezed into the dining room wearing a golden yellow dress bright enough to be mistaken for an entire forest of fall-colored leaves. Mother gasped and covered her open mouth. Father's face lost its color once again.

"Good evening." Angelique beamed as the butler seated her.

"Good evening." Luke returned her greeting since his parents were too stunned to speak.

"I detest a cold supper." Father bowed his head and said a short prayer of thanks for the food.

As soon as Father finished saying grace, Amos served the food the way he'd done most of Luke's life. His cousin wasted no time putting a fork full of carrots in her mouth.

"Are all your proper clothes dirty from your long trip, dear?" Mother's fork still lay next to her plate.

Angelique shook her head. "If you're referring to my black dresses, no, ma'am. I refuse to live a lie any longer."

"What do you mean?" Mother gripped her water goblet.

"My father had precious little time for me. I see no need to endure three more months pretending to mourn a man I barely knew—one who never cared for his only child."

Mother's eyes widened.

"I dislike hypocrites even more than cold food." Father smiled.

Angelique's grin revealed her dimples and emphasized her impish expression. "Then shall we plan some sort of party to introduce me to your neighbors? I haven't been to a dance in so long."

Luke took a bite of his ham and watched conflicting emotions play across Mother's face. No matter how much she despised Angelique's father, not observing an appropriate time of mourning was something his proper mother couldn't fathom.

"Well, there is the Parkers' ball next week." Mother's disdain for Jacques must have won out over her need for propriety.

"How perfectly lovely." Angelique attacked her food with a gusto unbecoming a young lady.

How perfectly awful. Luke couldn't think of anywhere he'd rather not be more than the Parker home. He slathered a piece of bread with butter, then popped a piece in his mouth. The fluffy morsel tasted at least a month old.

"I'm sure your cousin will be happy to introduce you to the other young people there." Mother grinned at him.

He gulped down his water to keep from choking on the bread. Angelique's expressive brown eyes twinkled in his direction. Introducing this beautiful cousin might cause him more kinds of trouble than he cared to think about much less deal with.

He couldn't think of a worse place to introduce her than at the Parkers' ball.

Chapter Four

Clarisse couldn't muster a smile as she settled onto the coach seat next to her mother and across from Titus and Jenette. Another ball to endure. If only she were as good at pretending headaches as Eugenia had been. She was happy for Marissa and Jonah but dreaded seeing Marissa's brother, Alton. The man knew how close she was to Eugenia, so he must realize Clarisse despised him for intending to marry Eugenia against her will.

"If only we had a breeze." Jenette vigorously fanned herself.

Titus turned toward his wife. "Are you sure you're up to going?"

"Of course, she is. All of you are, no matter how much you wish for excuses to stay home." Mama speared her son and daughter-in-law with a no-nonsense look the twilight shadows couldn't hide.

Jenette patted her husband's arm. "I'm fine. Don't worry so."

"That's my favorite job, my dear."

The loving looks Titus and Jenette bestowed on each other

made Clarisse's throat tighten. If only her beloved were still here to gaze at her like that.

"I expect each of you to be polite to Alton tonight no matter your collective opinion of the man." Mama shook her finger in the air toward all three of the unwilling passengers, shattering Clarisse's wistful thoughts of Garland.

"We wouldn't dream of slighting him." Titus's thin brown mustache twitched above his tight smile.

The silence in the carriage was more oppressive than the warm May night. Clarisse glanced out the window at the darkening landscape. Mama's continuing defense of Alton Parker troubled her. She feared Mama wouldn't be against an arranged marriage for her daughter since her parents had made theirs a companionable and happy one. Thankfully, Titus was so madly in love with his wife that he'd never agree to such a thing for Clarisse. She hoped and prayed she wasn't wrong about her brother.

A short time later, Clarisse exchanged rueful glances with Titus and Jenette as they followed Mama up the porch steps to the Parkers' columned brick house. She'd almost rather attend a wake. Only Jonah's parents' carriage sat in the drive. They would have a much harder time dodging Alton until other guests arrived.

Mr. and Mrs. Parker stood in the entry hall. "We're delighted to see you and your family, Cassandra." Mrs. Parker placed her hand on Mama's arm. "Thank you for sharing our happiness tonight."

"We wouldn't think of missing such an important event." Mama's glowing smile held no hint of the strained conversation that had occurred during their carriage ride.

Clarisse did her best to nod agreeably as her mother exchanged pleasantries with the Parkers. Jenette continued to employ her fan. Perhaps her sister-in-law's delicate condition would give them an excuse to leave early.

Marissa, with Jonah at her side, rushed in from another part of the house. "Pardon us for not being here to greet you, but Jonah wanted to make a special request to the musicians." She placed her hand in the crook of Jonah's elbow and smiled up at him as if they were the only two people around.

Jonah patted her hand without so much as a glance at her. Clarisse hoped he truly cared for Marissa and not just her rumored dowry. "We're honored you're here."

"Thank you all for the invitation." Titus made a slight bow.

"Yes, thank you." Clarisse forced the words past her stiff lips as Mama glanced toward her. Tonight would be a test or a testimony to her mother's years of effort to instill good manners in her daughter.

"Would you care to follow us to the dining room for refreshments?" Marissa took her eyes off Jonah long enough to look at the Matthews family.

"Something cool to drink would be wonderful." Jenette lowered her fan long enough to speak.

Marissa and Jonah turned toward the dining room. Titus and Jenette followed. Clarisse trailed behind the two couples. She hoped Jonah deserved his fiancée's unabashed adoration and had focused his attention on more than his business and finances these days. He'd been ambitious almost to a fault since Clarisse had known him. She wouldn't want such a dubious situation for herself.

For herself? How could she think about such a thing? She'd never betray Garland's love for her or the memories she so cherished. Never. Plus, she doubted any man in the county would be happy with her if her secrets were revealed. She gripped her fan and forced a smile as she entered the dining room. Then halted. Why hadn't she stayed with Mama?

Alton stood a few feet away from the flower-festooned table. Laden with punch and trays heaped with cakes, it looked almost ready to collapse. He raised a glass punch cup toward them. "Thank you all for coming to share my sister and Jonah's joy." His thin smile didn't reach his steely brown eyes or warm the tone of his voice.

"It's our pleasure." Titus seated Jenette in one of the chairs lining the walls. "Could I get you ladies some punch?"

Jenette nodded.

"Please." Clarisse took the wooden chair next to her sister-in-law. She wasn't thirsty, but she needed something to do with her hands other than fan herself. "I hope summer isn't going to be unbearable since it's so warm for early May."

"So do I." Jenette smiled her thanks as Titus handed her a cup of punch.

Before Marissa could take the chair next to Clarisse, Mr. Parker's hearty words of welcome to someone drifted into the room. "Oh. More guests have arrived. Please excuse us."

Alton escaped through the door. His sister and Jonah followed.

Clarisse strained to hear who was talking to Mr. and Mrs. Parker, but too many people spoke at once to be sure of anyone but her mother. To her horror, Marissa and Jonah soon escorted Mama, Luke Williams, along with a strange young woman, and Mr. and Mrs. Williams into the dining room. Luke must have made a sudden and complete recovery from the heartache Eugenia caused him, judging from the stunning redhead walking at his side.

Luke seated his parents and Clarisse's mother on the other side of the room next to Jonah's parents. "Could I get refreshments for anyone?"

"I'll tend to the ladies." Mr. Williams waved his hand

toward his son. "Go introduce Angelique to the other young people."

The redhead laughed as she took Luke's arm and propelled him across the room. Titus rose as they approached.

"Luke, please introduce us." She batted her lashes and beamed a full-dimpled smile at Titus.

"I'd like to present my cousin, Miss Angelique DuBois, recently arrived from New Orleans. Angelique, our neighbors Mrs. Jenette Matthews, her husband, Titus Matthews, and Miss Clarisse Matthews." Luke was stiffer than an over-starched shirt as he worked to avoid everyone's gazes.

For whatever reason, Luke didn't appear overjoyed about this cousin's appearance. Angelique's smile dimmed the instant Luke spoke the word husband along with Titus's name.

"Pleased to meet you." Titus made a slight bow.

"I'm so happy to meet all of you." Angelique took the empty chair next to Clarisse.

"I'll bring you some punch while you get to know our neighbors." Luke didn't wait to see if his cousin was thirsty before retreating toward the refreshment table.

"I've been looking forward to tonight ever since Aunt Evelyn mentioned it." Angelique's eyes shone.

"It is a special night." Clarisse struggled to sound cheerful.

"There you are, Miss DuBois." Alton marched toward Angelique the instant he entered the room. "Since you don't know anyone here, would you give me the honor of the first dance?"

Luke reached past Alton and shoved a cup of punch in front of his cousin, interrupting her lilting laugh. "I also brought you a piece of cider cake. Didn't you say that's one of your favorites?"

Angelique had no choice but to accept the offerings Luke thrust at her. "Thank you, dear cousin." The barely disguised look of disgust she shot at Luke did not match her honey-sweet tone as he slipped behind Alton to take the empty chair next to her.

"Mr. Parker, I'd be delighted to give you the first dance." Angelique deposited her cup and plate in Luke's lap and rose. "I'm not as thirsty as I supposed. Perhaps you would introduce me to some of the other guests who just arrived?"

"My pleasure." Mr. Parker beamed as he extended his arm and led Angelique over to the other side of the room.

Luke scowled and jerked to his feet so quickly, he almost dumped the refreshments on the floor. "I should see how my parents are faring."

Clarisse couldn't miss Mrs. Williams' perturbed expression as she spoke in low tones to her son. If only the lady had any inkling how unperturbed Clarisse was with her son's actions. Attempting a polite conversation with Luke was as appealing as walking through a briar patch minus her shoes and stockings.

Other guests continued to arrive. The dining room became crowded enough that Titus gave up his chair, as did Luke, who remained with his parents. The Parkers must have invited every neighbor they could, as well as a few people from Murfreesboro. Luke's cousin flitted in and out of the room with Alton Parker too often at her side. If Luke cared at all for Angelique, he should be doing his best to keep her from spending so much time with a man like Mr. Parker.

The instruments sounded for the first dance. Clarisse wished she could disappear. Her mother's pointed glance in her direction signaled Mama was doing more than conversing with her friends. Yet, Clarisse would do her best to dance with as few men as she could manage.

"May I have this dance, my dear?" Titus bowed to his wife as he held out his hand to help her to her feet.

"Of course." Jenette followed her husband into the parlor serving as the ballroom.

Other people paired off and went to dance, including several of the older married couples. Her pretense of wanting to finish her cake and punch had prevented her from accepting two invitations to dance. If Luke, his parents, and her mother hadn't been the only people left in the room, Clarisse would have been delighted. Ignoring Mama's watchful stare in her direction, she ducked her head as she forked the next to the last bite of cake. She'd soon be out of excuses for turning down young men.

LUKE TURNED his attention from his parents to glance toward the parlor. Why hadn't he thought to ask Angelique for the first dance? Since he hadn't, he needed to think of a way to watch over her as best he could now. Mother said she had cautioned Angelique about the younger Parker. But his cousin appeared to be immune to good advice.

The music paused, signaling the end of the first dance. He rose. He had to do something to watch over his headstrong relative. But what? The notes for the second dance began. He couldn't march in and demand she stop dancing with Alton, especially not in the man's home.

"Luke, I told you I'll see to the ladies here. Go enjoy yourself as any young man should." Father stood, then took Mother's plate for her. He scanned the room.

Luke followed his gaze. Clarisse sat alone, empty plate in her hand. He needed a good reason to make his way to the parlor and the dancers. Like it or not, the black-haired woman who averted her eyes when he glanced her way was the best method to achieve his goal. He crossed the room and halted by her chair.

"Allow me to take your plate and cup if you're finished with them?"

"Uh, yes. Thank you."

He couldn't miss how she'd peeked across the room toward her watching mother before handing him the plate and cup. Mrs. Matthews probably wanted to see Clarisse claimed by a partner as badly as his parents wanted him to choose one. Returning to stand in front of her, he forced a smile. "We're already missing the second dance. Could I have the next one?"

Her eyes widened. As furiously as she employed her fan, her jaw had probably dropped. Again, her gaze darted to her mother. "Yes, you may."

When she stood, he offered her his arm. "We could go to the parlor and enjoy the music until the next dance."

She placed her hand lightly on his sleeve. If not for their parental audience, he doubted she'd touch him in a thousand years. Unless she'd lied about not knowing what Eugenia suggested concerning the two of them and secretly approved of his invitation to dance. How he hoped she'd told him the truth the day she'd delivered that preposterous apology.

He leaned his head toward her ear as they walked into the hall. "I'll be happy to walk out on the porch later and explain myself."

Her eyebrows raised. "You have a reason for this?"

"Yes. A good one." He escorted her to an out-of-the-way corner of the parlor, then focused his attention on the dancers. Travis Glynne, the local attorney's son, had claimed Angelique. Much better.

The third dance was a waltz. Luke took Clarisse's hand as he guided her onto the floor. He smiled at her the way a partner should. She didn't smile back. Good. Since he didn't want to dance with any woman ever again, he hoped he'd found the one lady here who wouldn't expect more from him than he cared to offer.

He returned his attention to the other dancers. Parker had again claimed Angelique.

"I don't believe I've ever danced with such an inattentive man." The sarcastic tone of her words jerked his attention away from his cousin.

He peered down at Clarisse. "Do you truly mind that I'm not gazing into your luminous brown eyes and telling you you're the most beautiful woman in the room?" She was pretty with her delicate features, but some other man could enjoy her winsome smile and offer her such compliments.

"No, I don't." The way her cheeks colored made him wonder what she did or didn't mind.

He nodded. "I assumed so."

The dance ended. Parker took Angelique's elbow and led her toward the front door.

"Would you step out on the porch with me?" Luke released her hand.

"Yes. But only because I'm so curious about your strange behavior."

She followed him outside. Angelique and her partner stood on one end of the moonlit porch. After being sure Parker saw him with Clarisse, Luke halted at the other end with his companion. The gentle evening breeze refreshed him as he glanced over her head to be sure his cousin's escort continued behaving as a gentleman should.

"Your explanation?" She kept her voice low despite her insistent tone.

"Uh, yes. You deserve that." He turned his attention to the woman standing in front of him. The almost full moon didn't completely obscure her pleasant features. "I'm not happy

Parker is so interested in Angelique." He spoke softly enough for only Clarisse to hear him. "I'm sure you understand why."

"Yes, but what does that have to do with me?"

Clarisse's irritation pleased him much more than he cared to say. Perhaps she disapproved of her friend's suggestion. Or she truly didn't know the contents of the letter. Regardless, she sounded as if she didn't want to be with him any more than he wanted her company.

"Does your hesitation to answer me mean you're still thinking up a proper excuse for your behavior, or do you have a real explanation as promised?" She paused from fanning herself to stare straight up at him.

Her words jarred him from his thoughts. "Standing in the parlor scowling at Angelique while she glides by me on Parker's arm isn't an option. Dancing with you makes my watch care less obvious."

"Following her out to the porch isn't obvious?" Her dry laugh carried farther than he wished. Angelique and Parker stared in their direction.

"Not if our onlookers think you and I only have eyes for each other." Luke placed his hand lightly on Clarisse's shoulder, gazing down at her. She flinched but didn't move away.

Her laughter again pealed along the length of the porch. "I had no idea you have such a sense of humor."

"I don't. But I'm glad you think my remark about us is so absurd it's funny."

"Absurd. I'd say that's a good description." She resumed fanning herself despite the pleasant breeze making such an activity unnecessary. Was she nervous, bored with him, or what?

"Absurd, yes. But necessary." He glanced toward Angelique again. The moonlit night helped him see her. But not to his advantage when she could see him well enough to observe him watching her.

He quickly gazed down at Clarisse. "As I was saying …" He raised his voice enough to be overheard as he lightly brushed her cheek with his fingertips. She placed her hand over his just long enough to jerk his fingers away from her face. "I apologize for being so forward, but please allow me to ask you for a favor?"

"And what would that be?" Her almost whisper still matched his low tones. Good.

"I suggest a mutual alliance to protect Angelique from Parker. And perhaps from herself since she appears bent on ignoring Mother's warning to her about the man."

A soft giggle from his cousin interrupted whatever reply Clarisse might be intending to make. She cocked her head as if to listen to whatever was happening behind her while Luke stared directly at Angelique long enough to remind her she had an audience.

"Mutual as in our common concern for your cousin, nothing more?" Clarisse waited to speak until he refocused his regard on her.

"Yes. Plus, dancing with each other might help us make our parents happier about our limited social lives."

She sighed. "I suppose."

Her melancholy tone emphasized her dramatic sigh. He had good reasons for not wanting a romantic entanglement. Why did she seem so reluctant about receiving attention from a man? Her late fiancé would have never betrayed her or hurt her in any manner. Everyone in Rutherford County was aware of Garland's fierce love for Clarisse.

Parker led Angelique back inside. Luke fought the urge to trot after them. "So, would you help me be sure Angelique doesn't fall victim to Alton Parker's charms?"

She stared up at him. The shadows from the roof shaded her face, preventing him from seeing her eyes well enough to guess her thoughts. "If rescuing your cousin is your true motive, yes. But how do I know you're not taking advantage of my situation with my doting mother, who is determined I find a new beau?"

"You're accusing me of not being truthful?" He fought not to raise his voice.

"Why not? You did everything but call me a liar the last time I saw you." She tapped her folded fan on her arm.

He sucked in a breath. "Yes, I did. And I'm offering you my sincere apology. You've proved me entirely wrong tonight."

"I have? How?"

He was becoming much too good at saying things he shouldn't. Of course, she had no idea what he meant since she'd convinced him she didn't know about Eugenia's idea for the two of them. "Um ... well, your sincerity shines through with every word. I should have never doubted you've never read that letter."

"Apology accepted. I give you my word I'll try to help protect Angelique. I'd like your word you want nothing more from me than that."

"I promise. Protecting Angelique is all I have in mind."

"Good. We should go back inside if we intend to thwart whatever Mr. Parker might already be scheming." She opened her fan.

"Yes, we should." He extended his arm.

She placed her free hand on his sleeve. "We don't dare miss the important announcement Marissa's father is going to make tonight."

"And that would be?" He halted as they reached the front door.

"I'm sworn to secrecy. I'm a woman of my word, as you now know."

"Yes, I do." He opened the door for her to precede him into the entry hall.

He'd found a much-needed and willing ally to help him watch over Angelique. Now to figure out how to keep everyone in the county from assuming their sudden attraction to each other didn't mean what it appeared.

Chapter Five

Their driver helped Mama and Jenette into the enclosed black carriage. Clarisse settled into the seat next to her sister-in-law and across from her mother. This might be one of the more pleasant Wednesday afternoons she and Jenette had spent with Mama in a while.

"We should make calls together more often." Mama's face glowed. "I'm so glad both of you agreed to befriend Angelique. The poor girl has had such an unfortunate life."

"She has." Clarisse had no problem feeling genuinely sorry for Angelique, especially after Mama relayed what Mrs. Williams had told her in whispered tones at the Parkers' ball last week. Angelique's mother had died giving her birth. Clarisse couldn't imagine never knowing her mother. Or the heartbreak of having her father murdered only a few months ago.

Jenette nodded. "I admire Angelique's strength. Setting aside her mourning for the sake of her aunt and uncle."

Once they thoroughly covered what they'd been told of the young woman, Mama changed the conversation to the weather and other subjects Clarisse could discuss with no problem as the carriage rolled toward Oakridge. For the first time in days, Mama didn't mention Luke or make any hints about how delighted she'd been to see Clarisse spending so much time with him at the Parkers' ball. She hoped she wouldn't regret agreeing to help him watch over his cousin. Her entire family had been much too happy to see how many times she'd danced with Luke.

When the butler ushered them into the house, Mrs. Williams and Angelique greeted the three of them in the entry hall. "I've sent for refreshments. Do join us in the parlor."

Mama fell into step with Mrs. Williams. Clarisse and Jenette walked with Angelique. Since she hadn't seen or heard any sign of Luke, Clarisse hoped he was out with his overseer or doing anything else that would keep him away from the house this afternoon. She didn't mind helping him protect Angelique, but she'd rather do so without him as much as possible.

Mrs. Williams, Mama, and Jenette chose the chairs, leaving the couch to Clarisse and Angelique. "I'm so happy Aunt Evelyn asked y'all to come." Angelique's brown eyes sparkled as she looked around the room.

"So are we." Clarisse's words and smile were genuine. Perhaps her alliance with Luke wouldn't be the burden she feared.

By the time everyone finished their tea, Angelique fidgeted like a child as she glanced more than once toward the open window. "Would you like a walk in the front yard while the weather is so nice?" She shifted to look at Clarisse, then turned her gaze toward Jenette.

"I'd like to stretch my limbs as long as we stay in the shade." Jenette rose.

Angelique all but bounced from the room and into the hall. She snatched her bonnet from its hook and wasted no time tying the ribbon. Clarisse and Jenette followed her outside and down the porch steps.

"Such a beautiful day must be enjoyed outdoors." Angelique lifted her face toward the clear sky as she breathed deeply of the fresh spring air. "Aunt Evelyn and I have been walking some. Uncle Douglas, too, when he's up to it."

Clarisse strolled with her companions across the lawn toward the shade of a large oak. "What do you think of Tennessee so far?"

"It's so pretty here. So peaceful." Angelique raised her hands up in the air as if to encompass everything around her. Clarisse half expected her to twirl around like an enthralled child. "I love my dear aunt and uncle, who are working so hard to make me feel at home. Luke is too, as much as he won't admit it."

"I'm glad you're happy." Jenette grinned as if she were enjoying Angelique's company as much as Clarisse was.

"I am. Especially with my newfound family." Angelique's expression sobered as they halted in the shade. "From what my aunt says, y'all have known Luke for years. Has he always been such a serious person?"

Jenette nodded, looking nonplussed at Angelique's sudden change of subject. "Ever since I've known him. Clarisse has known him longer, though."

"Oh." Angelique turned her full attention to Clarisse. The mischievous sparkle in the younger woman's eyes set Clarisse's nerves on edge. She was much too pleased to know how long Luke and Clarisse had been friends.

"Luke and Titus played together as boys, so your cousin is like another brother."

Angelique's lilting laugh filled the large yard. "If I had a brother, I wouldn't have danced with him as often as you danced with Luke last week."

"Luke's a friend of the entire family. He asked me for a couple of dances too." Jenette opened her fan.

Sweet Jenette was the only one in the family who tried to understand how deeply Garland's loss still hurt and why Clarisse wanted nothing to do with other men. She wanted to hug her sister-in-law.

"I saw him dancing with you. But, Clarisse, do be careful of my cousin. Judging from the way he stared at you, his motives were far from brotherly concerning you."

"We're friends. He saw I had no partner. Gentleman that he is, he asked me to dance." Clarisse studied a yellow butterfly flitting nearby, wishing she could follow it off somewhere and dodge this uncomfortable conversation.

Angelique shook her head. "I'm sure he'd be with us now if he hadn't ridden to Murfreesboro to mail an important letter for Uncle Douglas."

Her new friend had no idea how happy the intended teasing remark made Clarisse. Luke didn't want to see her today any more than she wanted to see him. Let his cousin think what she wished about Luke's true intentions since she doubted any letter absolutely had to be posted today. She continued watching butterflies. Replying probably wouldn't do her any good.

"Luke says we'll go for a ride someday soon. Do either of you like to ride?"

Chills traveled up and down Clarisse's spine. She'd rather be teased about Luke than think about riding again.

"I won't be riding for a while." Jenette's glowing smile signaled her obvious pleasure concerning her situation. "I'm sure your aunt knows my news from Mother but hasn't told you yet. I'm in the family way."

"No, she didn't. Congratulations."

"Thank you."

Angelique turned her gaze to Clarisse. "I'm certain you'd be a better companion than my solemn cousin." Her eager expression appeared to beg Clarisse to accept her innocent invitation.

Taking in a deep breath, Clarisse focused on a pair of gray squirrels darting along the limb of the tree a few feet away. "I don't ride much anymore." How she hoped this new friend wouldn't press her for details. She hadn't been in a saddle since that awful day she and Garland had gone for their last ride.

"I'm sorry to be rude, but this afternoon heat ... Could we go back inside?" Jenette fanned herself as if it were a sweltering July afternoon.

"Oh, dear. I'm sorry." Angelique took Jenette's elbow. "We'll go in right now."

Dear Jenette. Her almost sister protecting Clarisse from having to explain why she didn't ride anymore. Perhaps also protecting herself since any mention of her brother Garland's death had to distress Jenette too. She positioned herself at Jenette's other side as they walked back to the porch.

Angelique ushered Jenette to a parlor chair the instant after they hung their bonnets on the hat tree. "Jenette was getting too warm. I've already told Amos to have someone bring her a cool glass of water."

"Are you all right, dear?" Mama focused on Jenette's slightly flushed face. "Do we need to go home?"

"I'm fine now." She smiled as if trying to reassure everyone. "Do continue with your conversation."

After looking Jenette over thoroughly, Mama and Mrs. Williams picked up their conversation. Evidently, they hadn't finished discussing Marissa and Jonah's engagement to their liking.

"I think they're well-suited to each other." Mrs. Williams refilled Mama's teacup. "Clarisse, would you like more tea?"

"Yes, please." She wasn't thirsty but sipping tea would be a good way to not have to talk about the happy couple. She'd say the couple deserved each other. Jonah had been so boorish that Eugenia had sent him away. Marissa had completely ignored Eugenia's disdain for a forced marriage to her brother, Alton. But Clarisse would keep such opinions to herself the way she did so many of her other thoughts Mama would be appalled to hear.

A servant came in with a glass of water for Jenette. She sipped as Mama told everyone about the house Jonah was already building.

"He'll be an excellent husband and take such good care of Marissa." Mama's brown eyes had their usual wistful look whenever she discussed an upcoming marriage.

Clarisse stirred her tea. If only she could have stayed home and read a good book.

"I liked meeting the entire Parker family." Angelique's aunt didn't mirror her smile as she shot a serious look in her niece's direction. "And all my other new neighbors too. Everyone has been so kind to me."

"We have wonderful friends." The sparkle returned to Mrs. Williams' eyes as soon as Angelique mentioned meeting other people.

"We do. Which is why I hope Luke will ride with me soon so I can learn more about my new home. If he can't, I've asked Clarisse to go with me."

Mama turned her full attention to Angelique. "That's an excellent way for the two of you to become better acquainted."

Oh, but it wasn't. How Clarisse wished she could speak her mind. But her mother was the least sympathetic member of her family when it came to understanding her grief over

Garland. Or her reluctance to ride again after his fatal accident. She picked up her empty cup, pretending to take another drink.

"Perhaps Clarisse could ride over to see you next week?" Mama's grin stretched across her face.

Clarisse gripped her fragile china cup, lest she drop it. Mama had been saying more and more often how Clarisse needed to return to a more normal life for a young woman of nineteen. Refusing such a request in front of Mama would ignite a firestorm of words once they were home if not in the carriage on the way.

"I'd like that very much." Angelique clapped her hands together while smiling at Clarisse. "Would next Wednesday be good for you?"

Everyone in the room turned their attention to Clarisse for her answer. Jenette couldn't rescue her this time. Ducking her head, Clarisse concentrated on setting her cup on her saucer. She hoped no one noticed her hand tremble. "Well, I—uh ... I suppose I could."

How she forced the words from her tight throat she wasn't sure. How she'd manage to go through with what she'd agreed to do, only God had the answer for.

Luke welcomed the chance to ride alone with his cousin. She'd made too many offhand remarks about Alton Parker this week. He'd take advantage of the almost perfect afternoon without a cloud in the sky. "Would you like to see one of my favorite trails through the woods or more of our property?" He posed his question as they neared the end of the long driveway leading from the house.

"I've ridden over a friend's plantation outside of New Orleans often. Let's ride in the woods."

"An excellent choice. I like listening to the birds and watching the squirrels."

"As do I. I want to learn all about my new home." Her eyes glittered as she glanced his way.

He returned her smile while wishing she owned a different color riding habit. Her outfit was only a shade or two darker green than Eugenia's riding clothes had been. Just the person he didn't want to be reminded of, especially since she was the last woman he'd ridden with. Along with Parker and his sister. More memories he'd rather not recall. "I'm glad you think of Oakridge as home now."

"I already prefer here to New Orleans."

From what he'd been told of her life in Louisiana, he could understand her sentiments. He turned his horse toward the woods. "I'll show you the trial to Hopeton, the Matthews plantation." A much better choice for him than the trail he'd taken to ride to Eugenia's house more often than he should

"I enjoyed visiting with the Matthews ladies yesterday. I think Clarisse and I might become good friends. Jenette too." She guided her horse beside his.

"Good. They're both fine ladies." He'd do all he could to encourage such friendships. "I'm assuming you met others at the ball last week."

"I didn't lack for dance partners, so I met more men than women. You watched so closely, I'm sure you know that." Her terse words sounded as if he'd irritated her.

"You didn't appreciate me keeping an eye on you?" He glanced over at her. Her lips quivered just shy of a frown. Since he wanted to caution her about Parker without aggravating her, he'd best diffuse this situation as best he could.

"I did not. You were so obvious Mr. Parker noticed you too."

The way her chin jutted out left no doubt about her exasperation with him.

He guided his horse around the bend. She followed until she could ride next to him again. He grinned into her serious eyes. "I made it a habit to watch out for my sisters for years. Since you're already like a little sister to me, you'll have to learn to put up with my insufferable habit the way they did."

"Insufferable is a good description."

He chuckled. He wouldn't tell her he'd had similar thoughts about her intrusion causing his parents possible stress. Not to mention the aggravation she caused him by having to escort and introduce her at social functions he had no interest in attending. "Does that mean you're not growing as fond of me as quickly as I am of you?" The trail narrowed as they rode into the edge of the woods. He took the lead, sure he'd soon hear her response. She'd never been at a loss for words so far.

The trail widened enough for her to come alongside him. "You're fond of me?" Her eyes widened as if he'd shocked her.

"Yes, I'd say I am." Which was the truth, the more he considered it just now.

She shook her head. "Why?"

"Why?" He stalled for time, thinking how to reply to the unexpected question he couldn't completely answer. He did and didn't like her. Her innocent beauty and vivacious nature were appealing. But not just to him. Which might lead to problems with someone like Parker. Her impetuous, headstrong tendencies that might cause his parents undue worries weren't endearing. "You're family. Caring for and watching over each other are what families do."

"Or should do." Her voice cracked. Looking down, she gripped her reins as if her horse were about to bolt.

"Yes, should do." Sympathy for her coursed through his

being. He would not, could not allow a cad like Parker to cause her further pain. He prayed for the right words to convince her to beware of the man, since whatever his mother had told her didn't seem to be sufficient. Prayed? His words to God had been few since he'd learned of Eugenia's betrayal.

He sucked in a deep breath as they rode into a small, sun-dappled clearing. "Since I am fond of you, I kept an especially close watch on you whenever you were with Alton Parker. Mother said she cautioned you to be careful of him."

"She did." Her chin jutting out again, she stared straight into his eyes. "Mr. Parker says he made some mistakes and has seen the error of his ways. So it's unfair for people to misjudge him or malign him now."

"Did he tell you what he did?"

"No."

"You're not the least bit curious?" Luke halted his mount. She reined in her horse. This sort of serious conversation should be had face to face, not while riding down a trail where he couldn't always see her expression to gauge her reaction. Poor planning on his part.

"No. You and your parents are giving me a second chance to overcome my painful past. Mr. Parker deserves the same courtesy."

"If he's truly changed his ways, yes. But his actions will have to prove his claims to me." He prayed for the right words to convince Angelique to be cautious. God hadn't answered his prayers in a while, but surely the Lord cared about an innocent girl who could be making a terrible mistake.

Parker couldn't be trusted to show his true colors. With his past gambling problems, he might possibly be as much of a scoundrel as Jacques DuBois. Especially the way the rogue had confronted Luke after discovering Eugenia knew about his card games and debts. Luke would never forget their heated conversation on the front lawn. He'd refused the man's demand for a duel and had to threaten to further expose his gambling problems to get him to leave.

"He said you'd disparage him. That the two of you were rivals for the same woman's hand. But she eloped with another man."

Luke sucked in a breath. The serpent in the Garden of Eden couldn't twist words any better than Parker if the man were already anticipating what Luke might tell his cousin. Ample evidence the scoundrel hadn't changed. He seemed to be already employing the same tactics on Angelique he'd used to win over Eugenia's unsuspecting father. But unbeknownst to Parker, this intended victim wouldn't inherit a plantation the way Eugenia could have. What did the man want?

"Since you have no answer, I assume Mr. Parker's words are true."

"Partly. We did pursue the same woman. But judging from your stiff posture and accusing tone, I'd be wasting my breath to tell you the whole truth. If or when you'd like to hear the full story, ask, and I'll tell you."

She shook her head. "I know how it hurts to have someone assume things that aren't true. So many people in New Orleans were sure Jacques DuBois' daughter had to be as much of a scalawag as he was. Or worse. I overheard more than once what people said behind my back." Her voice thick with emotion, she blinked as if fighting tears.

"I'm sorry. I promise you no one in Rutherford County will ever say such things about you to your face or behind your back. They will have to answer to me if they dare say one syllable against you." He shifted to pull his handkerchief from his pocket and offered it to her.

Sniffing, she dabbed at her eyes. "Thank you. I'd like to go home now."

He nodded. They rode in silence back to the house, giving Luke some much-needed time to think. He must protect Angelique from whatever scheme Parker appeared to already be planning. Why had the man targeted her so quickly? Probably because she was one of the few people who hadn't been told some sort of gossip about him after he'd somehow managed to pay his mounting gambling debts. Who had started rumors about Parker? Luke didn't know. The man had made enough enemies, the list of possibilities could be rather long.

But Parker's problems with his reputation weren't what concerned Luke. Since his naive cousin refused to hear or entertain the truth about the man, Luke had to be the one to protect her despite her misplaced sympathy for a cad.

Would Angelique listen to her new friend better than she listened to him? Enlisting Clarisse's help might have been one of the smartest things he could have done. But how to tell her what Angelique had said? Calling on her would be living a charade, making him as duplicitous as Parker.

Or would it, since she had agreed to help him protect Angelique?

Chapter Six

Luke held open the back door to the church building for his parents and Angelique. He hadn't been here since he'd learned Eugenia had eloped. A polished board creaked beneath his boot as if to announce the prodigal's return to the entire congregation. He slid into the family pew after the others had taken their seats. If only he could sit by the outer wall instead of the aisle where everyone could see him.

Steeling himself for the service, he stared at the stained-glass windows at the front of the sanctuary. So many of his prayers had gone unanswered this past year. Why had he come here?

The Matthews family claimed their pew across the aisle. Since Titus allowed the ladies to be seated first, Clarisse filed behind her mother. Jenette followed. Good. Luke would much rather have Titus in his peripheral vision than Clarisse. Yet, she was the reason he'd come today. After his conversation with Angelique a few days ago, he needed to talk to her.

Once everyone was seated, the pastor walked to the pulpit. "Join me in prayer."

Luke bowed his head, something else he hadn't done in a

while. The pastor thanked God for the beautiful day and went on to thank Him for a multitude of blessings, seen and unseen. Luke suppressed a groan. The last year of his life had been far from blessed.

"Please rise, and we'll sing *'Joyful, Joyful We Adore Thee'* while we continue to celebrate our God's goodness and love."

Fighting the urge to run to the door, Luke stood with the rest of the congregation. Joy had eluded him since he'd returned home from college last year and given up his dream of becoming an attorney. Eugenia had deepened his gloom by rejecting the love he'd offered. He mouthed the familiar words as Angelique's clear soprano floated from the other end of the pew. She sang with obvious enthusiasm as if relishing every sentence. He didn't.

"Melt the clouds of sin and sadness; drive the dark of doubt away ..." He hoped no one noticed his voice falter as he sang those words. Clouds and darkness too aptly described his state of mind. "Giver of immortal gladness, fill us with the light of day."

He stumbled through the rest of the verses as well as the next hymn, then sank into his seat. This used to be a place of solace and refuge. Not a reminder of all he'd sacrificed or lost. He should have found another place, another way to speak to Clarisse.

If only he could regain the peace he'd once had.

"We sang about joyfully adoring our Lord this morning. Rejoicing isn't hard when life is good. But what do we do if our lives become hard or unfair? Turn to Philippians, chapter four, verse four." Pastor Bentley paused long enough to allow everyone to find the verses. "Paul wrote this letter while a Roman prisoner, yet he tells us to rejoice. He had no earthly reason to be joyful, yet he was."

The pastor's seemingly contradictory words compelled

Luke to listen. Pastor Bentley went on to list other miseries Paul had endured. Luke had read from Philippians for years, but Paul's command to rejoice always fascinated him, but now in a way he'd never experienced. Luke's trials couldn't be compared to the hardships Paul had endured, yet Luke hadn't experienced joy in so long.

"I can't tell you why God allowed Paul's life to be so hard or why some of us in this congregation have suffered. Perhaps I'll ask the Lord about that in heaven one day. Paul rejoiced *in* the Lord. And in the Lord alone, regardless of his circumstances." Pastor Bentley's face lit up as he continued to talk about having joy in the Lord no matter the circumstances.

Luke's hungry soul drank in his pastor's encouragement. Coming to church for the wrong reason had been more right than he'd have supposed possible. He'd reread the entire chapter tonight before he went to sleep.

After the service, he followed his family down the aisle, pausing by the pastor standing at the open door. His parents introduced Angelique, then complimented the sermon before walking outside.

"Thank you for some very helpful suggestions." Luke shook the man's hand after his family was too far away to hear him. Mother would be glad Luke wanted to let go of his anger toward Eugenia, but he doubted Father would understand why Luke considered it a trial to take over the family plantation. Some things were better kept to himself.

"You're welcome."

Other people pressing around made it impossible for Luke to say more. He stepped aside as the Matthews family took their turn to greet the pastor. The woman he'd come to talk to smiled at Pastor Bentley before breezing past Luke and out the door.

Luke slipped past Titus and Jenette to catch up to Clarisse.

Her eyes widened when he reached her side at the edge of the churchyard. "May I have a word with you?"

"Well, I suppose so." She glanced around. "Only until my family is ready to leave."

"Thank you." He followed her to the welcome shade of the largest oak tree standing between them and the rest of the congregation. She walked around to the other side of the trunk as if to block them from sight. On such a nice spring day, others paused in small groups to visit the way so many did after the service.

He hoped everyone would soon be too engrossed in their own conversations to notice he and Clarisse had walked off together. "I tried talking with Angelique about Parker. It didn't go well." He sucked in a long breath. "I'd rather not go into details with so many people around. Could I call on you this week before the two of you go riding together?"

She clamped her open mouth shut. While she stared up at him in wide-eyed silence, he braced himself for the rejection she'd surely give him soon.

"C-call on me? As in, come to see me at my house?"

Knowing he shouldn't, he couldn't help grinning at the pretty, frustrated woman sputtering in front of him. He focused on the red bow on her bonnet tied beneath her chin rather than gaze into her perplexed, intriguing brown eyes. "Most men call on a woman at their homes."

Her eyes darted toward the rutted road leading up to the church. "Yes, of course they do. It's just that ... that I never envisioned a call from you as necessary when I agreed to help you." She licked her lips before looking up at him again, then took in a deep breath. "I suppose it's the only proper way for us to talk. Yes, you may call on me. But *only* to discuss our mutual problem with your cousin."

"*Our* mutual problem?" He shouldn't have said that but he

had to know why she now considered Angelique's predicament their problem instead of his alone.

"She's a sweet dear. I think she and I could become good friends."

"Thank you. Would tomorrow afternoon or Tuesday be best?"

"Tuesday after two o'clock. Mama and Jenette like to make calls on Tuesdays, and Titus often rides to Murfreesboro for the mail." She stared toward the carriages. "My mother will probably be ready to leave soon. I should go."

He doffed his hat to her. "I'll see you in a couple of days."

She nodded before walking away.

What had he done? He fought the urge to trot after her and cancel their meeting.

Except calling on her was the only proper way to speak with a lady. He must talk with her to prepare her for Angelique's misguided reasons to possibly befriend Parker. Perhaps if Clarisse were forewarned, she'd have time to think of the right words to dissuade Angelique from making a terrible mistake.

He waited until Clarisse was almost to her carriage before stepping around from the large tree. He didn't want anyone to see them walk off together if the substantial trunk had shielded them from view. Mother had liked Eugenia's suggestion for him to consider courting the woman enough that she'd welcome any kind of communication between him and Clarisse. As would Mrs. Matthews.

So, on Tuesday, he'd have the need to ride alone and think for a while. A perfect way to hide where he'd truly be going without telling anyone an outright lie. Since Clarisse chose the day she should be home alone, she, too, must want to keep their meeting a secret. Such convoluted measures would make for a good Shakespeare-type comedy if the situation weren't much too real.

* * *

Clarisse stared unseeing at the pages of her favorite poetry book. Usually, she savored an afternoon alone to sit in the parlor and read. Waiting for an unwanted call from Luke, who would arrive at any moment, made it impossible to concentrate on the words in front of her.

Her family had left, as she'd hoped, but she hadn't been able to think what to tell the butler when her guest arrived. Asking Moses to lie to her mother about a caller would be wrong and would work as well as trying to pick flowers in January. He wouldn't think of being so disloyal.

Setting aside her book, she rose to look out the window at the lush green lawn. Today wasn't too warm for late May. Perhaps if she walked in the shaded front yard, she could speak to Luke outside. They were probably on a fool's errand trying to keep Luke's visit a secret, but she'd try. She took her favorite bonnet off the hall tree and tied the ribbon.

Not long after stepping away from the porch, she spied a rider coming up the tree-lined drive. If only she were watching for Garland instead. She sighed. Luke raised his hand in greeting when he saw her. She walked toward a large chestnut tree away from the parlor windows to wait for him.

He ground-tied his horse before joining her in the shade. "Thank you for seeing me. I also appreciate you not wanting to be seen with me."

"You're welcome."

"Since you're riding with Angelique tomorrow, you should know about her sympathies for Alton Parker, despite my mother cautioning her about the man. I didn't want to risk

Angelique or anyone else overhearing us after church yesterday. She wouldn't be happy if she knew what I came to say."

She nodded. "She sympathizes with Mr. Parker?"

He went on to tell her about his conversation with Angelique. "I can't help wondering why Parker is so interested in a woman he's never met before. What he could he want with her."

"Titus recognized the DuBois name. Is she connected to their shipping company in New Orleans? His factor has done business with them at times."

"She is—was. Her late father was the last of the family line. Their attorney is in the process of selling everything the family owns."

"Oh." Clarisse pointed a finger toward him. "If Mr. Parker is familiar with the name, that is likely why he was so quickly attracted to your cousin. We both know how that man idolizes money."

"He'll be sorely disappointed." Luke shook his head. "Please don't mention that. We're trying our best to protect Angelique from gossip about her family's misfortune."

"Of course. From what your mother told Mama, your cousin has suffered so much." She blinked away the moisture in her eyes. After losing her father to illness and Garland to an accident, she had no trouble sympathizing with Angelique.

"She has. No matter how headstrong she's proving to be, I don't want her to be hurt by a rogue like Parker. Father gave serious consideration to telling Parker not to call on her. But if the rogue twisted that to his advantage, she might sympathize with him more than she already does."

"I'll do my best to see he doesn't cause her more pain. But why do you think she'll listen to me better than she did to you?"

He shrugged. "She didn't mention him saying anything against you. I had to be careful not to turn her against me since she thinks I dislike Parker because we both pursued the same woman."

Did the way Luke failed to mention Eugenia by name hint how much he might still be hurting over losing her? "I'm sure he never mentioned he'd have married Eugenia against her will to get the money to pay his gambling debts?"

Luke nodded. "My cousin didn't elaborate, but I'm certain Parker omitted that fact."

"Along with any other unflattering details about himself. I'll do my best to change her opinion of the cad."

"Again, I thank you. Also, for riding with Angelique tomorrow. As much as she likes to ride, she might do it every day if she could. She's eager to see as much as she can of her new home and delights to get out and enjoy the outdoors."

Clarisse's stomach churned at the mention of meeting Angelique tomorrow. Only with God's help could she find the courage to battle her memories of her last ride with Garland and go to Oakridge tomorrow on horseback. "I'm looking forward to talking to Angelique again." She forced the words from her dry throat, marveling at how normal her voice sounded.

"I'll go before any of your family returns." He grinned down at her. "My family hasn't mentioned anything about seeing us talking after church, so we did well there."

"That's good." How strange their conversation would sound if someone overheard them.

He tipped his hat. "I won't ride down the drive again in case your mother and Jenette might return sooner than expected. Good day."

"Good day to you." She strolled around the yard a while longer. Moses and the other servants were used to her walking alone. Keeping to her usual habits would make her afternoon appear more normal.

After walking back inside, she picked up the book she'd left on the couch. But thoughts of how she'd manage to don her riding habit tomorrow, much less ride to Oakridge, made it impossible to read one of her favorite poems.

Chapter Seven

Blinking in disbelief, Clarisse stared at her reflection in her dresser mirror while her maid finished pinning on her top hat. A stranger stood before her dressed in her deep red riding habit. She hadn't worn this outfit since … No. She forced herself to breathe evenly. If she kept thinking about that awful day, she'd never manage to walk to the barn. Much less mount her horse.

"I still says this color be perfect for you." Ruth grinned from behind her as she smoothed Clarisse's hair. "And I's so glad to see you ready to ride again."

Clarisse nodded. She appreciated her maid's sympathy but doubted her voice would cooperate to express such gratitude. Garland had often complimented the color of her habit when they rode together. "You may go. Theophilus should have Merry saddled by now."

"Yes, miss. I'm prayin' for you." Ruth kept her voice low before slipping out the door without waiting for Clarisse to respond. Since Mama wouldn't approve of how close Clarisse and Ruth were, her maid understood the need to be careful not to be overheard.

She squeezed her eyes shut as she prayed for strength. Garland had often said he admired her fortitude. Time to prove him right this afternoon. Plus, she didn't want to disappoint Angelique after all the heartache her new friend had endured. She let out the breath she'd been holding in and trudged out of her room.

When she reached the bottom stair, Mama and Jenette's voices came from the parlor. Clarisse halted by the door. "I'm going to see Angelique now."

Mama's face lit up. "Enjoy your afternoon."

"I will." Clarisse struggled to keep her voice from quivering. If only Angelique hadn't mentioned riding in front of Mama last week, making it almost impossible to say no. Her mother had been insisting more and more lately it was past time for Clarisse to set aside her grief and go back to a normal life. Perhaps riding with Angelique would help Mama not to be so concerned about her daughter's lack of a social life.

Clarisse swallowed hard as she walked up to the barn. Theophilus stood by the door with her horse, waiting for her. Her heart raced as he helped her mount the mare. Taking a deep breath, she steadied her trembling hands on the saddle horn. "Thank you for your help."

The groom nodded as he studied her. "Is you all right, miss?"

"Yes." She drew in another breath. "I will be." Only God knew how, at the moment. But with His strength, she would manage this ride she needed to take to help her friend. She gripped the reins and guided her horse away from the barn.

On the trail through the woods to Oakridge, she focused on what she might say to Angelique to keep her safe from Mr. Parker. If she weren't careful with her words, the friendship she hoped to forge might end before it started. She sorely missed Eugenia's companionship and wouldn't mind making a new friend.

Before she reached the circular drive in front of the Williams' pillared plantation house, the front door opened. Angelique, dressed in her dark green riding habit, waved as she stepped onto the porch.

"I've been watching for you. I'm so happy you're here." Angelique bounced down the steps. "Would you meet me at the barn? I told Aunt Evelyn I saw you coming, so she knows I'm leaving."

"Of course." Angelique's enthusiastic greeting warmed Clarisse's soul. Perhaps God was gifting her with the new friend she so wanted and needed.

As they rode past the carriage house a short time later, Angelique grinned as she lifted her face to the sun. "Tennessee is so pretty, especially with all the flowers this time of year. Spring is my favorite season, and I like it even more here."

Clarisse shoved aside memories of riding through colorful spring meadows with Eugenia as her friend exclaimed over the flowers. Today, she'd focus on the new friend whose enthusiasm reminded her of Eugenia. "I like spring too."

"Would you like to ride down the drive where we'll have some shade?" Angelique smiled over at her.

"That would be fine." Clarisse preferred the trees to open fields with fences or hedges to jump, but explaining why to anyone was more than she wanted to do. Or could do.

"Thank you again for coming to see me. I hope we can become good friends."

"I'd like that too." Which she would. If only Angelique had wanted to go for a walk or sit in her aunt's flower garden while they became better acquainted.

"I had few true friends in New Orleans. I'm hoping to

change that here." Angelique's eyes shone as she twisted to look at Clarisse. "I'd be happy for introductions to any of your other acquaintances."

"My friends have a habit of leaving." Clarisse gripped her reins as they neared the brick pillars at the end of the tree-lined drive.

Angelique's eyes widened. "You've been abandoned too?"

"I wouldn't call it *abandoned*." Looking down, Clarisse hunted for the right words. "Your cousin Beth has been a good friend since childhood. She married last year and moved to Nashville. My best friend Eugenia and her husband live in Illinois now." She'd not mention Garland since so few people understood how she could still miss him so badly two years later.

"Oh, I see." Angelique sighed as they turned toward the woods. "Deserted is the best description for my situation."

"I'm sorry."

"Thank you. And thank you for listening to me go on about myself like this."

"I don't mind." Listening to her talkative companion took her mind off her nerves. The trail narrowed as they entered a stand of trees. Angelique followed behind.

Clarisse shaded her eyes with her hand as they rode into a grassy clearing while Angelique came alongside her. A man waved to them as he rode out from the shadows at the other end. Clarisse stiffened.

"Do you recognize him?" Angelique squinted toward the rider, making his way to them.

"I think so." Clarisse shuddered as she reined in her horse. The closer the man came, the more certain she was of his identity. Of all days for Alton Parker to be out for a ride.

"Good afternoon, ladies." Mr. Parker tipped his hat to them as he approached.

Angelique grinned. "Good afternoon. I had no idea I'd enjoy seeing two friends today."

"Nor did I. Where are you two off to today?" His half smile was directed at Angelique alone. He didn't look any happier to see Clarisse than she was to see him. Since she and Eugenia were so close, the man had to wonder how much of the truth her friend had told her about him. How to hint at his past without making Angelique more sympathetic toward him might be difficult. But Clarisse had to try.

"Oh, we aren't going anywhere in particular." Angelique extended a gloved hand toward him. "You're welcome to join us."

He guided his horse next to Angelique's mare, putting her between him and Clarisse. "I was on my way to call on you, Miss DuBois, not knowing I'd have the pleasure of visiting with *two* lovely ladies today."

"We're happy to see you." Angelique batted her long lashes at him.

"Indeed, we are." Clarisse struggled to keep her voice pleasant as she glanced his way. His eyebrows quirked up as he gave her a perfunctory nod before returning his full attention to Angelique.

"Have you ridden to the meadow near here, Miss DuBois? There's shade along the creek. It's become one of my favorites during the few months I've lived here."

"That sounds nice, as warm as it is." Angelique focused her full attention on Mr. Parker. "We'll allow you to lead the way."

"Excellent." He guided his mount down the narrowing trail.

Angelique followed him, leaving Clarisse to trail behind them. She swatted at a fly, wishing she could do the same to Mr. Parker. In only eight months, the man had caused her a lifetime of problems. If he hadn't been determined to marry

Eugenia against her will, she and Paul might not have had to elope to escape the cad. And Clarisse might still be enjoying her best friend's company.

But since Luke had warned her of Angelique's misplaced sympathy for Mr. Parker, she was stuck as an unwilling chaperone. Stuck trying to protect her naive, too-trusting friend from the clutches of a man who was more interested in Angelique's supposed fortune than her.

"What do you think?" Mr. Parker halted his horse as they rode into the meadow.

Angelique reined in her mare beside her caller and stared at the array of white, yellow, and pink flowers scattered over the meadow. "It's so pretty. There's just enough breeze to make the flowers dance." She took a deep breath. "I smell honeysuckle close by too. Spring is wonderful here."

"The flowers aren't the only pretty thing to see." Mr. Parker gazed into Angelique's eyes.

Just as Angelique opened her mouth to reply, Clarisse pointed toward the creek a few feet away "You're so right about the beauty here. See how the trees form an arch over the water. It looks like a scene from a painting, welcoming us to enjoy the beauty."

Angelique peered in the direction Clarisse indicated. "Yes, it does. We should accept the trees' *invitation*." She urged her horse toward the creek.

Mr. Parker clenched his jaw as he rode beside Angelique. Clarisse maintained her spot on the other side of her friend.

"I never imagined the trees offering us an invitation." Clarisse inserted another inane remark as Mr. Parker again smiled into Angelique's eyes. "I like your picturesque way of seeing things."

"Quite picturesque." Mr. Parker squeezed in his comment,

obviously aimed at Angelique, judging by the way he continued gazing at her.

"Thank you." Angelique's cheeks tinged with color.

"It is lovely here. The shade feels good, just as you said it would." Clarisse focused her gaze on the creek as they rode along the bank. The tranquil scene soothed her.

They rode until the woods intruded on the idyllic meadow. Clarisse continued interjecting her observations about the landscape, the weather, or any other vapid comment as often as possible. By the time they turned their horses back onto the main trail, Mr. Parker's stiff posture and serious eyes signaled his obvious displeasure for the way his planned call had gone. *Good.*

When the trail forked, Mr. Parker halted his horse. "I'll bid you ladies good day since my home is to the right." He tipped his hat to them.

"Good day to you." Clarisse worked to keep her tone pleasant. The day would be much better once this man was out of sight.

"Getting to know two new friends at once is the perfect way to spend an afternoon." Angelique beamed at him. "We must all do this again."

"Yes, we should." His thin smile resembled a mask to disguise his less-than-enthusiastic-sounding tone. He tipped his hat again, then urged his horse toward his house.

Clarisse fought to keep her immense relief from showing on her face as she and Angelique guided their horses onto the other fork. Seeing Angelique happy and Mr. Parker miserable meant her afternoon had been well spent, no matter how much she'd dreaded riding again. Plus, she hadn't needed Luke to help her irritate Mr. Parker. The more she could do so alone, the less everyone would assume she and Luke might be more than friends.

"If I remember correctly from my ride with Luke, the trail to Hopeton is coming up soon." Angelique pointed up ahead of them.

"It is. But I'll ride with you to the beginning of your drive so you don't get lost."

"I'd appreciate that until I learn the woods better. I do hope we can do this again, and often."

"Yes, we should." *Should not.* But if preventing Mr. Parker from being alone with Angelique meant more discomforting rides, she'd repeat this outing.

They soon halted their mounts at the beginning of the drive to Oakridge. Angelique's smile shone into her warm brown eyes. "Thank you, too, for being such a willing chaperone. I never detected an ounce of jealousy from you even though Mr. Parker had intended to enjoy my company exclusively. You're already a true friend."

"You're welcome. I've enjoyed this time with you." She hoped Angelique understood a true friend would try to prevent her from getting too close to a man like Mr. Parker. "Since Mr. Parker is so happy to be with you, the next time you see him, you should invite him to church. I've never seen him there yet."

Angelique's eyes widened. "He doesn't attend church?"

"Not that I've seen." Sowing even one slight doubt about the man would be good. "None of his family does. Maybe an invitation from another newcomer would encourage them all to come."

"Perhaps you're right. I'll be sure to invite him if he calls again." Her smile returned at Clarisse's suggestion.

"You should." She wouldn't tell Angelique she and Eugenia had invited the Parker family to church more than once after they'd met them last fall. Saying anything too disparaging might make Angelique more sympathetic to Mr. Parker than she already was. Her new friend needed to learn the truth about the man's disdain for God for herself. The entire family had had ample time to come to church if they cared to do so.

Clarisse rode home in a much better mood than she'd been in when she left. Focusing on helping Angelique had kept the bad memories of Clarisse's last ride at bay better than she'd believed possible. Giving her friend one potential reason to rethink her opinion of Mr. Parker would be well worth the discomfort. She had good news to tell Luke the next time she saw him.

Which would be when? The more they talked together, the more likely someone would see them and come to the wrong conclusion about why they were speaking to each other so often.

Luke walked into church with happy anticipation this Sunday. Sunbeams streaming through the windows lit up the polished wood floor as if welcoming him inside. Trying to rejoice in the Lord alone this past week had given him peace. The peace of mind and soul he hadn't had since the day he'd learned Eugenia had eloped. His unfulfilled desire to be an attorney was still there. But since God hadn't removed that longing, he'd pray for a way to accomplish his dream.

The Williams family took their pew. Angelique had chattered the rest of the week about her wonderful ride with Clarisse and Mr. Parker. He and his parents had been most grateful an unintended chaperone had been with Angelique and her caller. Clarisse tossed him a quick, barely perceptible smile as she passed by him.

A discreet signal she had something to tell him? If so, what arrangements could they make for a clandestine meeting this week? He focused his attention on the pastor stepping up to the lectern. He hoped the Lord didn't mind if Luke had more than one purpose for coming this morning. Watching over his innocent cousin had to be something God wanted him to do.

After the service ended, he followed Clarisse at a discreet distance to the edge of the churchyard. She paused behind the same oak tree as last week. But today another young couple halted within a few feet of them behind another tree as if they, too, were seeking privacy at the beginning of the woods.

"I don't have much to say, so I'd hoped to quickly tell you about my ride with Angelique." She spoke barely above a whisper as she glanced toward the other people. "But I'd rather not risk being overheard by anyone."

"Should I call again on Tuesday?" He matched her low tone.

"No. Jenette says it's getting too warm to go visiting, and she'll ask her friends to come see her instead."

"Oh." This posed a problem he hadn't anticipated after how well last Tuesday's call had gone. "How or where do we talk alone then? I won't ruin your good reputation."

She chewed her lip as she glanced away. Before finally looking up at him, she sighed. "For almost eight months, Eugenia and Paul rode every Sunday afternoon they could and met in the woods. I suppose we could each go for a ride on Tuesday and end up on the same trail."

"Are you sure about that?"

She nodded.

Her solemn expression reminded him of someone planning to attend a funeral. Surely, meeting with him didn't pain her that much. "I'll meet you on the trail that goes to your house about two o'clock as long there's no rain."

"Yes, I'll—"

"There you are, cousin. Oh, Clarisse! I wanted to find you and ask if you'd like to ride with me again." The mischievous gleam in Angelique's eyes couldn't be missed as she stepped around the tree trunk. "Uncle Douglas and Aunt Evelyn are ready to leave."

"Then you'd best agree quickly with Clarisse on a good day to ride again." Instead of leaving the ladies to talk alone, he stood to the side. He'd have a word with his cousin while walking with her to their carriage.

"Could we meet on Wednesday again?" Angelique beamed at her friend.

His cousin's expectant expression reminded him of a child anticipating her birthday, which was coming later this month. He shoved aside thoughts of what kind of party she might want or the guests she'd like to celebrate with.

"Um, Thursday would be better for me this week if you don't mind."

Clarisse's smile didn't look completely genuine. Which didn't make sense after the way she'd talked about enjoying Angelique's company. He'd have to puzzle over that later. "We should go since Father and Mother are waiting on us." He doffed his hat to Clarisse. "Thank you for clarifying why Eugenia eloped."

He cupped Angelique's elbow in his hand and propelled her toward the parked carriages. "Clarisse and I are childhood friends and nothing more. You didn't see what you supposed when you found us."

She laughed. "Then what did I see last Sunday when you talked with her alone?"

"Not at all what you're thinking. And nothing for you to tell anyone else since the gossip about Eugenia Hampton has not completely subsided." He didn't try to soften his brusque tone. His cousin needed to know how aggravated he was with her.

"Eugenia is the woman you and Mr. Parker both pursued?"

"Yes, and I don't like talking about her or him."

"Of course not. I left the two of you alone last week. I won't say anything about you and Clarisse talking again today."

Her impish grin made him wonder if she'd be quiet about seeing him with Clarisse. Or not.

Chapter Eight

Clarisse checked her appearance once more in her dresser mirror before walking out of her room. Donning her riding habit had been easier today, but being sure her hat was pinned on straight didn't matter. She was meeting Luke in the woods to tell him about her ride with Angelique. Nothing more.

Mama had left to make a call, and Titus had ridden to check the fields with his overseer, but she should tell someone she was going for a ride. She peeked into the parlor. Jenette sat on the couch, bent over her embroidery hoop. Her sister-in-law raised her head when Clarisse walked into the room.

"Are you riding with Angelique again?" Jenette's glowing smile showed her happiness with such an idea.

"Not today. After our outing last week, I realized I've missed the woods Eugenia and I so enjoyed. So, I'm going for a ride on what was one of our favorite trails today. I'll ride with Angelique on Thursday."

"Good. I'm happy to see you back to doing something you used to like so much." Jenette's expression sobered as she took a deep breath. "Garland would be happy to see you riding again, trying to live again. He would be proud of you."

Clarisse's breath caught at the mention of her beloved's name. "Do you think so?"

"Very proud." Jenette's eyes misted.

"Thank you." Unable to say more, Clarisse hugged Jenette and made her way to the front door.

When she walked to the barn, she didn't have to force herself to put one foot in front of the other as she'd done last week. Jenette's words of praise weren't spoken lightly. She had been close to Garland and understood her late brother well.

Except for her brother's change of heart about slavery while he was attending college at the North. After much prayer and soul searching, Garland had shared his newfound abolitionist views with Clarisse and Clarisse alone. That she had come to agree with Garland, she shared with no one.

Her grief over losing Garland wasn't the sole reason she had no interest in a romance with any local man. No planter's son would want a woman with her opinions on how his family kept their plantation running on the backs of slaves who deserved to be free. She might not be welcome in her own home if her family suspected her true feelings.

Setting aside her serious thoughts, she smiled at Theophilus as he led her horse from the barn. "Thank you."

Not long after guiding Merry onto the trail leading from their house, she spotted Luke riding toward her as he rounded the bend. He raised his hand in greeting. She returned his salute with one of her own. Meeting a man who wanted nothing to do with her romantically was safe for her heart in so many ways.

"Good afternoon." He guided his horse alongside hers. "Again, I appreciate your willingness to keep our meeting a secret."

"You're welcome." His warm smile emphasized his gratitude. Much better than the way he'd scowled at her weeks ago when she'd delivered Eugenia's note of apology. She welcomed this return to the easy friendship they'd enjoyed since he and Titus had played together as boys.

"You have something to tell me about your ride with Angelique?" He cocked his head while waiting for her reply.

"Nothing I couldn't have said quickly after church if there hadn't been other people too close by."

"And if my cousin hadn't interrupted us." He swatted at a spider web hanging from the branch overhead. "She saw us talking together the Sunday before too. Since neither of my parents has mentioned us visiting after church, I think she's kept her word about not saying anything about us."

"That's good." A cardinal sang from a nearby tree. Company she didn't mind. Not that she minded the man riding beside her since he truly was an old friend. "After Mr. Parker left us, I suggested Angelique should invite him to church. Eugenia had said the man wants nothing to do with God, so he'll probably lose interest in Angelique as soon as she invites him to come to church."

"I daresay you're right. That was a brilliant idea for Angelique to discover for herself the truth about the kind of man he is." He smiled straight into her eyes.

"I hope so." She glanced down as she guided Merry around a fallen log. How she wished Garland was the one looking at her with such a delighted expression. "The man had Angelique's rapt attention with every disarming word he spoke."

"I gathered that from our family dinner conversation. She thoroughly enjoyed her ride with him and you." Luke's countenance sobered.

Clarisse laughed despite Luke's serious expression. "That's

amazing. I've never come so close to being rude in my life. I did my best to keep Mr. Parker from talking, even interrupting him at times."

Luke grinned as he shook his head at her. "I can't imagine you ever doing such a thing. Eugenia, yes, but ..." He looked away. "I-I didn't mean that the way it sounded."

"I know. Eugenia did what she had to do to try to fend off Mr. Parker."

He sucked in a shaky breath. "Yes, you do know. Which is why we must do what we can to protect my cousin. Thank you for helping her even when she doesn't see she needs it."

"I don't mind. That's why I told her we'd ride on Thursday this week. If Mr. Parker assumes Angelique rides with me on Wednesdays, perhaps he'll call on her another day. Thursday would be excellent, don't you think?"

The light returned to his blue eyes. "Yes, it would be." He beamed at her. "You are a wonderful friend. The best kind of friend my cousin could have."

"Thank you." She focused her attention on a pair of gray squirrels chasing each other along the branches in front of them. Much better to watch their antics than think too deeply about the intensity of Luke's gaze when he'd said she was a wonderful friend before mentioning Angelique.

He took his reins in one hand before pulling his watch from his vest pocket. "I should return home unless you have more to tell me. I have ledgers to go over with Father if he's not still resting."

"I've nothing more to add." She welcomed him checking his watch. What others would consider rude while conversing with a lady was a good sign to her. He still must not want to be with her more than necessary.

"Then I'll wish you good day and head toward Oakridge." He tipped his hat before riding away.

Clarisse took her time returning home. She'd forgotten how peaceful riding alone through the woods could be. Inhaling the earthy scents while listening to the birds sing was a near-perfect way to enjoy an afternoon. Especially since no one was around to question why she preferred solitude to socializing. Other than Garland, Eugenia had been the one person who understood her. Perhaps Angelique would one day be as good a friend as Eugenia.

When Clarisse entered through the back door, Mama and Jenette's voices drifted from the parlor at the front of the house. Her mother was giving Jenette an enthusiastic-sounding report of her visit with Mrs. Parker this afternoon, in particular, how Alicia and Jonah planned to wed in August. Of course, the Matthews family was already invited.

Going upstairs to change clothes without greeting her family would be rude no matter how much she didn't want to hear the latest news about anyone with the surname of Parker. So much for her almost idyllic afternoon. She forced a smile as she stepped into the parlor.

"I hope you enjoyed your call, Mama. Would you send Ruth up to help me change?"

"Jenette tells me you went down one of your favorite trails and plan to ride with Angelique this week too. I'm glad to see you resuming your normal activities."

Clarisse smiled and nodded. "I'd like to change so I'll be ready for supper on time." She left before Mama could say more about happenings at the Parker house. Let Mama relish the wedding date news and how Clarisse was returning to a more normal life instead of thinking about why Clarisse hadn't yet mentioned her planned ride with Angelique. Or using this announcement as a time to hint her daughter should also renew her interest in finding a good husband one day.

By the time Clarisse walked into the dining room, the rest

of the family had taken their chairs. She'd postponed hearing more talk of the Parkers as long as possible. Mama's beaming smile included Clarisse, Jenette, and Titus the instant the last amen sounded after Titus said grace.

"As I was telling Jenette a while ago, the house Jonah started building last spring will be finished soon. He and Marissa plan to wed in August."

"That's wonderful news." Jenette cut a bite off her pork chop. "I won't be going out in public by then, but I'll be happy to give them my good wishes if Alicia wants to call on us."

Titus buttered a roll instead of looking at Mama. "As will I since I'll go to the wedding only if Jenette is feeling well."

"They'll all understand why Clarisse and I may be the only ones there from our family." Mama's smile never dimmed as she reached for her water goblet.

Clarisse popped a bite of sweet potato into her mouth to keep from saying anything. If only she had a valid excuse for missing the upcoming ceremony. But attending a wedding was better than enduring a ball that lasted late into the night with dance partners she had no interest in. Since the Williams family would probably be invited, Luke would be there, giving her one unattached man who would be safe to talk to.

No. She'd speak with him only if needed. The now dry-tasting sweet potato threatened to choke her. She gulped water from her goblet to wash it down and wash away any other unbidden thoughts of Luke.

* * *

THE INSTANT LUKE STEPPED INSIDE, female voices from the parlor greeted him.

"This will be the best birthday party of my life." Angelique's distinct giggle punctuated her words.

He shook his head. The words he'd dreaded hearing the night Angelique had come were especially troubling now with his concerns for her. He took his time wiping every speck of dust from his hat before hanging it on the hall tree.

Perhaps they were so engrossed in their plans he could slip past the parlor door and upstairs to speak to his father without them noticing. He peeked into the parlor from the edge of the doorway. The ladies huddled with their heads turned away from the doorway. He'd sneak past before either of them noticed him.

"Is that you, Luke?" Mother called to him just before he reached the bottom of the stairs.

"Yes, mother."

"I assume you're parched after your ride. Clara just brought in water from the well."

Respect and manners wouldn't allow him to ignore his mother's invitation. He trudged into the parlor. "A glass of cool water would taste good." He seated himself in the chair across from the couch his mother and cousin occupied.

"Aunt Evelyn says we should have a small early supper with a few friends then a ball later with almost the entire county invited for my birthday."

The look of sheer ecstasy on Angelique's face reminded him of his boundless happiness the day Father gave him his first knife. He'd grown to love her like a little sister. How he wanted to see her stay so genuinely happy.

"We should ask the Matthews family to dinner. You can tell Clarisse in person Thursday." Mother smiled as she patted Angelique's arm.

"I'll do that. We should also invite the Parkers for supper."

Mother's smile vanished. Luke gulped his water to keep from voicing his disapproval of his cousin's idea. He and Clarisse still had much work to do to reveal the true Alton

Parker. At least Clarisse would soon learn about the upcoming party from Angelique, giving her time to think about what to say or do to help protect her new friend. He'd take the time to do the same.

Angelique looked from Mother to Luke. "How can I ask Mr. Parker to come to church if I don't see him? Plus, we might be able to invite the entire family while they're here."

"I suppose you're right." Mother's still serious expression signaled the opposite of her words. "Since your uncle's health is so fragile, we should limit supper to those two families."

"That's a good idea." Luke emptied his water glass, then rose. "I'll leave the planning to you ladies. Father said he'd like to go over the ledgers with me this afternoon."

The sparkle returned to Mother's eyes. "He's feeling well enough today for that. Go upstairs and tell him you're home."

Father greeted Luke at the top of the stairs. "I heard you talking with the ladies. Let's go into my—*our*—office and look at the figures you wanted to show me."

"Yes, sir." Luke matched his steps to his father's as they descended the stairs, ignoring the corrected reference about the office. A law office was still the only one Luke wanted, but he wouldn't mention that and ruin Father's good day.

"If you need us, we'll be in our office." Father halted long enough to glance toward Mother and Angelique, still seated on the couch in the parlor.

"Thank you, dear." Mother nodded toward her husband.

Luke slid the pocket door closed while his father seated himself in the chair behind his desk. A sight Luke welcomed more than he dared say. "I assume you know about Mother and Angelique's plan for a birthday party."

Father nodded as he opened the drawer containing his ledger.

"Angelique wants to invite the Parkers to the small supper

before the ball." He took the chair across from Father as he went on to explain how she'd used the need to invite the family to church as her excuse to ask them to the dinner.

"Be glad she's not an attorney. A woman with such a sharp mind would be a formidable opponent in court." Father's eyes twinkled.

"Yes, she would. Which makes convincing her that Parker doesn't have her best interests in mind that much harder."

Father opened the ledger. "Along with her tender heart."

"Yes. I'm glad she's made one good choice befriending Clarisse."

"Might that lady also be a good choice for you?" Father smiled straight into Luke's eyes.

Luke forced himself not to look away. "Only as a friend I've known since childhood."

"That remains open to debate as much as the two of you appear to like talking to each other." He peered down to open the ledger on his desk.

Rather than respond, Luke swallowed his words of protest. Saying anything would probably make Father's misperceptions worse. He didn't want to know if his parents had somehow seen him talking to Clarisse after church or if Angelique had told them about it.

Either possibility meant the large oak tree in the churchyard hadn't shielded them from view as they'd supposed. Worse, the need to partner with Clarisse to watch over Angelique at her upcoming party would mean the whole county might as well be watching them that night.

Chapter Nine

Clarisse shielded her eyes from the afternoon sun as Mr. Parker turned his horse down the trail leading to his house. Oh, the joy he'd parted company with Angelique and her on their ride this Thursday afternoon the way he'd done last week. He twisted to wave one last time. Angelique waved back. Clarisse lifted her hand as the man rounded the bend and disappeared from their view.

"Shall I accompany you to your driveway again today?" She turned to look at Angelique, still grinning in the direction of her out-of-sight caller.

"I'd like that if you don't mind. I shouldn't be such a bother to you soon." Angelique turned her glowing smile in Clarisse's direction.

"You're a friend, not a bother."

"Thank you so much. It's been an exquisite afternoon with two friends."

"Exquisite?" Angelique's unique way of describing places or events amazed her. The flowers had danced last week.

Angelique laughed. "Yes. Perfectly wonderful is an inadequate depiction. Mr. Parker saying Marissa wants my family to come to her wedding is exquisite. Especially since I couldn't detect any animosity toward Luke from Mr. Parker."

Clarisse settled for a forced smile as her reply. How she longed for the day Angelique would allow Clarisse or Luke to tell her how duplicitous Mr. Parker could be. She sincerely doubted such a man had let go of his hard feelings toward Luke.

"Plus, I invited both of you to my upcoming birthday party and asked Mr. Parker to come to church and bring his family."

"Yes, exquisite does sound better." For entirely different reasons on Clarisse's part. She had again thwarted Mr. Parker's intentions of calling on Angelique and spending time alone with her in the Williams' parlor.

Angelique rode in the direction of Oakridge. Clarisse followed her.

"The crops needed rain, but I'm glad the rain came yesterday instead of today." Angelique waited until Clarisse came alongside her again to say more.

"So am I." Mr. Parker admitted he would have called on Angelique yesterday if not for the weather. An entirely different reason to be thankful for the rain. So good her sweet friend couldn't know her true thoughts. Yet she prayed for the day Angelique would want to know.

"As I told Aunt Evelyn, I'm going to have the best birthday I've ever had. Every guest will be happy to be there and genuinely happy for me."

"Yes, we will be."

Angelique's expression sobered as she dodged a low-hanging branch. "My father never hosted any event without using it to further business relationships. Or to find a prospective husband for me after I turned sixteen."

"I'm sorry." Clarisse straightened after leaving the low branch behind her.

"Thank you. Now I have a family much like yours." The sparkle returned to Angelique's eyes. "Not that my uncle and aunt don't want me to find a good husband, but they've both told me to pray for the right man. And waiting until I'm nineteen like you or later will be fine with them."

"That's good." If only Mama were as happy as Angelique assumed. Clarisse was too particular about potential spouses, according to her mother. But she wouldn't mention that or why she was so choosy. Voicing her opinions about slavery would probably cost her this new friendship and every other one she might forge.

She had the courage to form her own opinions but not the bravery to voice them. Only God knew how or when the right time to be completely truthful with everyone around her would come. Until then, she'd continue her silence.

"I'm so blessed with my new family. God is truly working something tragic for my good." Angelique's contented sigh floated into the quiet woods surrounding them.

"Yes, He is." The trail narrowed. Clarisse took the lead, glad she didn't have to say more. Being quiet by nature had its advantages. Her talkative new friend didn't act the least bit bothered about Clarisse's habit of saying little.

Angelique chattered on about her party the rest of the way. Her aunt insisted on a new gown for her. Their seamstress was already working on it. "Could we ride again next week? Monday or Tuesday would be better for me since my new dress should be ready to try on sometime after that." She halted her horse near the stone pillar marking the beginning of her driveway.

"Let's meet on Monday." Clarisse would save Tuesday for riding with Luke if necessary. No. She should change her mind this instant and choose Tuesday. But she couldn't. Just in case Luke might have something important to tell her.

"Excellent. I hope we'll be able to talk about seeing the entire Parker family at church." Angelique flashed Clarisse a glowing smile.

"Until Sunday." Clarisse waved as she turned Merry back onto the trail.

Clarisse prayed for Angelique the remainder of her ride home. She truly would like to see Mr. Parker and his family sitting in a church pew. Everyone needed to hear about God's love for them. Miracles did happen. Which would be so much better than seeing her sweet friend's hopes dashed to pieces.

With Angelique still on her mind, she walked toward the house. The sight of Titus and Jenette strolling hand in hand at the edge of Mama's flower garden brought her back to her current surroundings. Each gazed so intently at the other that neither of them realized she was less than fifty feet away. Their quiet words spoken only to each other didn't carry to her ears well enough to make out what they were discussing. Rather than interrupt their moment, she stepped behind the trunk of a large oak.

How she wished for someone to concentrate only on her the way Titus did with Jenette. She sucked in a shaky breath as she slumped against the tree to keep from losing her balance. Where had such an unbidden idea come from?

She closed her eyes, willing her mind to clear. She still loved Garland. Would always love him. But Jenette said she was sure he'd be happy Clarisse was riding again, living again. Did living again include finding a new love? The more she pondered such an idea, the more certain she was an unselfish man like Garland wouldn't expect her to never love again.

She sighed. Even a good man like Luke would never be more than a friend if he so much as suspected her inmost thoughts. He valued the family plantation enough he'd left college and set aside his own plans to help his ailing father run things. She never wanted to be the mistress of such a place. Plus, she'd helped Eugenia to elope. Luke would not ever want or love her.

Her eyes jerked open. She straightened. Why had Luke come to mind? Especially since being more than his friend was impossible. She peeked around the tree toward the flower garden. Titus and Jenette were not in sight.

She marched toward the house. The sooner she could get her mind on something else, the better off she'd be. Mama, Titus, and Jenette's voices drifted from the parlor when she walked into the dining room. If she were quiet, she could slip upstairs without being noticed. Sorting through her jarring thoughts about renewed love and Luke had left her in no mood for talking to anyone.

Mama stepped into the hall just as Clarisse reached the bottom of the stairs. "Did you enjoy your ride with Angelique?"

"I did. Would you please send Ruth up to help me change?"

"Of course. I'll look forward to hearing about your pleasant afternoon at dinner."

Clarisse smiled and headed upstairs, thankful for a good way to postpone conversation. She needed time alone to consider the wayward longings that had overwhelmed her while watching Titus and Jenette.

She sighed as she stepped into her room. No man in Rutherford County would have a woman with her beliefs. Wishing for something different would only cause her pain. Better to resign herself to spinsterhood.

* * *

Luke stood at the outside of the family pew, waiting for Angelique and his parents to slip into their seats. His cousin paused next to him, allowing Mother then Father to seat themselves instead of taking her usual spot by the window. He motioned for her to precede him, glad society demanded a lady sit first. As excited as she'd been to invite the Parker family to church, she'd probably spend much of her time watching for them instead of preparing for worship.

His prayer that her tender heart wouldn't be crushed this morning was genuine. No matter his opinion of one Parker in particular, the entire family needed to hear about the Lord. That he could sincerely pray for his former rival had to be a miracle from God Himself. Achieving his goal to become an attorney would take another act of God. Waiting while not losing heart got harder with each passing day, especially since he'd left college a full year ago.

The Matthews family filed into their pew across the aisle, bringing his thoughts back to the present. Instead of her usual discreet, half-smile, Clarisse beamed as their eyes met. No. Her ear-to-ear grin had to be aimed at Angelique. Not him. Better to focus his attention on the stained-glass windows at the front of the church. He'd come to worship the Lord, not to be noticed by Clarisse or any other woman.

Angelique spent the next several minutes peering around him, trying not to look too obvious about what she was doing. With their pew toward the middle, she wouldn't be able to see who sat in the back without making a spectacle of herself. Pastor Bentley walked up to the pulpit. She straightened her drooping shoulders and stared straight ahead. When they rose to sing "*Rock of Ages,*" her voice faltered at times.

Caring about someone's spiritual well-being was admirable. But unless Parker changed for the better, his sweet cousin might be endangering more than her heart. He prayed again for a way to convince Angelique not to want to see the rogue again.

When the service ended, Angelique rose. The instant she

stepped into the aisle, she turned to see who was behind them, blocking Mother and Father from exiting the pew.

"I don't see him, dear." Mother placed her hand on Angelique's arm. "I'm sorry."

"Thank you."

Luke allowed his family to greet the pastor, then precede him outside. His parents halted in the shade to visit with a couple of neighbors. He followed his still-silent cousin to an oak not far from their parked carriage. Strange, how Clarisse hadn't tried to get his attention to signal if they needed to find a secluded place to talk. He fought to smile only on the inside when she walked toward him and Angelique.

"I assume we're still going for a ride tomorrow?" Clarisse halted beside Angelique and focused her attention on her friend.

"Yes. I'd like that." Angelique's expression brightened. "Luke, won't you join us?"

No. He shouldn't. One quick look at Clarisse changed his mind. She might have something to tell him that she could hint about tomorrow. "Only if you ladies talk about more than ball gowns and parties. If not, I'd rather fall off my horse than listen to such topics."

Clarisse's face paled.

He couldn't have had a worse moment to blurt out words without thinking, especially since she'd witnessed her fiancé's fatal riding accident.

Clarisse ducked her head, but were those tears she was blinking away?

"Please forgive me for my tactless remark." Luke held his breath as he waited for her to acknowledge his apology.

An eternity later, she glanced up at him. Pain still evident in her solemn, brown eyes, she nodded. Mrs. Matthews walked past them on the way to her carriage. Clarisse stared in her mother's direction. "I'll see you tomorrow." She followed her mother.

Shaking her head, Angelique's eyes followed her retreating friend. "Please explain." She kept her voice soft while the Matthews' driver helped Clarisse into the carriage. "What caused my dear friend such pain?"

"Her fiancé died from a terrible accident. His horse missed a jump over a hedge and threw him. He died moments after he hit the ground. Clarisse was riding with him and saw everything."

Angelique gasped. "How awful."

"It was. From what Mrs. Matthews has told Mother, Clarisse hadn't been in a saddle since that day until she rode with you."

"Oh, my." Her eyes widened.

"She must think a lot of you." Much more than she now thought of him as careless as he'd been with his words.

Angelique turned her regard back to Luke as the Matthews carriage departed. "Yes, she must. God has gifted me with a very special friend."

"He has. She's very special." Something else he shouldn't have said. The smile spreading across Angelique's face confirmed his mistake.

"I'm sure she is a *very* special friend to you." Angelique tossed the teasing words at him before heading toward their carriage.

Luke matched his steps to hers. Refuting her hint would make her tease him more. Plus, he had more important things to caution her about to help prevent Clarisse from enduring more pain. "Please don't tell anyone about my flippant words or how I accidentally hurt Clarisse. She wouldn't want someone bringing up Garland's accident, no matter how they might frame the conversation."

"I understand."

"Thank you."

During the carriage ride home, his parents talked about the pastor's wonderful sermon about God's indescribable peace without any mention of the Parker family's absence. Angelique intently listened to her aunt and uncle—so much so that she said little.

Luke added a few words occasionally, lest anyone guess his true thoughts were focused elsewhere. He prayed the verses about peace that passed understanding would comfort Clarisse despite how his insensitive words must have dredged up such terrible memories for her.

Since Angelique had kept her word and not mentioned Clarisse during the entire ride home, Luke walked into the dining room, ready to enjoy lunch. While Father said grace, Luke sent up another prayer for consolation for the friend he'd so recklessly wounded.

"I so appreciate all of you understanding my concern for the Parkers despite your low opinion of their son." Angelique directed her smile to all of them as she passed the platter of ham to Luke.

"You're welcome, dear." Mother ducked her head to butter her bread.

"I'm praying I have another opportunity tomorrow to invite Mr. Parker to church."

Father's hand paused halfway to his water goblet as he focused his attention on Angelique. "Do you have plans to see him tomorrow that we don't know about?"

She shook her head. "Oh, no, sir. But I'm praying he joins Clarisse, Luke, and I on our ride."

"I see." Father gulped his water as if he were parched from a summer day's walk.

Mother's silver eyebrows arched as she smiled toward Luke. "You're riding with Angelique tomorrow?"

"Perhaps." He ducked his head, pretending an immense interest in what would now be the tasteless food on his plate.

"I'm sure Clarisse is looking forward to you joining us." Angelique pointed her spoon at him the instant he lifted his eyes toward her.

Since he'd just put a forkful of carrots in his mouth, Luke shrugged. He doubted Clarisse was looking forward to seeing him tomorrow or any other day. Angelique must realize that too. Did she hope to help him make amends with Clarisse, or did she have other motives? Probably both since Parker had joined her and Clarisse more than once.

"You must come. Three of us inviting Mr. Parker to church might be very persuasive if we see him tomorrow."

"You could be right." Mother's grin included Angelique and Luke.

By the time the meal ended, Angelique had set her trap so well that Luke would have no choice but to ride with her and Clarisse. If Clarisse galloped her horse toward home the instant she spied him, he wouldn't blame her.

Chapter Ten

Clarisse rode toward the trail to Oakridge, eager to see Angelique while not looking forward to possibly seeing Mr. Parker. She prayed he wouldn't join them. Since they hadn't ridden on a Monday yet, he might think today would be a good day to see Angelique alone in her parlor. Her goal to talk with Angelique about not seeing Mr. Parker in church couldn't be accomplished if the man she wanted to discuss joined them.

She sucked in her breath as she caught sight of two riders rounding the bend a few yards ahead of her. Despite the trees obscuring them from full view, she had no doubt Luke was the man riding with Angelique. So much for time alone with her new friend. Unless Angelique might listen better if she and Luke both tried to reason with her about Mr. Parker.

"Good afternoon." Angelique halted her horse next to Clarisse. "I assume you don't mind if Luke rides with us."

"Not at all." Clarisse was sure her smile included Luke. She didn't mind reassuring him she'd accepted his apology yesterday.

"Thank you." Luke relaxed his grip on the reins.

Angelique shifted in her saddle. "I'd like to ride to the creek and the beautiful meadow we went to the first time Mr. Parker joined us."

"That is a beautiful place. Do I need to lead the way?" Clarisse worked to keep her tone pleasant, sure that Angelique had chosen one of Mr. Parker's favorite spots, hoping to do more than enjoy a ride with only Clarisse and Luke.

"I'm getting better at knowing where I am, but you should probably lead."

Clarisse turned her horse toward the desired destination. The day couldn't come soon enough when her sweet friend dreaded coming across Mr. Parker as much as Clarisse did.

"If we see Mr. Parker today, I'm hoping that three of us inviting him to church might help persuade him to come."

Angelique's words knifed Clarisse's conscience. Regardless of her opinion of the man, God loved him. Mr. Parker needed to know that life-changing truth. But she still didn't want to see the man who had intended to marry Eugenia only for her dowry. She'd talk to the Lord about her feelings later.

Or not.

Mr. Parker himself came into view the instant they rounded the next bend.

"Mr. Parker, how nice to see you." Angelique spoke from behind Clarisse. Her happy tone couldn't be missed.

"I'm glad to see you too." The man glanced past Clarisse, aiming his thin smile at Angelique. His hard eyes betrayed his displeasure at seeing her companions.

"We're heading to the meadow you like so well. Please join us." Angelique guided her horse alongside Clarisse.

"I'd be delighted." He tipped his hat toward both women.

"As would I." Angelique beamed at him.

"Since we have two excellent chaperones, I'd like very

much to ride next to you where possible." His subtle gaze scanned more than Angelique's face.

Her cheeks colored. Without a glance at her friends, she urged her horse alongside Mr. Parker. Luke rode up next to Clarisse. His stiff posture and clenched jaw all but shouted his displeasure.

"I'm also looking forward to seeing you at your birthday celebration next week." Mr. Parker stared so intently at Angelique, he barely ducked in time to miss a low-hanging branch.

Before Angelique could reply to Mr. Parker's remark, Clarisse said the first thing that came to mind, "As am I. I can hardly wait to see your new gown." If Luke didn't want to hear about new dresses, perhaps Mr. Parker wouldn't want to either. She'd be as annoying as possible. Luke shouldn't mind that, considering the circumstances.

Angelique laughed. "It's going to be the prettiest one I've ever had."

As they continued on the trail, Clarisse inserted inane comments or interruptions as she'd done on their previous rides. The way Luke grinned over at her whenever they were side by side signaled he appreciated her rude efforts.

"Oh, it's just as beautiful as the last time." Angelique reined in her horse when they reached the edge of the meadow, still decorated with flowers, waving grass, and sunshine.

Mr. Parker halted beside her. "Yes, it is." He smiled straight into Angelique's sparkling eyes.

"God's beauty never ceases to amaze me." Luke guided his horse to the other side of Angelique.

Mr. Parker's body stiffened at Luke's mention of God, but his taut smile didn't fade.

"Some of my favorite places to pray are outdoors." Clarisse

stopped on the other side of Luke, rather than end up too near Mr. Parker.

"Mine too." Angelique continued looking over the scene.

"Riding in the shade along the creek should feel good today." Mr. Parker urged his horse forward without waiting for anyone to agree with him.

If Angelique noticed the man's quick change of subject, her expression didn't show it. Her smile never dimmed as she came up alongside him. Clarisse and Luke trailed behind them. She worked to keep her expression pleasant. Judging by Luke's tight grip on his reins, he was fighting the same battle.

As if by unspoken mutual agreement, she and Luke continued mentioning God whenever possible as they rode along the creek. By the time they were in the woods again, Mr. Parker's stiff smile looked as if he'd painted it on.

The man halted his horse as they reached the trail leading to his house. "I'll bid you all good day."

"I'm looking forward to seeing you at my party. I'd be even happier to visit with you after church and hear your opinion of the pastor's sermon." Angelique's kind, pleading brown eyes should melt Mr. Parker's heart.

The cad's expression sobered as he gazed toward the trail in front of him.

"Yes, we'd all like to hear what you think," Luke spoke up as Mr. Parker tightened his reins.

"Indeed, we would," Clarisse added her words. The best she could do at the moment, no matter how much Angelique might wish for a more enthusiastic invitation.

"Perhaps one day. Good afternoon." He tipped his hat to Angelique before heading his horse onto the trail.

Angelique sighed as she stared at Mr. Parker's retreating form. Then shifted to look at Clarisse. "Thank you for trying to help me."

"You're welcome."

They rode in silence until they neared the trail to home. Angelique reined in her horse. "I'm glad I'll see you Sunday."

"I'm always happy to see you too."

"Thank you. I'd dearly like to know why Mr. Parker isn't interested in God."

Clarisse shrugged. "Who knows what his reasons are? Eugenia's father still refuses to see his need for God."

"Perhaps I'll ask him why the next time I see him."

Perhaps not. Clarisse swallowed the words Luke's serious expression signaled he'd also like to say aloud since neither of them wanted her to see the man again. "I'll bid you goodbye since you have Luke to ride home with."

"Enjoy the rest of your ride." Angelique smiled at her as Clarisse turned Merry onto the trail to Hopeton.

"Clarisse, wait. Please." Luke stared straight at his cousin as Clarisse halted her mare. "You can surely find your way home alone now and allow me a short time with Clarisse."

Angelique's laughter pealed through the woods. "Of course, I can."

Luke shifted to look into Clarisse's eyes. "May I escort you home?"

"Well, uh, I'm accustomed to riding to Hopeton alone with no problem. I—"

"But not today." Angelique cut off the remainder of Clarisse's intended protest. "Refusing the offer of such a good *friend* would be absurd."

"All right." Clarisse doubted she could have refused Luke after looking into his pleading eyes anyway. Perhaps agreeing only after Angelique's prodding would emphasize her continued desire for Luke's friendship and nothing more.

* * *

Luke rode next to Clarisse, rejoicing in silence, until he was sure his cousin was too far away to hear their conversation. His apology yesterday hadn't been adequate. She deserved better, regardless of how much Angelique might tease him later about him seeing Clarisse home. "Thank you for being so gracious after how I hurt you yesterday. I didn't think before I spoke."

"We've been friends long enough for me to know that."

"I suppose we have, but I do appreciate you forgiving me so readily. Another reason I've come to admire you since you started helping me protect Angelique." A compliment he shouldn't have said. He'd asked for this time alone to offer a better apology and thank her for befriending his cousin. Nothing more.

"You've come to admire me?"

"I have." Her wide-eyed look of surprise was quite becoming. The trail narrowed. He allowed her to precede him while he redirected his wayward thoughts back to what he wanted to tell her. "As I was saying …" he glanced over at her as he came up alongside her again. "Angelique says God has gifted her with an amazing friend. I agree."

She shook her head.

The more awestruck her expression, the prettier she looked as she continued to stare at him. "I can't imagine how hard it must have been for you to ride with Angelique. But you set all that aside in order to help someone you barely knew. I'd call such a selfless act admirable. "

"I hadn't and don't think of it like that." Her expression sobered as she glanced toward the trees at the edge of the trail. "Angelique has become a precious friend. I don't want Mr. Parker to deceive her any more than he has."

"For that, I thank you too." As quickly as she changed the subject back to Angelique, she must not want to talk about why she hadn't ridden in so long. "Especially since the more we're seen together, the more people are going to assume our childhood friendship is turning into something more serious."

"Which makes me wonder why you're escorting me this afternoon when Angelique will go straight to your parents with the news we're riding together alone?"

Her direct gaze probably meant to demand an answer served instead to emphasize her beauty. Her deep red-wine-colored habit was perfect for her expressive brown eyes and black hair. Worthy of a painting done by the best of artists. He sucked in a breath as he refocused his thoughts. "Would you want anyone to overhear me tell you I have such high regard for you?"

"No."

A pair of gray squirrels scampered across the branch ahead of them. She diverted her attention toward the chattering animals. A most welcome interruption for him. Perhaps for her. He'd wanted to thank her and praise her, but he hadn't intended to not be able to take his eyes off her as he explained himself.

"We have created an unintended problem for ourselves trying to help Angelique." She guided her horse around the next bend, again taking the lead a moment.

"A problem we can't solve until after we convince my sweet cousin we have good reason not to trust Parker."

"True." She reined in her mare by the brown brick pillars marking her driveway. "I'll bid you good day. If we ride much farther, someone in my family might also see us together."

Luke shrugged. "Can you imagine my mother not telling your mother about our ride after church on Sunday?"

"No."

"Then I might as well accompany you down your drive, don't you think?" How could he have blurted out such a thing? Surely, she'd refuse him since they were only friends.

"Um ..." She licked her lips as she focused on some point ahead of her for much longer than he wished. If she were going to refuse him, he'd like for her to do so more quickly. "Allowing people to think we might be fond of each other will make it look more natural for us to be together while watching over Angelique at her party next week."

"Yes, it should." He shouldn't have agreed at all, especially not in an instant.

She urged her horse toward the drive. Instead of galloping his horse in the other direction the way he should, he rode alongside her. What had come over him? He must not take leave of his senses like this again.

As they approached the house, Titus and Jenette glanced up from the chairs they occupied on the front porch. Their broad smiles left no doubt how happy they were to see him with Clarisse. Luke halted his horse next to a chestnut tree and raised his hand in greeting. Clarisse reined in her mare.

"We've definitely achieved our goal to look more natural together." He forced the words from his dry throat.

"We have. Sooner and better than I'd intended."

Her clipped tone might signal she regretted her decision as much as he lamented his. He hoped so. "I'll bid you goodbye before someone wonders if I might be courting you."

The color drained from her face. "A good idea. I'll see you Sunday."

He tipped his hat to her before turning his mount away from the house. Away from her. Let her think how to explain to Titus and Jenette they hadn't seen what they'd assumed. He'd need his solitary ride home to concoct his own story.

After leaving his horse with the groom, Luke took his time entering the house. He paused as he walked in the back door. No voices came from the parlor or anywhere else in the front of the house. Angelique was probably changing clothes. Father might be resting. If he were careful, he could make his way upstairs to his room and not have to face anyone until time for supper.

Once inside his room, he slumped against the closed door. He still had no idea how to explain or excuse his ride with Clarisse. The ride he'd asked for, and she'd agreed to. What had come over him? He had no idea. Wasn't sure he wanted to figure it out. What he did know? He'd never risk being betrayed by a woman again. Which meant he must be much more careful with Clarisse than he'd been this afternoon.

The instant he entered the dining room, Father's eyes twinkled. Mother beamed at him. He should have been the first one to the table, not the last. Another mistake.

"Angelique told us you saw Clarisse home." Mother's smile intensified as Luke seated himself across the table from his grinning cousin.

"I did. I'll explain after we pray."

Everyone stared at him as soon as Father finished asking the blessing.

"I made a casual remark about falling off my horse after church while Angelique and I were talking to Clarisse. I needed time with her to apologize better than I did yesterday. She graciously forgave me."

"Of course she did." Angelique grinned across the table at him as she took the bowl of green beans Mother passed to her. "As you said, God has gifted us with a very special friend."

No. He hadn't said exactly that. But pointing out the truth wouldn't do any good. Everything he'd done this afternoon shouted louder than any denial he could utter. "Did you get a chance to mention we all tried to encourage Parker to come to church?"

"Not yet." Her eyes shone as she told Father and Mother

about seeing Parker, plus how Clarisse and Luke had helped her encourage the man to come to church.

Luke didn't think he'd ever been happier to listen to a conversation about Alton Parker. Anything was better than giving his family more time to discuss how he'd escorted Clarisse home. His explanation about wanting to apologize must have been a sufficient excuse.

He still needed to determine a satisfactory reason to explain the afternoon to himself. He'd said much more than he planned. Much more than he should have.

Clarisse took in more than one deep breath as she followed her family up the porch steps. The Parkers' carriage was already in the driveway when the Matthews family arrived. Another evening to endure Mr. Parker's presence for Angelique's sake. The man had not come to church again. She'd done her best to commiserate with Angelique after the service. Tonight, that wouldn't be necessary.

Avoiding Luke as much as possible was what was essential. He'd visited with other friends after church, leaving her to talk with Angelique alone, which probably puzzled her family after Luke had seen her home last week. But no more than she'd confounded herself for allowing Luke to escort her. She'd never know true happiness with any planter's son. So, enjoying Luke's company the way she'd done that day must not happen again.

"Welcome, dear friends." Mrs. Williams greeted them as soon as the butler opened the door. Mr. Williams extended his hand to Titus. Angelique and Luke stood with them.

Angelique enveloped Clarisse in a hug as her aunt and

uncle greeted Mama, Jenette, and Titus. "I'm so glad you're here."

"So am I." Clarisse returned her friend's smile as soon as she stepped back.

"We can visit with the Parkers in the parlor for a few minutes. Marissa couldn't come. She's spending the evening with Jonah's family but her parents and Alton are here." Mrs. Williams led the way, minus her customary smile.

With only enough seating for the ladies, the men stood, leaving the younger Mr. Parker to hover near the chairs Angelique and Clarisse chose across from the couch. Luke positioned himself much closer to Clarisse than she wished.

"Your gown is exquisite. The moss green silk with the ivory sash looks perfect on you." Clarisse offered her genuine compliment, just as Mr. Parker opened his mouth.

"Thank you. Aunt Evelyn suggested the color."

The loving look Angelique exchanged with her aunt warmed Clarisse to her very soul. Judging from her friend's glowing smile, she wondered if Angelique was almost too happy to sit still. A much-needed reminder that suffering through a formal meal and a ball all in one day was worth the trouble.

The butler soon stepped in to tell Mrs. Williams dinner was ready to serve. She rose. "Shall we go to the dining room now?"

Mr. Parker extended his arm to Angelique. Smiling into his eyes, she placed her hand on his sleeve. Luke offered his arm to Clarisse. Her barely upturned lips couldn't compare to Angelique's broad grin, but Luke didn't look offended. Good. She didn't want a repeat of the almost adoring looks he'd given her at times during their ride last week.

Mrs. Williams seated her next to Angelique, with Jenette on Clarisse's other side. After the ladies were seated, Luke and Mr. Parker took their places across the table from them. Not the arrangement Clarisse would have chosen. But the way Mr. Parker clenched then unclenched his jaw when Titus took the chair next to him seemed to signal the rogue disliked his hostess's choices more than Clarisse did. Luke's clever mother was doing her best to surround Mr. Parker with as few admirers as possible.

With so many people at the table, conversation flowed as swiftly as a bank-full creek after a rain. Clarisse could say enough to be polite without anyone wondering why she was so quiet. The usually loquacious Mr. Parker had a hard time putting in more than a sentence or two at a time. Her meal tasted much better than she'd anticipated.

After their early supper, the men congregated in the library. The ladies went upstairs to check their hair and dresses. Clarisse and Jenette followed Angelique to her room.

"This is the absolute best night of my life." Angelique twirled in the middle of the room like a giddy child.

"We're glad you're so happy." Jenette smiled as she walked over to the cheval mirror in the corner.

The three of them visited until time to go downstairs and wait for the other guests to arrive. Angelique soon joined her family in the entry hall to greet people. Clarisse followed the others back to the dining room with chairs now arranged around the wall and the table laden with punch and cakes.

"Would any of you ladies like refreshments?" Titus stood next to Jenette's chair as he made his offer to Clarisse and Mama.

"Only some punch." Jenette employed her almost ever-present fan.

Mama watched the other people entering the room. "I don't want anything right now."

"Neither do I." Clarisse kept her eye on Mr. Parker without appearing too obvious.

The cad remained standing not far from where his parents were seated. As the room filled with people, he showed little interest in the other single ladies. Possibly for good reason. Since Clarisse didn't notice any unattached woman gazing his direction, she couldn't help wondering if someone had been spreading gossip about the man. Which, in his case, would be true if it concerned his gambling and debts. Luke hadn't been the only man Mr. Parker struggled to repay.

After the last guest arrived, Luke wasted no time stationing himself by Clarisse. Mr. Williams rose. "Our family is honored to have everyone here tonight. We are thrilled you've come to help our dear Angelique celebrate her eighteenth birthday. We thank God for sending her to us and for giving us so many friends."

The instruments soon began the music for the first dance. Luke extended his hand to Clarisse. "May I?"

"Yes, you may." She placed her hand in his long enough to stand as Mama beamed her direction.

How unlike the last ball she'd attended. She'd danced with Luke then only to appease her mother. Tonight, she walked into the parlor, her hand resting on his sleeve without an ounce of trepidation. Mama and everyone else could think whatever they liked. She and Luke had a purpose her family and his would be proud to support if they had any idea about the pact they'd made. They'd have to deal with people's other misconceptions about them later. How? She wasn't sure. She'd concern herself with that problem another time.

"Angelique requested a waltz. She says it's her favorite." He took her hand in his as he led her onto the floor of the parlor turned ballroom.

"I'm sure Mr. Parker won't mind holding her hand a while." She kept her voice low, lest someone overhear her sarcastic tone.

Luke nodded. "Your idea to be seen together more was a good one. I haven't seen a single arched brow whenever anyone looks our way. Perhaps Angelique won't be so suspicious if they step outside, and we follow them again."

"I hadn't considered that." Or how she didn't have to pretend to enjoy moving to the music with Luke, his fingers lightly resting on the small of her back. Being seen more with him might have been a good idea. But standing with him in the night shadows on the porch wouldn't be good for her wayward heart. Yet, if they were to continue watching over Angelique, she and Luke would have to follow his cousin and Mr. Parker outside, if necessary.

Moments after the musicians played the final notes, Jonah Browning's brother Amos claimed Angelique. Exactly what she and Luke wanted. His broad smile indicated his agreement.

"Would you do me the honor, Miss Matthews?" Travis Glynne, the local attorney's son, appeared at her side from where she couldn't say. Being so focused on Angelique that she hadn't noticed him was all right. But not seeing him because she'd been concentrating so much on Luke as he gazed into her eyes was totally wrong.

"I'd be delighted. "She forced a smile.

The music for the next dance began. She allowed him to lead her onto the floor. Away from Luke and the other woman he'd asked to dance. To her utter delight, Mr. Parker ended up with his mother as a partner. Mr. Glynne asked Angelique for the third dance, leaving Mr. Parker adrift and standing at the edge of the room, watching the other couples. Her vivacious friend shouldn't lack for callers after tonight. The pattern repeated itself once more before Mr. Parker managed to ask Angelique for another dance. When the music ended, he guided her toward the front door onto the porch.

"Would you like to get some fresh air?" Luke smiled down at her.

"Yes, I would." She placed her hand on his sleeve as they walked toward the door. No one in the room appeared surprised to see them leave the parlor together. Their ruse was working well. Too well.

Luke all but slammed the door shut as they walked onto the shadowy porch, looking to see where Angelique and Mr. Parker had stopped. The sliver of a moon provided just enough light to see Mr. Parker's hand drop from Angelique's shoulder.

Clarisse walked with Luke to the opposite end of the porch from where his cousin stood. They halted with her back almost to the other couple, allowing Luke to face her and see his cousin at the same time.

"We came out here at just the right time," Luke whispered almost in her ear as he leaned his head toward her.

His nearness made her breath catch. She concentrated on the reason she and Luke had come outside instead of the shivers running up and down her spine. "We did. He was too forward with Eugenia from the day they met."

"I don't doubt it."

Matching Luke's low tones, she mentioned how some of the other ladies looked to be as reluctant to dance with Mr. Parker as she would be. "I can't help wondering if someone has been talking about him."

"More than one of the men he bragged to has female relatives they might have warned about him."

As Luke had been kind enough to do with Eugenia, but she wouldn't bring up a memory that probably still pained him. "Any number of people could have said something about him by now."

"Yes, that's—"

"We're going back in the house, dear cousin. You won't have to whisper your sweet endearments to Clarisse any longer." Angelique's teasing tone dripped with sarcasm as she and Mr. Parker stepped toward the door. When Mr. Parker's hand touched the knob, she halted to look directly at Clarisse and Luke. "Unless we should stay out here to properly chaperone the two of you?"

"We'll be fine. Go enjoy the ball you wanted so badly."

"Oh, I will."

As warm as her face felt, Clarisse had never been so thankful for an almost moonless night. Sweet endearments? She and Luke had more misperceptions to untangle than they'd planned once they succeeded in rescuing Angelique.

* * *

Luke groaned as he bent to splash water from his basin onto his face. The yawning man facing him in the washstand mirror appeared to be half asleep. No more rest than he'd managed last night, his mattress might as well have been stuffed with pebbles instead of feathers. He had important things to do today and needed to be alert and look his best.

But thoughts of Clarisse and how much he'd enjoyed her company last night had robbed him of sleep. Like Eugenia, Clarisse wanted nothing more than his friendship and had said so often. Yet he'd enjoyed her company much more than he should. He dare not make the mistakes with Clarisse he'd made with Eugenia. One heartbreak was more than enough. He wouldn't risk another one with Clarisse or any other woman.

By the time he walked into the dining room for breakfast, he'd banished any wayward thoughts of Clarisse. Father seated Mother. Luke pulled out Angelique's chair and then stepped around the table to take his spot. "Your birthday party was more successful than you'd hoped."

"It was. I'm so thankful for my wonderful new family." Her glowing smile included everyone

"We're all glad you're here." Father bowed his head. He thanked God for their meal and for bringing Angelique to Oakridge. "I expect you'll want a restful day after dancing with so many men last night." Father's eyes twinkled as he passed the platter of biscuits to Angelique.

"I don't have plans for today." She ducked her head as she buttered her bread.

"Nor do I. But I'm so happy you had such a wonderful night." Mother passed the platter of eggs to Luke.

"After being with so many people last night, I'm going to enjoy a solitary ride to Murfreesboro and pick up the mail." Luke ladled eggs onto his plate. "I didn't get a chance to tell you last night that Travis said his father has been quite ill."

Mother's fork paused in midair. "I'm amazed he didn't mention that about Adam to your father or me."

"Travis was much more interested in dancing with Angelique. We spoke for only minutes." Luke grinned at his cousin. How nice to tease *her* for a change. Better still, he could mention a good man who deserved her attention.

"I don't doubt that." Father gave Angelique an indulgent smile.

Angelique bit into her biscuit rather than reply. Which might or might not be good. Luke would be sure to tell her later what a fine man Travis was.

"Mr. Glynne is feeling better. He almost died from pneumonia. His recovery has been slow. Travis is now running their plantation. That's why he was close enough to come to Angelique's ball last night."

"We'll pray for Adam." Mother cut up a piece of bacon.

"I'll check on him and give him our regards after I see if we have mail." Luke focused his attention on his food. He wouldn't tell anyone about the note Travis had delivered to him from his father.

"As warm as this morning already is, you may wish you'd picked a different day." Father reached for his water goblet.

"Perhaps. But I haven't ridden for the mail in a while, and I'd like to see how Mr. Glynne is doing."

Luke left a short time later. Clarisse hadn't been the only person he'd talked with outside last night. Travis had come to do more than celebrate Angelique's birthday. The short letter from Mr. Glynne asked Luke to help him temporarily while he finished recuperating.

Thus the need for a quiet trip to Murfreesboro alone. He prayed for wisdom and guidance as he rode. Mr. Glynne's offer was the closest Luke had come to seeing his prayers answered to practice law. But his parents might think otherwise. As their only surviving son, they'd indulged what they considered a whim to study law, sure he'd outgrow it and realize his true calling was to grow cotton. Until Father's heart started causing him problems, and they'd insisted Luke return home.

Luke had suggested they find a man capable of being a manager as well as an overseer. Father and Mother had insisted Luke's loyalty and duty lay with the plantation his grandfather and father had worked so hard to build. Out of love for his parents and concern for his father's health, Luke had complied with their wishes.

But honoring his parents as God decreed didn't lessen his longing to be an attorney. Didn't the Lord also want to give Luke the desires of his heart? Was it wrong to want something different from what his father and grandfather had devoted their lives to? His heart's home was in his law books, not a cotton field.

Luke picked up a letter from Father's factor and one from Angelique's attorney. Two good reasons and excuses for coming to town. Next, to see Mr. Glynne, the man who had inspired and encouraged him when Luke decided he wanted to study law.

A few minutes later, Luke knocked on the door of his friend's two-story house at the edge of town. The butler grinned as soon as he saw Luke.

"Mr. Glynne asked to see me."

"Come on in, Mr. Williams. The mastah been lookin' for you."

"Thank you." Luke handed his hat to the man.

"The mastah tell me to take you to his office soon as you get here." The servant led the way down the hall and slid open the pocket door for Luke to enter.

"Luke, my boy. So nice to see you." With the aid of a cane, Mr. Glynne struggled to his feet. He walked around his desk and extended his hand.

"Likewise, sir." Luke shook hands with him. Travis had told Luke his father's health problems had taken a toll on him, but nothing Travis had said prepared Luke for the shock of how frail Mr. Glynne appeared. He'd lost a considerable amount of weight. If not for his thick mane of gray hair, the man would be almost unrecognizable from a distance. His heavy breathing indicated standing was almost more than he could do for long.

"Please, be seated." Mr. Glynne sucked in several labored breaths as he made his way back to his chair. "As you can see, I'm still recovering. Dr. Maney says it's a miracle a man my age survived pneumonia. Most don't."

"Thank God you did, sir." Luke shuddered as he gripped the arm of the leather chair on the other side of the desk. He didn't want to think about his mentor not sitting in front of him.

"Indeed. I'm here only by the grace of God." His warm smile broadened, lighting up his wrinkled face the way Luke had become accustomed to. "I need help until I get my strength back. I can't think of anyone better to assist me than you."

"How can I help *you?* You know more about the law than anyone from here to Nashville."

"The doctor says I must be careful not to do too much too soon." Mr. Glynne leaned toward him. "Did Travis tell you he's running our plantation?"

"Yes, sir. I encouraged him to call on my cousin since he's living closer now."

Mr. Glynne chuckled. "I heard about your stunning cousin after Travis met her a while ago at the Parkers' ball. I suspect my wife and I will hear more about her the next time we see our son."

"Angelique is a beauty inside and out. We're glad she came to us." Luke had no problem complimenting the cousin he now dearly loved.

"I'm sure you are." Mr. Glynne took another deep breath. "Back to the reason I asked you to come. I need your help. I can't pay a clerk when I can work so little. So, my loyal clerk had to seek employment elsewhere and moved to Nashville." He paused to catch his breath, laboring as if he'd walked across town. "Would you consider helping me for two or three days a week until I can work the way I've always done? I'd pay you by the job. You could stay at our house the one or two nights necessary."

"Sir, I'd be honored, but..." He shook his head, unable to finish the rest of the sentence.

Mr. Glynne nodded. "But your parents, specifically your father. Douglas has not changed his mind about your choice for your life's work?"

"No. They're more certain now than ever that I should be a planter instead of an attorney. Father's health has improved since I came home last year to help him."

"As it should when you're the one who's really running the plantation."

"Yes, sir. Which means he and Mother refuse to think about me one day practicing law instead of planting cotton."

"Working for me temporarily might be a good way to help them begin to change their minds and see you as the lawyer you are." Mr. Glynne propped his elbows on his desk as he steepled his fingers.

"I'd like that, sir." More than he could put into words.

"I need you two days, perhaps occasionally three, a week to see I don't overtax myself. One of my clients asked me to rewrite his will. You could do that from home."

Luke's pulse quickened. A piece of his dream might be in his grasp. Father could spare his help two days a week. Especially since they had such a good overseer. "I'll do it, sir."

"Bravo, my boy. Thank you."

"You're welcome." Luke marveled how his voice could sound so calm while he was jumping and shouting for joy on the inside.

"To assuage your father's feelings, I'll write him a letter explaining why I must have your assistance and why you couldn't refuse my request." Mr. Glynne's blue eyes glittered like a child who realized he'd get his way. "My health has not hindered my gift of persuasion, especially concerning an old friend like Douglas."

"I'm accepting your offer regardless of what my parents think, but I won't turn down your assistance to help them see why I agreed to help you."

"Honoring your parents is right. As is helping an old friend." Mr. Glynne's expression sobered as he opened the top drawer of his desk. "Let's get down to business." He placed a document of several pages on the desk in front of him. "Gerald Hampton came by yesterday insisting I rewrite his will as quickly as I could manage."

Luke's throat tightened at the mention of Eugenia's father's name. "What does he require?"

"He had intended to leave his plantation to Eugenia once she found a suitable husband to care for her and the property."

"Yes, sir. I was aware of that." How, he wouldn't say since Alton Parker had been the one to brag about one day controlling two profitable plantations.

"All right. Gerald wants his estate left to his three oldest children, share and share alike. They can sell everything if they desire or hire a good manager and split the profits. The choice will be theirs."

Too afraid to trust his voice, Luke nodded. A myriad of memories threatened to choke off his words if he tried to speak. Eugenia had turned her back on so much. For what?

"As I said, you could take care of this at home. Gerald could come to your house to sign it with your father as a witness. Then, you can bring it to me by next Thursday?" Mr. Glynne's words jerked Luke's thoughts back to the present.

"Yes, sir. That should work well."

They discussed other jobs Mr. Glynne needed help completing. Luke stayed for lunch the way he'd done for several years. When he left, he carried Mr. Glynne's letter for his father in his jacket pocket, as well as one for Mr. Hampton, explaining Luke would rewrite his will.

"Thank you again, sir." Luke grasped Mr. Glynne's wrinkled hand as they stood on the porch.

"You're welcome. Promise me again you won't read what I wrote to your father."

"I promise, sir."

"Good. Enjoy your ride home, Luke Williams, attorney at law. You'll soon be one of the best in the state."

"Only because of you, sir."

Mr. Glynne beamed at him. "Tell Douglas and Evelyn hello for me. I look forward to meeting your cousin one day."

"Yes, sir."

During his ride home, Luke thanked God for answering prayers he'd been tempted to give up on. Answering in a way he hadn't imagined possible. A nearby mockingbird sang as if rejoicing with him. As Mr. Glynne said, helping an old family friend didn't mean he couldn't also honor his father and mother.

Thoughts of his parents and what he'd soon face at home slammed into him as if someone had tried to knock him off his horse. He sucked in air. Since God had given him a small way to begin fulfilling his dream, God would surely help Mother and Father realize Luke could help Mr. Glynne without neglecting them or Oakridge. His words of thanksgiving turned to pleas for wisdom and strength he didn't possess.

Chapter Twelve

Luke returned to a quiet house. He checked the parlor. No one there. Father's office sat empty when he went in to lay the letter from his factor on his desk. He should find Angelique and let her read the letter from her attorney. Amos stepped into the hall as Luke headed toward the stairs.

"The massa and mistress be resting still. Miss Angelique is in the flower garden so she don't bother them."

"Thank you. I'll change out of these dusty clothes, then see if she'd like some company."

A short time later, Luke walked toward Mother's flower garden at the edge of the backyard. Angelique sat, book in hand, on a black wrought iron bench beneath an oak tree. As Travis had told his father, the young redhead was stunning. Her favorite yellow dress fit her bright personality to perfection. Two months ago, he'd wished she'd never come. Now, he'd battle with anyone who tried to hurt her.

"I hope the shade and the breeze make you a little more comfortable in this June heat." He spoke before approaching her. No use startling her from her reverie.

"They help some. Did you enjoy your time alone?" She motioned for him to sit next to her.

"Yes. Your attorney wrote you and Father has news from his factor, so I'm glad I went to Murfreesboro today."

Angelique reached for the folded letter as soon as he slipped it from his shirt pocket. She read it in silence. "Everything I grew up with will soon be gone." She swallowed hard. "*Monsieur* Chirac has successfully sold our house and most of Papa's remaining assets. He should soon have enough to settle the debts with a small sum left over for me." Laying the paper in her lap, she closed her eyes and leaned against the back of the bench.

"Are you all right?"

"I will be. I didn't expect such wonderful news to also be a little sad. I have a few good memories from there, but New Orleans will never be home again."

Luke patted her arm, not sure what to say or if he should speak at all.

"My loyal nurse told me about Jesus when I was a little girl. The day I became a Christian, I asked God to change my father and give me a loving family." She sighed. "But Papa wanted nothing to do with God." As she opened her eyes, her lips turned up in her customary smile. "So, the Lord answered my prayers in a way I never believed possible."

"I'm glad He did." Luke would save his story of the opportunity God had given him until after he talked to his parents. Angelique shouldn't be dragged into what might be an unpleasant discussion. "If you ever have any legal questions about what Mr. Chirac is doing, I studied law for two years in college. I'll be happy to help you."

Her mouth formed a perfect O. "Why haven't you told me this before?"

"I've never had the opportunity until now." Especially

since his main concern was to convince her Alton Parker was not the kind of man he claimed to be. Or lately, assure her that he and Clarisse were only friends.

She stared at him as if he were a stranger. "Then why are you managing Uncle David's plantation instead of working somewhere as a lawyer?"

"Father needs my help for now. Like you, God is answering my prayers in His own time in His own way."

"You sound so certain. How or why?" She cocked her head as she continued to study him.

"I'll explain more later."

She laughed. "Judging from the way your eyes are shining, later should be quite interesting."

"Yes, it could be." He rose. He'd hinted at more than he intended. "Father is probably up by now. I'll go see if he'd like to read his letter before supper."

"I'll be inside after a while. My shady spot here is more comfortable than a stuffy parlor inside on such a hot day."

"I'll see you at supper."

His parents' soft voices drifted into the hall as Luke approached their bedroom. He knocked on their door. "May I come in?"

"Yes." His mother replied.

Luke stepped inside. "You both look rested."

"We are." Father's good color and strong voice emphasized his words as he sat on the bed to put on his shoes.

"I put a letter from your factor on your desk. I had a good visit with Mr. Glynne after I picked up the mail. He says to tell you hello."

"How is he?" Mother smoothed her white hair as she peered into the dresser mirror.

"Better. He's trying to regain his strength and is only able to work two or three days a week."

"I'm glad he can work at all." Father seated himself in the side chair beside the bed.

"As am I." Luke took a deep breath. "He asked me to come in to help him two, perhaps three days, a week until he completely recuperates. I told him yes."

Father gripped the arm of his chair. Mother almost dropped the brooch she was pinning on her dress.

"I wouldn't think of refusing to help an old family friend." Luke prayed as he stared at his silent, solemn-looking parents.

"But we planted more cotton this year than we ever have." Father unwrapped one finger at a time from the chair arm.

"Yes, sir. And it's coming along well. I'll be working at home some days instead of going to Murfreesboro."

"You talk as if this arrangement is already settled."

"Yes, sir. It is. I'm happy to help you and Mother. But I can honor your wishes and assist a friend in need as well." He'd never stood his ground like this before. Neither of his parents appeared pleased.

"We shall see." Father's clenched jaw signaled his displeasure.

"Yes, sir, we shall. Mr. Hampton wants some changes made to his will. I'll be doing those at home. I'll ride to his house tomorrow and give him Mr. Glynne's letter explaining I'm now assisting him. Mr. Hampton can come here next week to sign the will so you can be his witness."

The oppressive silence blanketed the room like choking dust. Luke didn't flinch under his parents' stern glares.

"I'll ride to Murfreesboro next Thursday to take the new will to Mr. Glynne to keep." He slipped his mentor's letter from his inside jacket pocket. "Mr. Glynne wrote this to you and Mother. He insisted I shouldn't read it. I've kept my promise to him." He handed the folded piece of paper to his father. "I'll see you both at supper soon. Angelique knows nothing about Mr. Glynne's offer."

Mother nodded before crossing the room to look over Father's shoulder to read the letter. Luke took his leave. He'd made his case without the aid of whatever Mr. Glynne had written. He'd honored his parents all his life. But a man of twenty-two had a right to a life of his own, to pursue his own dreams. He'd prayed for the last year for a way to become an attorney if it was God's will. Since God had given him this opportunity, the Lord must approve of what Luke wanted.

* * *

CLARISSE WALKED down the aisle of the church, searching for Angelique. She again sat next to Luke, probably hoping to catch a glimpse of Mr. Parker walking in. Unless God worked a miracle in the man's heart, Angelique would soon be disappointed again. How Clarisse longed for the day Angelique would befriend a better man.

Before sliding into the pew, Clarisse smiled at her friend. Angelique grinned back. As did Luke. Did he have something he needed to share with her? Angelique had spent too much time with Mr. Parker a few days ago. Clarisse would be sure to walk away from other people visiting outside later in case he wanted to talk.

After the service, she strolled to the large red oak at the edge of the churchyard. If anyone in her family saw her, they didn't appear to mind. She suspected they'd noticed she and Luke visited often now after church. Perhaps the two of them should start talking about ways to one day convince so many people they were only friends.

"We're so glad to see you." Angelique hurried toward Clarisse, tugging on Luke's sleeve as if to propel him along.

The poor man did not look happy to accompany her. Good. His smiles had been much too warm while they danced Wednesday night, especially when they'd gone outside to watch over Angelique.

"Luke has some wonderful news. If he won't tell you, I will." Angelique laughed as she halted next to Clarisse.

"My version will be much less wordy than yours." Luke aimed a mischievous smile at his cousin before returning his full regard to Clarisse, standing in front of him. "Mr. Glynne has been very ill. I went to see him Thursday. He asked me to help with his law practice a day or two a week."

"Which is absolutely wonderful. I'll be bragging one day that I know the best lawyer in the state." Angelique tapped Luke's arm.

"I'm glad you can work for Mr. Glynne." Everyone knew Luke had left college to come home and help his ailing father. How like this man to also want to aid someone else.

"Also, could I ask you to ride with me tomorrow or Tuesday? While we danced, Mr. Parker asked if he could call on me this coming Wednesday." Angelique glowed.

Clarisse worked to control her expression while thinking how best to reply. Telling her friend her true thoughts might push her even closer to the scoundrel she still refused to see for who he was. And away from Clarisse or Luke. "Let's ride tomorrow. Something unforeseen could come up on Tuesday, and I'd miss seeing you all week." She hoped Luke understood her veiled hint that riding with him might be what could happen on Tuesday.

"All right. I'll see you tomorrow afternoon."

"There you are, Miss DuBois." Travis Glynne joined them, stopping to stand beside Angelique. "I enjoyed celebrating your birthday with you. Thank you for inviting me."

"You're welcome."

Angelique's smile wasn't as bright as the ones she bestowed on Mr. Parker, but she didn't look upset to see Mr. Glynne. Clarisse would pray for how to show Angelique what a fine Christian man he was.

"Might I call on you so we can become better acquainted?"

"Well, I'm riding with Clarisse tomorrow and—"

"But you're free every other day but Wednesday. Travis is an old family friend. Mother and Father would love to see him too." Luke smiled into his cousin's eyes.

"Which day would be best for you, Mr. Travis?" Angelique stared straight at Mr. Glynne as if Luke were nowhere near.

"Could I come Thursday afternoon?"

"I'd be delighted."

"Thank you. I'll look forward to Thursday all week."

"How is your father? Luke tells me he's been ill." Clarisse wanted to know about his father, but she also wanted to keep Mr. Glynne visiting with them.

"He's getting stronger every day."

"We'll pray for him. I'll tell the rest of my family too."

"Thank you."

The four of them talked until Angelique spied Luke's parents walking toward their carriage. "Uncle Douglas must be getting tired. Luke and I should go. Good day, friends."

"Good day to everyone." Mr. Glynne tipped his hat to her and Angelique before walking away.

Luke lingered at Clarisse's side. "Would you meet me in the woods Tuesday afternoon?" He kept his voice low.

"Yes." She'd much rather ride alone with him than have him sitting with her in the parlor in plain sight of her family. But she shouldn't have agreed to ride with him without any hesitation.

"I'll see you then." Luke tipped his hat before following after Angelique.

* * *

After dismissing her maid, Clarisse checked her hat and hair in the dresser mirror. She was meeting Luke and shouldn't care about her appearance. If he had the slightest idea how much she'd helped Eugenia to elope, he'd never want to see her again. She marched herself into the hall and down the stairs. No use wasting more time staring at her reflection.

Mama and Jenette sat in the parlor with their embroidery when she walked toward the front door. She paused in the doorway. "I'm going for a ride."

"Again?" Mama glanced up from her project.

"Yes. I've come to enjoy my solitary outings as much as riding with Angelique."

Her mother smiled. "Enjoy your afternoon."

"I shall." Clarisse headed to the door before Mama could say more. So far her mother was so happy to see Clarisse returning to her former routine that she didn't seem to mind how often Clarisse rode alone or went for walks on Tuesdays. Perhaps she and Luke should vary the days they met.

Her uncooperative heart sped up when Luke came into view on the trail a while later. She waved as he rounded the bend. He waved back.

He guided his horse alongside hers. "Thank you for meeting me. I want to tell you one thing I'm doing for Mr. Glynne."

"You do?"

He nodded. "You must promise not to tell anyone what I'm about to say. But you should hear this from me in case the wrong person somehow finds out and says things they shouldn't."

"I'd never repeat anything you tell me in confidence, but your cryptic words don't make sense."

"I'm sorry. I'll try to explain. I rode to Mr. Hampton's house this past Friday. He recently insisted Mr. Glynne rewrite his will. He didn't mind when I told him I'd do it for him since I'm working for his attorney now." He stared straight ahead while sucking in a shuddering breath that sounded as if he'd run to her house without stopping.

His silence was maddening. "I'm sure Mr. Hampton still likes you, but why do I need to know you spoke with him?"

"He's disinheriting Eugenia and leaving everything to his three oldest children. I don't imagine that shocks you."

"No. Titus and Mama have called on him a few times to check on him. He grows more bitter and angry every time they see him." But she still had no idea why they were having this conversation.

"I'm surprised he received them since he now has such a low opinion of you. The more he's thought about what Eugenia did, the more certain he is you knew about her plans and chose to keep her secrets."

Which she had. A blue jay scolded them from a nearby branch. The bird's nest must be close by. The squawking bird probably sounded more pleasant than Mr. Hampton had. How to answer Luke without him rebuking her more loudly than the bird or galloping his horse away from her? "I didn't want her forced into a loveless marriage with Alton Parker any more than you did. So, I didn't betray her confidences just as I'll not betray yours. Which I'm still not sure why you think I should know."

"Mr. Hampton is so angry with you now, I fear he might tell someone else any manner of misleading or false things to harm your reputation." He halted his horse.

She reined in Merry. "Mama says Mr. Hampton has become a recluse and sees no one these days. He refused to see her and Titus the last time they called on him."

He stared straight into her eyes. "Except for the Parker men who ride over occasionally. Alton has come alone some too. Mr. Hampton still regrets the scoundrel didn't become his son-in-law."

"Mr. Parker wouldn't hesitate to spread gossip about me, but his words hold little weight around here, especially with anyone who knows me."

"True, but I want you to know as a precaution."

"Thank you. I appreciate your concern." Which she did. But his gaze reminded her of the way Garland had regarded her. She urged her horse along the trail again. If Luke had nothing more to say, she should think of an excuse to head home. But the words refused to leave her lips.

He guided his horse alongside hers. "I appreciate the way you listen. The other work Mr. Glynne wants me to do will be much more agreeable."

"I'm sure it will. Angelique could hardly contain her happiness for you during our ride yesterday." Clarisse changed the subject to something more pleasant since she couldn't bring herself to end this time together. "She admires you even more after learning you left college to come home and help your father."

Clarisse wouldn't mention Angelique wasn't the only one who also thought more of Luke now. His concern for her reputation touched her more than she cared to admit. Especially to him.

The trail narrowed. He allowed Clarisse to take the lead until they could ride together again. He took in a couple of deep breaths. "If Father's health continues to improve, I hope to spend more time as an attorney than as a planter."

He didn't want to spend his life as a planter? Her pulse quickened at such an unexpected revelation. But even attorneys owned slaves. Mr. Glynne had a housekeeper plus a butler who also acted as his driver.

"I'll also ask you not to repeat what I just said, please. My parents don't understand why I'd choose a law practice over a plantation."

Oh, but she understood. Neither her family nor Garland's parents would have accepted his wish to not be a planter if he'd lived to tell them about it. Something else she couldn't, wouldn't tell him. "I won't say anything."

"Thank you. I wanted to caution you about the possibility of unwarranted gossip and not burden you with my problems with my parents."

"I don't mind listening to a friend who needs someone to talk to." She meant every word, but shouldn't have blurted them out. Becoming his confidante might make them closer friends. A risk she shouldn't be willing to take.

He reined in his horse as they reached a fork in the trail. "I should return home. Mr. Hampton is coming tomorrow to sign his will. I need to look over it and be sure I didn't misspell a word or make some other mistake before I deliver it to Mr. Glynne on Thursday."

"I'll let you be on your way. I know my way home." She added the last sentence lest he offer to escort her again.

He smiled as he tipped his hat to her. "I'll be in Murfreesboro until Friday or Saturday, but I'll see you in church Sunday."

Until Sunday. She clamped her mouth shut to keep from saying the words out loud. "Perhaps Mr. Parker will surprise us and come Sunday too." Not that she would be straining to see if the man walked in, but she had to say something that wouldn't convey how glad she'd be to see Luke on Sunday.

He nodded. "We can pray he does. Good day."

"Good day to you."

He took the trail to Oakridge. Instead of watching him until he disappeared around the bend, she urged her horse toward Hopeton. She took her time riding home, using it to think about her perplexing conversation with Luke. As she'd told him, she wasn't worried about whatever Mr. Parker might say about her. Luke baring his soul to her did concern her.

She wanted to help him protect Angelique. She hadn't anticipated the need to protect and guard her own heart from the man she admired more every day.

Chapter Thirteen

Luke ushered Mr. Hampton into Father's office on Wednesday a few minutes after two o'clock. "Please, be seated, sir. After you read over the will, I'll have my parents come witness your signature."

"Excellent." Mr. Hampton took the chair on the other side of the desk from Luke.

"I'll be happy to send for something if you'd like a drink of water or any other refreshment."

"Thank you, but no." Mr. Hampton turned his attention to the document in front of him.

A forceful knock on the door sounded loud enough for anyone downstairs to hear. The butler welcomed Parker and ushered him inside. Angelique's enthusiastic greeting floated through the office door as she led the man to the parlor.

Mr. Hampton glanced up. "Did I hear Alton coming in?"

"Yes, sir. He's been calling on Angelique."

"I see." Mr. Hampton returned his attention to his will.

"If you'd rather, he could be your second witness. My mother is not fond of being involved in anyone's legal matters." Part of the truth. Her opinion of Mr. Hampton had suffered as soon as Luke had told her the man intended to force Eugenia to marry a man like Parker. A man too much like Angelique's father. She'd be glad if someone else would be the necessary witness.

"As I've said, I still value Alton's friendship. That's a wonderful idea."

"I'll get my father and Mr. Parker whenever you'd like."

"I'm almost through reading this. I'm sure it's all in order considering I have such good attorneys." Mr. Hampton grinned.

"Thank you, sir. I'll be back in a few minutes."

Luke went upstairs to get his father. Then went to the parlor. "Could I interrupt for a moment?"

Angelique's look of disdain could wither grass. Parker's eyes narrowed a moment before he put on his usual counterfeit smile. "Mr. Hampton is in my office, ready to sign his newly revised will. He'd be honored if you'd witness his signature, Mr. Parker."

The man's face lit up. "Of course. Excuse me a moment, Miss DuBois." He followed Luke into the office.

Luke smirked on the inside while working to maintain a serious expression as Parker added his signature along with Father's. The cad who had intended to one day oversee everything Mr. Hampton owned now stood to witness Mr. Hampton leaving it all to his other children. Gloating probably didn't make the Lord happy. He'd have to pray about that later.

Plus, Mr. Hampton had expressed so much sympathy for his almost-son-in-law that Luke had begun to wonder if the rogue's visits might be intended to convince Mr. Hampton to leave him some sort of token amount to make up for his daughter's betrayal. Luke could never prove his suspicions in court. But Mr. Hampton's words had inferred such the day Luke had informed him who would rewrite his will.

Tomorrow, he'd talk to Mr. Glynne about the Parkers to test his employer's assessment of the family before telling him of his suspicions about Alton. If Mr. Glynne was taken in by his other clients the way Mr. Hampton was, Luke would keep silent and pray Mr. Hampton didn't alter his will again later.

Parker shook hands with Mr. Hampton. "I'm glad to be of service to you, sir."

"Thank you, Alton."

"You're welcome. If you gentleman will excuse me, I'll return to the parlor."

A few minutes later, Luke saw Mr. Hampton to the door while Father returned upstairs. "Good day, sir. I'm glad I could be of service to you."

"Thank you for being so quick to help me." Mr. Hampton headed out the door toward his carriage as if he had to be somewhere else in a matter of minutes.

Wishing he could pause and listen to the conversation in the parlor, Luke settled for going into the library across the hall. He slid the pocket door halfway shut, being sure to make as much noise as possible while doing so. Whatever Angelique and Mr. Parker were discussing, they kept their voices too low to be overheard. Not a good sign, considering who his cousin was conversing with. He grabbed a law book off the shelf. Best to appear to be in here for a reason.

The clock on the fireplace mantle tolled three times. Mr. Parker still sat in the parlor. Luke checked his pocket watch twice. The rogue finally left at about three-thirty. Luke forced himself not to move from his chair as he listened to Angelique bid her caller goodbye.

Angelique marched into the library moments after the

front door closed. "He's gone now. You may close the book I doubt you were reading."

Luke smiled as he placed the open book on the table by his chair. He had no intention of going back on his promise to be insufferable. "Would you like to hear about the case law I was studying?"

"No. I'm going to my room to freshen up before supper. And I'm quite happy you'll be in Murfreesboro tomorrow when Mr. Glynne comes to see me." She whirled before stomping into the hall.

He'd accomplished more this afternoon than helping Mr. Hampton. Angelique wouldn't think so, but his parents would. If only they'd be as happy for his work as an attorney today.

Angelique was the last one to enter the dining room for supper. While Amos seated her, she smiled only at her aunt and uncle. Luke would much rather endure her anger than suffer through seeing her with Parker. Father said grace as soon as Angelique took her chair.

"Did you enjoy your visit with Mr. Parker?" Mother passed the bread to Angelique.

"I did. He told me about where he's from in Virginia since I've never been there."

"I hear it's very pretty. So pretty a native Virginian might consider returning." Father cut up his chicken.

Angelique's smile faded at Father's veiled hint. "Mr. Parker is quite enthralled with Tennessee. He said fall here is glorious in its splendor."

To hide his own amusement at Father's clever line, Luke ducked his head to cut up his potatoes. His cousin would soon be aggravated with someone other than him.

"Mr. Parker assured me he plans to come to church soon." The sparkle returned to Angelique's eyes as she buttered her bread.

"I hope he does, dear." Mother's tender tone left no doubt her words were sincere.

Luke kept his attention focused on his plate. If the man ever came to church, Luke doubted his motives would be sincere. Another thing he had to pray about. God cared about Alton Parker's soul. Luke should too.

"He asked if he could call me by my first name. I said he may." Her direct gaze toward her uncle and then to her aunt appeared to indicate her determination to have her way in the matter regardless of their ideas.

Father set his water goblet down with such force the water sloshed. "He may not."

Angelique clamped her open mouth shut as she stared at her uncle. "He's a good enough friend you allowed me to invite him to my birthday supper. I see nothing wrong with his request."

"I do. As your legal guardian, I'll not allow Mr. Parker or any other man you barely know to be so familiar so soon."

Her chin jutted out. "What of your old family friend, Mr. Glynne, when he calls on me tomorrow?"

"I'll personally escort Travis to the door if he disrespects you like that. Which he won't. His father would be appalled if his son showed such a lack of manners."

"Oh." Angelique popped a bite of bread in her mouth.

"Yes. Your aunt will be reading in the library tomorrow while Travis is here, or I'll be looking at my ledgers in my office."

"Unlike your father, dear, we care what happens to you." Mother's tender expression emphasized her loving, conciliatory words.

Angelique ducked her head as she stabbed a carrot. "Yes, ma'am."

She said little the rest of the meal, leaving Luke and his

parents to discuss the hot weather and lack of rain without her input. He wasn't happy to see Angelique so upset. But giving his parents someone else to be concerned about might mean they'd be less apt to think as much about Luke irritating them by leaving to help Mr. Glynne tomorrow.

* * *

CLARISSE WALKED out of the church with Angelique. They halted in the shade of a large hickory tree. Her friend had again watched in vain for Mr. Parker to come. But Clarisse wouldn't talk about that unless Angelique brought it up.

"What day would you like to ride this week?" Clarisse fanned herself.

"Any day but Wednesday. Mr. Parker asked to call on me again despite everything Luke did last week." Angelique grimaced as her cousin headed toward them.

"Oh?" Clarisse grinned on the inside. The more obnoxious Luke could be to Mr. Parker, the better.

"Yes. Could we ride tomorrow so I can talk to you about it?"

"Tomorrow will be fine." As would any other day, unless Luke intended to go to Murfreesboro again. If so, reserving Tuesday to see him would be best. No. She should stop saving days for him. Especially after their last ride.

Luke soon joined them, stopping next to Clarisse. "I assume you ladies plan to ride as usual."

Angelique folded her arms in front of her, almost dropping her fan. "We do. But you are not welcome to come with us tomorrow."

"You don't say?" His eyebrows quirked up in what appeared to be mock amusement. He grinned at Clarisse. "Since my cousin so disdains my company, I'm forced to ask if I could call on you Tuesday afternoon because I'm going to Murfreesboro on Thursday again. May I?"

Clarisse stared up at him, trying to think how to reply to such an unexpected public request. "Um, well I—"

"Of course he can." Angelique giggled. "Even *friends* call on each other."

"Yes, they do. Tuesday would be good for me." Clarisse fanned herself.

"I'll see you then." His beaming smile indicated he was happier than he should be.

Before Angelique or Luke could say more, Mr. Glynne walked up to them. "I thoroughly enjoyed visiting with you, Miss DuBois. Could I call again on Friday?"

"Yes, you may. Friday is excellent."

"Thank you."

Clarisse talked with her friends until she saw Jenette and Mama walking to the carriage. "My family must be ready to go home. I'd best go now."

"I'll see you tomorrow," Angelique called to Clarisse as she turned to leave.

Monday afternoon, Clarisse and Angelique met at what had become their customary spot on the trail between their houses.

"Could we ride in the shade of the creek along the meadow?' Angelique turned her mount without waiting for Clarisse's reply. "My family must wonder why I still want to ride on a hot July afternoon. But I need to talk to you alone instead of in the parlor where someone might overhear me."

"Oh?" Clarisse followed her friend. Her loved ones probably wondered the same thing about her in this heat.

"All of my family cautioned me not to befriend Mr. Parker. But the man has truly seen the error of his ways. How do I get them to see that?" Without offering Clarisse a chance to give an answer she didn't want to offer, Angelique went on to tell how irritating Luke had been when the man called. Plus, how her uncle wouldn't allow Mr. Parker to use her first name and insisted someone was in the library or his office whenever she received a male caller. "I doubt they would be so vigilant if Mr. Glynne were my only caller. They truly don't like Mr. Parker."

Clarisse prayed for the right words. She couldn't allow her companion to think she approved of Mr. Parker but didn't want Angelique to become angry enough with her to end their friendship. "Have they told you why they think so little of Mr. Parker?"

"Aunt Evelyn said he gambles. She's also troubled he doesn't attend church."

"Those are both valid concerns."

"Yes, but he no longer gambles at cards. And last week, he assured me he'll come to church soon."

"Your uncle and aunt care about you and are probably waiting to see if he keeps his promises. Some people are notorious for not keeping their word." She hoped what she said would remind Angelique of the father she'd said lied to her so many times. But mentioning him specifically, along with Mr. Parker, might antagonize her friend.

"Yes. But too many people misjudge someone the way they so often did with me."

"True."

Angelique reined in her horse as they rode into the meadow. "The grass isn't as green, and the flowers are fading with the lack of rain, but this is still such a pretty peaceful place."

"It is." Clarisse liked this spot too. Just as she and Eugenia had often enjoyed pretty places on their rides before. Garland, too, before … No, she'd not think of Garland's terrible accident today. Her concern needed to be with her naive friend.

Unlike Eugenia, Angelique didn't realize Mr. Parker's words were no more than empty flattery. He'd tried to ingratiate himself with Eugenia, also asking to be on a first name basis with her. As long as the man appeared to be repeating the same pattern with Angelique, Clarisse could only conclude the scoundrel had some kind of nefarious motive for befriending Angelique. How she wished she could discover what it was.

"Shall we ride along the creek in the shade?" Angelique urged her horse forward. "I suppose you don't like hearing me telling you how insufferable Luke is or disparaging him in any fashion." She glanced over at Clarisse, a mischievous twinkle in her eyes.

Clarisse did mind. Perhaps more than she should. But she wouldn't tell anyone such a thing. "He loves you like a little sister. He was awful with his sisters. Especially so with Beth, since she's three years younger."

"I suppose since Beth is your friend, you could tell some tales on Luke, but you won't." Angelique laughed as she pointed a gloved finger at Clarisse.

"I don't repeat what other people tell me unless I have good reason to do so." She wouldn't tell Angelique how much of their conversations she reiterated to Luke. But watching over Angelique warranted it.

"I believe you. Eugenia was such a good friend. You had to have known she was thinking of eloping with that wheelwright. But you couldn't have told anyone since the whole county was so shocked that people still talk about it."

"Eugenia was and is a good friend." Clarisse didn't like the direction of this conversation. Allowing Angelique to think

Clarisse wouldn't repeat her words to anyone wasn't right. But protecting her friend, who still refused to see the truth about Mr. Parker, was of utmost importance.

She prayed for the day she could be truthful with this dear companion. The day Angelique would finally see the real Mr. Parker who still seemed bent on deceiving unwitting people.

Chapter Fourteen

Tuesday afternoon, Luke left his horse with the Matthews' groom. He shouldn't be here for Clarisse's entire family to see. When he walked around to the front of the columned house, a dark green enclosed carriage sat in the drive. He groaned. If he weren't mistaken, someone in the Browning family, most likely Mrs. Browning, had come calling. He lifted the brass knocker, wishing he'd ground-tied his horse and could ride away unseen instead.

"Welcome, Mr. Williams." The butler ushered him inside.

"I'm here to see Miss Clarisse."

"Yes, sir."

Clarisse stepped into the hall before Luke could hand his hat to the servant. "Good afternoon. Mama is visiting with Mrs. Browning. Would you like to walk in the yard?"

"Yes, that would be nice."

She took her bonnet off the hat tree. The one with the red ribbon she often wore. It matched her white dress trimmed in red roses around her neck, sleeves, and hem. The dress she'd had on the day she delivered Eugenia's letter to him.

"Shall we talk in the yard or Mama's flower garden?" She fluffed the bow as she waited for his reply.

He forced a smile. With God's help, memories of her delivering Eugenia's letter no longer angered him. But he shouldn't be able to recall the dress Clarisse had worn that day. "Whichever you prefer."

"I'd rather get some exercise and walk in the yard."

He should have suggested the garden at the back of the house out of sight from the parlor windows overlooking the lawn. But he hadn't. Perhaps the talkative Mrs. Browning had so much to say that neither she nor Mrs. Matthews would be looking out the windows much.

He opened the door for her. Cupping her elbow in his hand, he assisted her down the steps. The right thing for any gentleman to do. But so wrong when walking next to her infused his soul with contentment. He dropped his hand to his side the instant her slipper touched the green grass.

"I assume you have something important to tell me since you're willing for so many people to see us." She halted in the shade of a chestnut tree off to the side of the house and away from the windows.

Good. She still didn't want anyone watching them. "Yes. I had an interesting discussion with Mr. Glynne last week. He knows one of the men Parker owed. Mr. Glynne doesn't trust Parker any more than we do."

She sighed. "Yet Angelique is still blinded by his charms."

"As is Mr. Hampton." He told her about telling Mr. Glynne of his suspicions that Parker might be preying on Mr. Hampton's sympathy and hoping to get money from the old gentleman. "When Mr. Hampton came in wanting to rewrite his will, Mr. Glynne persuaded Eugenia's father not to leave Parker so much as a token sum, saying his children could easily contest the will."

Clarisse gasped as both hands covered her mouth. He stooped to retrieve the fan she dropped. "That man is worse than we feared."

"I'm afraid so." His fingers brushed hers when he returned her fan to her. The temptation to take her hand almost overwhelmed him. No. If he didn't concentrate on the problem he came to discuss, he'd be in the sort of trouble he'd sworn to never risk again.

"Does your father know?" Her welcome question refocused his thoughts.

"No. Since Mr. Hampton is a client, I can't repeat his problems to them."

She shook her head. "But you're telling me."

"The more you know, the better you might be able to help me persuade Angelique of her mistakes." Which was part of the truth. The other part, he couldn't tell her he felt more comfortable confiding in and talking with her by the day. "I know you won't repeat what I say."

"Of course not."

"My parents fear forbidding my stubborn cousin from seeing the man might push her into his arms instead of away from him. We all suspect she'll disobey Father's order not to allow Parker to use her first name."

"From what Angelique told me on our ride yesterday, she's quite upset with all of you."

He nodded "She's voiced her sentiments to me more than once." A welcome breeze caressed the bow beneath her chin, directing his contemplations far away from his cousin.

"I'm glad Mr. Glynne is calling on her too. But I don't understand her lack of enthusiasm for him." Her furrowed brow emphasized the concern she voiced.

"Neither do I. Every woman I know would be flattered to have two men interested in her simultaneously."

"Not every woman." She ducked her head.

"Is that so?" Judging from her sad tone, he shouldn't have blurted out such a question. "I'm sorry if I misspoke. I've become too adept at that lately."

"It's all right." She stared into his eyes. "No man can truly know what any lady is really thinking unless she chooses to tell him."

"And you don't want to do so. I'll respect your feelings."

"I appreciate that." She looked in the direction of her beige brick house. "I'll keep praying for Angelique."

"As will I. I'll also continue thanking God she has a genuine friend like you."

She shook her head. "I don't feel genuine when she has no idea how often I repeat what she tells me to you."

"That's why I call you a genuine friend. You want to do whatever you can, anything necessary to help her. You understand the true meaning of loving someone the way you love yourself."

"Thank you. I also consider you that sort of true friend."

"I'm honored." He bowed and kissed her hand then jerked upright as if he'd almost fallen into a roaring fire, which he had. What had come over him? Kissing her ungloved hand.

Clarisse stared wide-eyed past him. He looked to see Mrs. Browning gawking their way before allowing her driver to assist her into her carriage.

"If you never want to see me again, I understand. I admire you as a true friend and nothing more. What I meant as only a token of our mutual friendship will be misinterpreted by Mrs. Browning and soon everyone in the county." Not the sort of complete, abject apology Clarisse deserved. But he couldn't say he was truly sorry for kissing her hand.

"We've added another tidbit of gossip to the collection we've already started." Her lips turned up in almost smile.

"Yes, we—*I* have." Her puzzling reaction left him struggling to think much less say anything. She didn't sound or appear to be the least bit angry with him. Did she accept his fumbling excuse for the kiss being a token of friendship? The disappointment welling up, making his chest tight, shouldn't be there.

"Depending on whom Mrs. Browning calls on next, your family could hear about this afternoon before mine does." Clarisse returned Mrs. Browning's wave as the carriage rolled down the drive toward the gate.

"True. One can hope she has a bout with some sort of ailment, since my mother says the woman is a hypochondriac."

Clarisse laughed. "We are an awful pair, aren't we, for wishing such a thing?" She sobered. "But I hope we aren't awful for talking behind Angelique's back so often."

"No. We aren't. We're protecting an innocent young lady from a prowling beast she doesn't realize is stalking her."

"I wish I knew why Mr. Parker is so interested in Angelique." She clasped her hands in front of her.

"I'd like to think only for her supposed fortune, but the fear it's something more is beginning to haunt me. Especially the more I learn of his devious ways." He wouldn't mention the man challenging him to a duel after the scoundrel learned Luke told Eugenia of his gambling debts.

She nodded. "I'm glad I'm not the only one."

Her quick assent to his suspicions sent shudders through him. "Dealing with Parker is a far worse problem than whatever gossip will soon be floating around about us."

"Definitely. I'd rather deal with a few rumors about you and me instead."

"As would I. I should be going before we give someone any more to gossip about. Feel free to tell your family whatever you think necessary to explain or excuse my call and my behavior."

"My family would like to see you come more often, so, any excuse or denial I offer only serves to make them think they're right about us becoming more than friends." Her eyes twinkled despite the seriousness of her tone.

"True, which is why I'll wish you good day and be on my way." He tipped his hat to her then turned to walk toward the barn and his means of escape from the new problem he'd created by kissing her hand.

* * *

CLARISSE SPENT the rest of the week mulling over her time with Luke. Since he was such an honest man, his explanation for why he'd kissed her hand must be true. She shouldn't have been disappointed he'd called his kiss a token of friendship. But she was, then and now. She must control her heart's wayward wishes for more from him.

On Sunday, she stepped from the family carriage, intent on ignoring Luke as much as possible. She'd ride with Angelique this week while he was in Murfreesboro. She had nothing to tell him on Tuesday, so he had no need to call on her this week.

As Titus ushered her into the pew across from the Williams family, Angelique smiled at her. Luke stared straight ahead. Wonderful. She returned Angelique's smile with one of her own, glad Luke wouldn't think she was including him.

Angelique's eyes widened as she discreetly glanced at the pews toward the back. Clarisse followed her friend's gaze for a moment and almost lost her balance. Mr. Parker slid into the pew closest to the door. Clarisse focused her gaze on the stained-glass windows at the front as she took her seat. No use drawing attention to the man and causing a commotion. Angelique probably wouldn't hear a single bit of the sermon. Clarisse prayed Mr. Parker would listen to every word of every hymn sung and every syllable Pastor Bentley uttered.

When the service ended, Angelique all but pushed past Luke to get to the aisle. Clarisse took her time, allowing her family to go ahead of her. Not a good idea. She stepped into the aisle at the same time as Luke and ended up walking by his side toward the pastor standing at the back door.

As if by mutual agreement, each of them gave Pastor Bentley a quick compliment on his sermon before stepping into the churchyard to search for Angelique. "I see them behind the large chestnut tree near the hitching rail." Clarisse directed Luke's gaze.

Luke grinned. "I'm glad she wore her bright yellow dress today." He matched his steps to hers as they headed toward his cousin.

"We're so happy to see you here," Clarisse spoke the moment she and Luke reached their target, interrupting Mr. Parker in mid-sentence. Amazing how adept she'd become at being rude.

"Indeed we are." Luke's tone didn't sound as enthusiastic as his words

"Thank you. I was asking Miss DuBois if I could call on her this week to discuss the pastor's remarks."

"What a wonderful idea. Why don't we all go for a ride and enjoy each other's company again? Luke and I would be pleased to help Angelique answer any questions you might have. Wouldn't we?" Clarisse tossed Luke what she hoped looked like the brightest smile he'd ever received.

"Um, yes. We would. Any afternoon before Thursday would be excellent with either of us. Am I right, Clarisse?"

"Oh, yes." Clarisse aimed a fake grin in Angelique's

direction before her friend could open her mouth. "Would any of those days be good for you?"

"Well, I suppose …" Angelique glanced toward Mr. Parker. "What day do you prefer?"

Judging from Mr. Parker's clenched jaw, none of them were good for him. "Tuesday would be all right."

Clarisse suppressed a chuckle. Luke's twinkling eyes indicated he might have done the same. "Jenette is already walking toward our carriage. I'll see everyone on Tuesday."

Luke fell into step with her as she turned to go. He inclined his head toward hers after they were a few feet from Angelique and Mr. Parker. "What a superb performance and suggestion." He whispered almost in her ear.

She laughed softly as they paused a few feet from the carriage. "Yes. One Eugenia would be quite proud of as well, as she could always think of something clever to say." She clapped a hand over her mouth. "I shouldn't have mentioned her to you."

"She isn't my favorite person to talk about, but she would be quite pleased the way you thwarted Parker so well."

"Pleased is an understatement no more than she thought of that rogue." She sighed. "But I do pray the man listens to us or someone about God."

"Praying for him is difficult. But I'm trying." He glanced toward his family's carriage. Their driver was helping his mother inside. "Angelique's conversation will soon be cut short by someone other than us."

"Yes, it will."

Mama quirked an eyebrow in their direction before allowing the driver to assist her into their carriage.

"Until Tuesday." Luke walked with her to her family's coach.

"I'll see you then."

He tipped his hat before turning to leave. As the driver helped her up, Clarisse steeled herself for whatever Mama or the others might say about her and Luke. How often had she or Luke used the word *we* or *us*? She hadn't spoken in such familiar terms to anyone but Garland. Anyone overhearing them would assume she and Luke were engaged to be married.

The tangled threads of the ruse they were weaving got more difficult to unknot by the day.

* * *

Luke stepped into a quiet house after his abbreviated ride to the fields. Their competent overseer had everything well in hand. The cotton was thriving. Lord willing, they'd have a bountiful harvest. He had time to go upstairs and change clothes, then enjoy reading some law before everyone came down to eat.

Going over statutes or court rulings would help keep his mind off yesterday afternoon. The ride with Clarisse, Angelique, and Parker had been uneventful. The cad artfully dodged every reference the ladies or he made about God, leaving Luke to suspect the man's true motives for coming to church this past Sunday were not good.

Yet, he'd again offered to escort Clarisse home after Parker had left them. He'd had nothing necessary to tell her and had fumbled his words more than once, attempting to pretend he needed to speak with her. Blurting out words he had no business saying was becoming too normal whenever he saw Clarisse.

Bidding her goodbye at the beginning of her long driveway had been the only sensible thing he'd done. He dare not allow himself to be in a situation where he might kiss her hand again. Or her tempting lips, if she'd allow.

Jerking off his dusty clothes, he marched downstairs to

grab a book as soon as possible. Too many thoughts of Clarisse these days had nothing to do with telling her anything concerning Angelique.

A short time before supper, a soft knock on the library door interrupted his studying. "May I come in?" The door slid open before Luke could answer his father's question. "Your talk with the overseer went well?"

"Yes, sir." Luke closed his book and laid it on his lap. "We might see over thirty bales per acre this year."

"Good. Very good." Father took the chair across the coffee table from Luke, a too-serious look on his face for hearing such a welcome report. "Are you going to Murfreesboro tomorrow?"

"I am. Mr. Glynne needs me to attend the county court meeting for him on Friday morning and take care of a few other things tomorrow."

"How much longer will Adam require your help?"

Luke gripped his closed book as he prayed for the words to say. Words he should have already said after the discussion he'd had with his mentor last week. "Mr. Glynne's lungs are damaged to the point Doctor Maney says he may never completely recover. In light of that, Mr. Glynne wants me to continue helping him indefinitely."

Father clenched and unclenched his jaw. "I suspected as much when I read the letter Adam wrote to me."

"As I told you, I promised Mr. Glynne not to read that letter."

"He explained he was close to death and how badly he needed your help ..." Father's voice trailed off as he glanced away toward the bookshelf lining the wall behind Luke. The room was so quiet the ticking clock on the parlor fireplace mantle sounded as if it might be in the library instead.

"Which is partly why I agreed to work for him." He might

as well speak his mind no matter how little enthusiasm Father exuded for what Luke needed to say.

"Only partly?" Father jerked his attention back to Luke.

"Yes, sir. Mr. Glynne has managed a successful law practice while taking care of a prospering plantation for years now. I see no reason why I can't do the same. Nothing has gone amiss here the last two weeks when I've been in Murfreesboro."

"Not yet. We hired this overseer only six months ago."

You hired him. Luke swallowed his words of contradiction. Father had listened little to Luke's opinions about who should be the new overseer, despite how much he kept insisting he needed Luke's help to manage the plantation. "He proved himself well during planting this spring." Luke braced himself for whatever might come next while praying for the day his father would accept Luke's dream could be different than his and his father's dreams.

"An overseer doesn't completely prove himself until he's handled planting and harvest. You know how I feel about that."

"Yes, sir." No use arguing that point when they had a more serious disagreement Luke was past ready to settle. "I'll pack my saddle bag after supper and leave right after breakfast tomorrow."

He wouldn't mention he'd bring more than he needed for two days and leave those clothes at Mr. Glynne's house. If he were to need to stay longer someday, he'd be prepared. He longed for when his primary residence was in Murfreesboro and he'd come to Oakridge two or three days a week instead.

Helping Mr. Glynne renewed his hope for seeing an answer to his many prayers to practice law. Waiting on God's timing was not easy. Especially since the father he loved and wanted to honor showed no sign of changing his opinion of the profession Luke wanted to pursue.

Chapter Fifteen

Thursday morning, Luke bid his family goodbye as soon as they finished breakfast. The hour-and-a-half ride to Murfreesboro gave him time to think. Too much time, as often as Clarisse came to mind. He must be more careful. Like Eugenia, she'd said more than once she only wanted his friendship. He dared not repeat the same mistake he'd made with her best friend.

The sooner they could convince Angelique that Parker cared only for her supposed fortune, the sooner he and Clarisse could end the charade they were becoming too adept at playing. The notion of not dancing with her or riding with her brought a dull ache to his chest that shouldn't be there. If only he could think of a way to show his cousin the real Alton Parker and end the game he and Clarisse were playing. Something else he needed to pray for more fervently.

Two chattering gray squirrels chasing each other around a nearby tree trunk diverted his thoughts. Time to focus on the next two days. Which to him would be as carefree as the creatures now running from branch to branch over his head. A widow wanted to sell her land. A man needed to file for a judgment to collect a debt owed to him. Friday would be the best day. He'd be on the courthouse steps to buy his own land in Murfreesboro.

Another thing he hadn't told anyone but Mr. Glynne. He didn't like keeping things from his parents. He hoped and prayed for the day he could again confide in them. But he couldn't turn down the chance to get a parcel of abandoned land for a good price. As Mr. Glynne said, the land would wait and be there for the day God changed his parents' hearts concerning Luke's wishes.

When Murfreesboro came into sight, his heart sped up. Home. This was, *would be,* home. He rode to Mr. Glynne's house.

His boss opened the door before Luke finished looping the reins around the hitching post by the front porch. "Good morning. Come in and refresh yourself before you go to my office."

"Thank you, sir."

He stayed long enough to put his clothes in the Glynnes' spare room and go over the clients scheduled to come in today. By nine-thirty, he was gathering up the necessary papers to head to Mr. Glynne's office on the other side of town.

"Thank you again for coming to my aid." Mr. Glynne, still leaning on his cane, walked onto the front porch with him. "Keep this key to the office door. It's a spare. Consider it yours." He pressed it into Luke's hand.

Luke stared at the brass key that symbolized such immense trust. "I don't know what to say."

"No words needed, my boy. Perhaps, Lord willing, that office will be yours one day."

"Sir, I ..." He shook his head, unable to voice his thoughts.

"Lord willing, my boy. I do believe He's willing, or He

wouldn't have given you such abilities and talent. You have an almost natural knack for legal affairs like I've seldom seen."

"Thank you more than I can say, sir."

Mr. Glynne placed his free hand on Luke's shoulder and looked him in the eyes. "Thank you. Without you, I'd have to lock that door for the last time and sit on my porch watching the town and my world pass me by."

"I'll do my best, sir, to be worthy of your trust."

The elderly man grinned. "You're already worthy, my boy. Now go on to the office. We've stood here talking long enough."

"We have indeed." He lifted his satchel of papers in a salute then took the porch steps two at a time. Never had he been so happy to go to work.

Luke pondered his mentor's words of encouragement the rest of the day. His own father didn't trust his judgment or abilities to the extent Mr. Glynne did. The elderly gentleman's encouraging words about Luke's talents being a gift and sign from God strengthened him to wait for the day Father finally accepted it was right for Luke to follow a different path than he and his father had traveled.

* * *

THE NEXT MORNING, Luke woke at dawn before anyone but the Glynnes' cook was stirring. From the window of his borrowed room, he watched the golden rays of the rising sun until they peaked above the still-sleeping town. He dressed, then waited until he heard Mr. and Mrs. Glynne moving about to step into the hall.

"Good morning. Did you rest well?" Mrs. Glynne smiled at him.

"I did. And you?"

"Very well." She led the way to the dining room.

Mr. Glynne seated his wife before taking his place at the other end of the table. Luke took what was his now customary place in the middle. Without the leaves in, the arrangement made for an intimate meal with the three of them.

After Mr. Glynne prayed, he passed Luke the platter of eggs.

"Thank you for having me so often."

"It's our pleasure. With our daughters and now Travis all in their own homes, we enjoy having a young person here." Mrs. Glynne beamed at him as she buttered her biscuit.

"Today's the day you become an official landowner. To today." Mr. Glynne lifted his water goblet in a salute.

"To today." Luke raised his goblet.

"Possibly another sign from God that you can buy a nice parcel of abandoned land for a good price and negotiate, too, with the neighbor who wants to sell his tract next to it."

"Yes, sir. I do believe you're right. The small monetary inheritance from my grandfather should pay for what the one piece is worth with some money left to go toward the neighbor's land."

"You can build a nice house there one day with plenty of room for a carriage house and a yard. Do you have a lady in mind to share it all with?"

Clarisse's beautiful face and smiling brown eyes came to mind in an instant. Luke almost choked on the bite of egg he'd just put in his mouth. He swallowed. Having good manners and not speaking with his mouth full gave him time to direct his thoughts to where they should be. "I don't have anyone in mind at the moment."

His hosts exchanged knowing glances but didn't contradict him. Had they somehow learned how much time he'd been spending with Clarisse from Travis or someone else? If rumors were circulating all the way to Murfreesboro, he and Clarisse would have more people than they'd anticipated to convince neither of them loved the other.

"We will keep our promise not to tell anyone about your purchase." Mrs. Glynne's words returned Luke's thoughts to the present.

"I appreciate that. I'm looking forward to the day I can tell my parents about it."

"As are we, my boy. We're praying for them to accept your choice of vocation."

"Thank you."

Not too long after breakfast, Luke walked toward the Glynnes' front door.

"You'll beat Sheriff Crocket and his deputy to the courthouse, leaving this early." Mr. Glynne again walked onto the porch with Luke.

"I'll wait. I want to be sure I'm the first man there in case someone else is interested."

"Good idea. Be on your way, and Godspeed to you."

"Thank you, sir."

Luke forced himself to walk at a normal pace to the courthouse. This morning, he'd take his first step to becoming a resident of Murfreesboro. His happy heart soaked in the sights of the houses and cabins he passed on the way to the main square and the courthouse.

As Mr. Glynne had said, Luke had to wait for the sheriff to arrive. When no other man came to bid on the abandoned property, Luke breathed a silent prayer of relief and thanks.

"Mr. Williams, you are now the owner of the land formerly belonging to Mr. Paul Stuart. None of us will ever understand why the man left everything the way he did, but he did you quite a favor. Congratulations." Sheriff Crocket shook Luke's hand.

"Thank you, sir."

"I assume a man of your means will build a much more substantial house there than the cabin young Stuart constructed."

"It will be a while since I'm only helping Mr. Glynne for now and don't have my own practice."

"We'll look forward to the day you do. Adam speaks very highly of you."

"I'm honored to know Mr. Glynne." Luke tucked the precious signed paperwork into his satchel. "If someone mentions this land, could I ask you not to say who bought it?"

The sheriff's eyebrows arched up to collide with a stray piece of brown hair on his forehead. "I never had anyone request that before."

"I'd like to let the gossip about this property die down a while longer before announcing I own it."

"That makes sense."

"Thank you. I'll bid you good day. I have work to do for Mr. Glynne now."

"Have a good day." Luke took his time walking back to his temporary home with his mentor. He'd had to think long and hard about buying Paul Stuart's abandoned land when the sheriff had posted notice of the sale in *The Courier*. Perhaps since Eugenia had apologized for hurting him, she'd be happy he'd benefited from the land her now husband had abandoned in order to elope with her.

As well as Clarisse knew Eugenia, he should ask her about his supposition. No. He wouldn't and couldn't do such a thing. She only wanted his friendship. Sharing his innermost thoughts with her was out of the question. Plus, Clarisse nor Titus might not be happy Luke had bought Paul's land. Titus had been as close to Paul as Clarisse was to Eugenia.

* * *

FOR ONCE, Clarisse was glad no one in the congregation appeared surprised to see her walking out of the church beside Luke after the service. Her need to talk to Luke about her conversation on her last ride with Angelique outweighed looming future problems. Without a word to her, he walked toward the spot where Angelique stood talking with Mr. Parker. Amazing, the man had come to church again.

She paused as she placed her fingers on his sleeve. "I need to speak with you alone before we join your cousin."

He grinned. "Lead the way to wherever you'd like." He patted her hand with his free one, preventing her from letting go of his sleeve.

She chose a shady spot within sight of the couple they wanted to watch, then slipped her hand off his arm. "Angelique and I had a very interesting conversation on our ride this past Friday."

"Can you tell me about it here, or do I need to call on you before I return to Murfreesboro?"

"We should meet in the woods. This conversation must be private with no risk of being overheard." She peeked over her fan toward Angelique and Mr. Parker.

"Tuesday would be best for me. I need to meet with our overseer tomorrow."

"Then I'll see you Tuesday." She turned to walk toward Angelique and Mr. Parker.

Luke snagged her arm. "If I'm to meet you Tuesday, I can't ride another day with Angelique and Parker the way we did last week."

She laughed. "Then I shan't have to be as rude as I was last week and invite us along on another outing we wouldn't be welcome on."

"True." He matched her steps as they headed toward the two they were surveying.

Before they could join Angelique and Mr. Parker, the man tipped his hat to Angelique as he made his way to his horse. She was still staring after him when Clarisse and Luke walked up to her.

The glowing smile she bestowed on them made Clarisse's heart wrench. How could her sweet friend be so deceived? "I'm so glad Mr. Parker came again."

"So are we." Despite the sincerity of her words, Clarisse wished to take them back. She couldn't keep saying *we* whenever she was with Luke. She mustn't continue speaking for him as if they were so comfortable and familiar with each other.

"Since neither of you were present, we didn't make plans for the four of us to ride this week." Angelique's beaming grin didn't dim.

Clarisse hid her frown behind her fan at Angelique's use of *we* referring to herself and Mr. Parker.

"That's all right. I need to use my time at home this week to tend to plantation business." Luke's measured words sounded as if he, too, were concerned about Angelique referring to her and Mr. Parker together.

After making plans to ride with Angelique on Wednesday, Clarisse noticed Mama heading toward the carriage. "I should go now. I'm looking forward to seeing you soon, Angelique." She added her friend's name lest she also say something similar to Luke.

* * *

CLARISSE RODE toward the usual clearing to meet with Luke a little earlier than normal. Perhaps he had sensed her urgency

Sunday morning to speak with him about Angelique. A welcome breeze rustled the leaves as she reined in her horse to watch for him.

He joined her a few minutes later. He must have realized how important this meeting was. If not, she didn't want to think about the possibility he might be impatient to see her. As eager as she was to see him. No. She'd concentrate on the real reason she needed to talk to him.

"You have something important to tell me?"

She nodded. "I assume you know Mr. Parker called on Angelique Thursday last while you were in Murfreesboro?"

He urged his horse along the trail where the trees would hide them from view. "She informed me as soon as she and my parents greeted me on my arrival home Friday evening. She's still quite eager to prove all of my family wrong about our assumptions concerning the man."

"Did she tell you she recently told Mr. Parker how meager her inheritance will probably be? He assured her he doesn't care how little or how much her fortune is."

Luke's eyes widened as he glanced over at her. "No. She knows Mother would be distressed to know Angelique shared something so personal with that man. Especially as hard as Mother works to protect Angelique from gossip."

"I feared as much." She tightened her grip on the reins. "Did you notice Travis Glynne didn't speak to her after church?"

"I did."

Clarisse sighed. "He called on her Friday before she left to ride with me. She told him she didn't want more than one gentleman calling on her at a time. Ever so sweetly were her words to me."

"My parents will not be happy to hear any of your news." He groaned. "If Parker told Angelique the truth about not caring how much money she has, that means your suspicions about another motive for him calling on her are right."

"Yes, but what else can he want other than money?"

"I don't know. But I noticed he still has few ladies willing to dance with him." The trail narrowed. He took the lead.

Clarisse guided Merry alongside him before replying. "Perhaps because of our assumption someone is gossiping about him?"

"Any of the other men he owed could have dropped hints about him."

"Anyone other than you since you're not the sort of man to do that."

"Thank you." He beamed at her compliment.

Clarisse couldn't return his smile. "You wouldn't think of talking about someone behind their back. But what am I doing now and have been doing since May? I've told you so many things, Angelique confides in me, thinking I'd never repeat our conversations."

Luke reined in his horse to look directly in her eyes. "You're helping to protect Angelique from untold heartache, not betraying her. Imagine what might happen to her if you keep silent."

She stared past him and watched a mockingbird land on the branch a few feet ahead of them as she pondered his words. "Yes. But only if we're wrong about him not changing his ways."

"Any man can change if he allows God to help him. But until he disavows his old ways to me, I can't trust him."

"Why would he have to speak personally with you?" She turned to study him again.

"I'd rather keep those reasons to myself."

"All right. I don't trust Mr. Parker since he appears to be doing some of the same things he did with Eugenia."

"Exactly. I'll need to see him change to believe him." He urged his horse along the trail again.

Chirping birds and chattering squirrels soothed her as they rode along in silence. Companionable silence? Perhaps. Luke had become a much closer friend than she'd intended.

"Please pray for God to open Angelique's eyes soon." Luke spoke after she guided Merry around a fallen log to come alongside him again.

"I have been already. I fear she's taken up with a man who is more like her father than she realizes."

"Much more. And again, I'll not explain how I know that." He jerked on the reins. "I should escort you to your drive now."

"All right." Judging from his stern expression and the ominous tone of his voice, Clarisse doubted she wanted to hear the explanation he'd refused to give her.

Chapter Sixteen

Since Eugenia's betrayal, Luke had never wanted to attend another wedding. But sitting next to his beaming cousin as the carriage rolled toward the Parkers' plantation house filled him with another sort of dread. His parents, seated across from them, also feared that Parker's reasons for calling on Angelique weren't good after he'd told them about his last conversation with Clarisse. The happier Angelique sounded, the worse his stomach burned. He'd much rather be in Murfreesboro as usual this first Friday of August.

"I'm so happy for Marissa and Jonah. To think they only met at the Matthews' Christmas ball last year. Everything about their love is so special."

Luke wondered if Angelique would bounce off her seat. "I think they're well suited to each other." The slight shake of his father's head indicated he agreed with Luke's comment.

She had no idea his words weren't complimentary. He wouldn't elaborate. Marissa hadn't impressed him when he came upon her the first time while she was riding with her brother and Eugenia. If he'd met a more vapid woman, he couldn't remember one. Jonah had tried to order everyone about since they were boys. The two deserved each other.

He'd pray about his uncharitable thoughts later. For now, he needed to concentrate on his too-joyful cousin naively heading to her own ruin with Parker unless God intervened soon. How he wished he understood why the cad was so intent on pursuing Angelique. If he could discern the man's true motive, perhaps he could thwart him better. His parents believed forbidding Angelique to see Parker would risk her eloping with him. Luke agreed. As did Clarisse.

"What has you in such deep thought that you look just shy of a frown?" Angelique interrupted his gloomy musings. "I can't imagine having anything but happy feelings on a day like this."

I can. He forced a smile rather than speak his mind. "You're right. I'll calculate how many bushels of cotton we might pick tomorrow." What a hypocrite he'd become. Saying one thing. Doing the other. All in the name of protecting a woman who refused to believe she needed anyone's watch care.

Not telling his parents about buying land in Murfreesboro was less deceptive. Or was it? He hadn't hidden his desire to work and live in town from them. They'd be shocked to learn what he'd done only because they'd disapprove. Another situation he'd like for God to intercede in.

Too soon, their carriage halted in the circular drive behind several other conveyances already parked in front of the Parkers' house. Titus offered his mother his arm to assist her up the porch steps. Clarisse trailed behind them. One person he could commiserate with. As close as she'd been to Eugenia, Clarisse didn't want to be here anymore than he did.

Mr. and Mrs. Parker, along with Alton, stood at the door, greeting guests. "We're so glad you came to share our joy." Mr.

Parker bowed slightly to Mother as she and Father stepped into the front hall.

"We wouldn't think of missing such an auspicious occasion." Mother's smile didn't include the younger Parker standing beside his father.

"Ang—Miss DuBois, may I escort you?"

"I'd be delighted."

His parents exchanged uneasy glances as Angelique placed her hand on Parker's outstretched arm and walked away with him. They couldn't have missed hearing how the cad had caught himself before using Angelique's first name. Another reason to distrust him when he refused to adhere to Father's wishes.

Luke sought out Clarisse as he followed his parents into the crowded parlor. As quickly as she glanced his way, she must have been watching for him. He made his way to her side.

"I'd like to say hello to Angelique, but getting across the room to where she is looks to be almost impossible with so many people." Clarisse's thin smile appeared forced.

"I hope she'll want to step outside for some air before or after the wedding supper. If she does, I'll see that you get to talk to her."

They continued their empty chattering until the ceremony started. Clarisse stiffened as Marissa descended the stairs, holding to her father's arm. She blinked a couple of times. Did today remind her she'd once planned to be a happy bride? He should have assumed she might not want to come today for reasons other than her friendship with Eugenia.

The wish to comfort her surged through his being. Without thinking, he patted her arm. She didn't jerk away. Her woeful glance up at him couldn't be disguised by the half smile turning up her full lips.

He stayed with her during the entire ceremony and the

supper afterward. Leaving her to be so miserable alone was impossible. "Would you like to go outside?" He offered his invitation as soon as he could.

"Shouldn't we wait to see where Angelique and Mr. Parker might go first?" Her whispered words were so soft he had to lean in to hear her.

He shook his head. "You should get away from all this. We'll worry with them another day."

"Thank you." She placed her hand on his sleeve as he extended his arm to her.

He led her out to the shaded front yard. She let out a shaky breath as they halted under an oak tree. "How did you know how badly I wanted to leave all that?"

"You've acted unhappy since the ceremony began. I'm assuming from painful memories of your own?"

She nodded. "Yes, and like you, I'd rather not explain why."

"It's enough I saw the tears in your eyes."

Her lips formed a beautiful *O* shape he had to look away from. "You did?"

"I did." He should never have admitted to observing her to that extent. But he had. "Friends watch out for each other, don't they?"

"Yes, they do."

Her beaming face warmed his soul while chilling his heart. He'd eased her mind. But his rebellious heart ached for more than the friendship she wanted while longing to comfort her during the wedding. Another reason they needed to find a way to help Angelique as soon as possible. The charade they played now endangered his heart.

"I think I see them coming down the steps. Should we invite ourselves to ride again with them next week?"

"No. I'm going to Murfreesboro on Wednesday since I

couldn't go today. I'll need Monday and Tuesday to tend to Oakridge business."

"Oh. So, you won't call on me or meet me in the woods?" She cocked her head as she gazed up at him.

Did he imagine the disappointed tone of her voice? Her genuine frown was no delusion of his fancy. "I'll see you in church tomorrow and the week after."

"All right. But we should walk over to them."

"We should. My cousin will think there's something wrong with us if we don't aggravate them in a well-mannered fashion when they're talking together."

She laughed. "Is that what we do?"

"I'd say it's a good description, wouldn't you?"

"Yes, it is." She placed her hand on his arm before he extended it to her.

They strolled toward Angelique. Several people visiting together smiled or nodded in their direction as they walked. The happiest expressions were on their mothers' faces.

* * *

CLARISSE RODE toward her usual meeting place with Angelique, glad to get out of the house for a while. They'd chosen Thursday since Mr. Parker planned to call on Angelique tomorrow. She hoped God didn't tire of her many prayers for Him to intervene and show Angelique the truth about Mr. Parker.

The sooner, the better, for so many reasons. She'd gone for a ride Tuesday afternoon to keep to her usual routine and not make Mama suspicious about why she'd stayed home. But her solitary outing had not refreshed her as she'd claimed when she returned. She'd missed seeing Luke much more than she should.

Angelique waved the moment she caught sight of Clarisse, then urged her horse around the bend to meet up. "I'm so happy to see you."

"I'm glad to see you too." Clarisse guided Merry alongside Angelique. "I'm assuming we'll stay in the shady woods since it's so hot today."

"We should. New Orleans' heat is worse with the humidity. But I'd ride almost anywhere to talk to you today."

"Is something wrong?"

Angelique laughed. "Not wrong. But Aunt Evelyn says she's been married too long to talk and talk about a wedding that was almost a full week ago."

"I suppose so." Clarisse glanced down to smooth her skirt. She wanted to chat about weddings less than Mrs. Williams did.

"Marissa was radiant. Her gown was perfect. Don't you think it was an almost exact replica of the one Rachel Jackson wore for General Jackson's first inauguration?"

"I hadn't thought of that, but yes." She could discuss a wedding if Angelique focused on the fashion aspects.

Angelique exhaled a long sigh. "I'm dreaming of the day Uncle Douglas gives me away."

"Looking forward to marrying a good man is nice." Clarisse forced the words from her dry throat. She had to say something but not anything that would make Angelique think Clarisse approved of Mr. Parker as the man for her.

"Only nice?" Angelique stared at her as if Clarisse had stated the moon turned green last night. "Don't you envision the day you say yes to a man who will be your lifelong love?"

"I did once."

"But not now?"

"My fiancé died in a tragic accident. I've never found

anyone like him since then." Clarisse's hands trembled as she gripped the reins.

"I'm so sorry. Why didn't you tell me this before?"

"Like you, I don't enjoy talking about painful things in my past."

"I understand." Angelique dodged a low hanging branch. Clarisse followed behind her.

"Which is why I'd rather talk about Marissa and Jonah's exquisite wedding last week and my future hopes." The sparkle returned to Angelique's eyes.

"What kind of man do you wish for?" Clarisse welcomed the change of subject. Perhaps she could yet think of a way to help Angelique see Mr. Parker would not give her the life of love she longed for.

"Someone who listens. Who loves me just as I am ..."

"All good traits for any man. Plus, he should be a man of God," Clarisse added her comments the moment Angelique paused. "God doesn't want us to marry an unbeliever."

"True, but a man who is trying to understand what faith in God is could be considered."

Prickly shivers radiated up and down Clarisse's spine as Angelique voiced what had to be a veiled hint about Mr. Parker. "If I were acquainted with a man who was sincerely seeking God, I'd wait until he put his faith in God before planning a wedding."

Angelique reined in her horse. Clarisse halted Merry beside her. "You know full well I'm talking about Alton Parker. Luke says he has valid reasons not to like him. Do you?" Angelique's no-nonsense tone signaled she wanted only the truth.

"Yes. I do. I didn't care for the way he treated Eugenia. I'll tell you more whenever you're ready to hear it."

"Like Luke, you don't believe he's changed. Why?"

Thoughts of how Luke had told her Mr. Parker had tried to convince Mr. Hamilton to leave him a small sum came to mind as a good reason. But she couldn't betray Luke's confidence about one of his clients. Clarisse prayed for the right words she could say. Words that would probably cause her sweet friend pain no matter how gentle Clarisse could manage to make them. "He was fully aware Eugenia didn't love him but convinced her father to choose him for her husband and force her to marry him."

Angelique's face paled. She recoiled as if Clarisse had slapped her. "Oh, my. If anyone but you said such terrible things about Alton, I wouldn't believe them." Her lip trembled. She ducked her head. "I think I'd like to go home now. I have much to think about."

"Do you want me to ride with you until the trail forks to Oakridge or leave you alone to think?"

"I-I'd like to be alone."

"Every word I told you is true. I'll pray for you. Please understand I want to help you, not hurt you."

"I don't feel as if you've helped me right now." Angelique swiped at a tear with her glove. "I'll see you Sunday."

"Until Sunday." *If* her friend would speak to her then. Clarisse stared at Angelique's slumping shoulders until she disappeared around the next bend. How she prayed Angelique would take to heart the words of caution she'd finally allowed Clarisse to voice.

She didn't rush while returning to Hopeton. Perhaps God had begun answering her many prayers for Angelique to realize Mr. Parker wasn't who he pretended to be. If only she hadn't had to hurt her friend in the process. Luke would understand. She'd ask him after church what day they could talk.

Chapter Seventeen

The next Tuesday afternoon, Clarisse rounded the bend heading toward the spot on the trail she usually met Luke. He was there waiting in the shade for her. Perhaps Angelique had told him about her ride with Clarisse last week, and he wanted to speak with her as badly as she did with him.

"Good afternoon." He grinned as she came alongside him.

"I didn't expect you here already." Especially since she'd left early enough, she'd assumed she'd be the one watching for him.

"Angelique hasn't been her usual perky self lately. I suspect it's due to more than Parker not being in church this week. She won't tell any of us what is bothering her. Do you know?"

"I do." Clarisse told him about her last conversation with Angelique, including how she'd told her friend about Mr. Parker wanting to marry Eugenia despite knowing she didn't love him. "I'm glad she spoke to me at all Sunday and agreed to ride with me Thursday."

"I doubt she'd speak another syllable to me if I said anything against Parker." He let his reins go slack.

"True. I don't know why she listened to me instead."

His expression sobered. "Parker doesn't detest you the way he does me."

"He's not fond of either of us." She brushed away a spider web in front of her. If only she could so easily banish Mr. Parker from Angelique's side. "How is your work going in Murfreesboro?"

"Quite well." His countenance lit up the moment she mentioned his other job. "I like dividing my time between Oakridge and Mr. Glynne's law office. This sort of life suits me."

"That's good."

"Very good. Practicing law is an answer to prayer I've waited so long to see."

His obvious contentment stirred longings she'd suppressed the almost two years since the life she'd planned with Garland had been torn from her. What did God want her to do with the rest of her life? Marriage wasn't a possibility unless the Lord sent someone who would accept her unpopular views. And accept she'd like to do what she could to help end the problem of slavery.

"The Lord used you to start answering our prayers for Angelique." Luke interrupted her unsettling thoughts.

"I hope so. I'm praying Mr. Parker doesn't twist what I told her and turn her against me."

"I fear Parker is capable of almost anything." He took the lead as the trail narrowed.

His words chilled her despite the late August heat, especially since he knew more about the rogue than he was willing to divulge. Clarisse followed him until they could ride side by side again.

"Since Angelique is still speaking to my family and you, I'm taking that as a sign she's sincerely thinking about what you told her." Luke's warm smile and tender expression reminded her of how Garland had gazed at her when trying to reassure her.

But the man riding beside her would never be more than a good friend. "I'm hoping you're right. I've come to love Angelique like a younger sister."

"As have I."

They continued down the trail a while longer. Having exhausted the things Clarisse needed to say to Luke, she cast about in her mind for a polite excuse to end their time together. "Titus rode to Murfreesboro to check for mail and should be home soon. My family will be expecting me back too."

"If you don't mind, I won't escort you to your drive today. I need to read over some case law yet this afternoon."

"I've been riding in these woods long enough to find my way to Hopeton." She grinned at him, glad he couldn't see her home. But not as happy as she should be for a solitary ride. "I'll see you in church."

"Good day." He tipped his hat to her before she turned her horse toward Hopeton.

On her way home, Clarisse mulled over her discussion with Luke. She'd miss talking things over with him once they succeeded in helping Angelique realize the truth about Mr. Parker. Luke listened to her the way Garland had done.

She sighed. Maintaining their friendship meant never telling Luke all her true thoughts. She had no one to completely bare her soul to since losing Garland. The groom waved to her as she neared the barn.

Titus rode up as Theophilus helped Clarisse dismount. "What a perfect time to find you here."

Her brother's beaming smile roused her curiosity. "It is?"

"Yes." He reached into his saddle bag. "We have mail from Illinois."

Clarisse clapped her gloved hands together. "We do?"

"We do." He handed a letter to her. "Eugenia enclosed this note addressed to you alone and said it should be read before the other one. The letter she and Paul wrote together is to all of us. Contrary to her instructions, I read it before leaving Murfreesboro. I had to know how they're doing. I'll share that letter with Jenette and Mother later."

"I can't possibly wait until I'm in the house to read this." After walking a short distance from the servants working around the barn, Clarisse unfolded the precious piece of paper.

"I'd like to know what she says, if you can share it." Titus remained by her side.

She nodded, already concentrating on her friend's words. "She and Paul are very happy. They bought a farm with a small cabin already built. We aren't to mention to anyone the cabin has only a dirt floor for now. She's also written to her father but wonders how he'll receive her letter. And, oh, my..." Clarisse gasped and almost dropped the letter.

"What is it?" Titus leaned toward her.

Heart pounding, Clarisse stared up at her brother. "Every word Paul's father said about Mr. Parker holding a gun on Paul is true. You were so right to try to speak up for Mr. Stuart. He did aim his pistol at Mr. Parker as the cad told everyone, but only after riding up to see Mr. Parker pointing his weapon at Paul's heart."

"The exact story John Stuart told me when he and Mr. Parker returned to the Hampton plantation."

Clarisse continued reading Eugenia's account of how John Stuart and Mr. Parker had found her and Paul on the road two days after they'd eloped. "Mr. Parker intended to kill Paul and force Eugenia to go back with him." The lump in her now tight throat prevented her from saying more. She handed the letter to Titus.

"You want me to read this?"

She nodded.

Titus quickly perused the page. "I'm even more thankful she got away from that man." He gave the letter back to her.

Clarisse folded it. "I must tell Luke about this tomorrow since he's going to Murfreesboro on Thursday. We must put an end to Angelique's infatuation with Mr. Parker." She prayed for guidance about what to do.

Titus quirked an eyebrow as he studied her. "We, meaning you and Luke?"

She clamped her open mouth shut. Titus appeared to have understood more than she'd said. Much more than she'd intended to convey. "Yes."

He smiled. "You'd call on a gentleman alone? His parents like you, but I can't see Mrs. Williams setting aside propriety to that extent."

"Being sure Luke knows how dangerous Mr. Parker might be is more important than propriety or explaining everything to you."

"All right." His expression sobered. "I'll tease you about Luke later."

"And I'll tell you why your conclusions about us are wrong later."

"That should be an interesting discussion. For now, I've come up with a way to tell Luke about Alton." The mischievous glint in his eyes made her wonder if she wanted to hear his solution.

"How?" She fought the urge to poke him. How could he find anything amusing about how badly she needed to talk to Luke?

"I'll go see Luke. He told me a while back he has pups for

sale. He'll be surprised to see me since I didn't express an interest then, but that shouldn't cause any problems between boyhood friends."

"That's a wonderful idea." The urge to poke him disappeared.

He nodded. "A better one than you ruining your reputation by calling on him."

"I appreciate your help."

"I'm happy to do what I can for Angelique. We should go in and change clothes so we aren't late for supper."

They walked in silence to the house. Titus caught Clarisse's elbow as they reached the back door. "I'll tell Jenette about Alton's antics later. Mentioning them to Mother would do no good."

"I'm sure you're right since Mama is still appalled Eugenia dared elope with a wheelwright."

Titus grinned as he opened the back door for her. "Explaining why she should change her mind would be quite complicated, considering how much we helped Paul and Eugenia."

Voices coming from the parlor indicated Mama and Jenette were in there. Clarisse peeked in the door. "Would you send Rose up to help me change clothes?"

"Of course." Mama smiled as she glanced up from her embroidery.

Clarisse retreated to her room, glad she had some time to think and pray alone before having to pretend in front of her mother that nothing was amiss. Poor Angelique had no idea the kind of man she was dealing with. Luke did.

She wasn't sure which of them might be in more danger, considering what Mr. Parker had tried to do to Paul and Eugenia.

Chapter Eighteen

Luke sat behind his father's desk, going over the plantation ledger while Father rested upstairs. The slight breeze coming from the open window behind him did little to ease the heat of the afternoon. He'd much rather be in his law office in Murfreesboro. Not *his* yet. But every time Luke came to help him, Mr. Glynne reminded him it would be one day.

A knock on the front door interrupted his work. Parker wasn't supposed to be here until Friday while Luke was gone. He inclined his head toward the closed sliding door to better hear who might be calling today.

"Good afternoon, Mr. Matthews." The butler's greeting wafted through the door.

Mr. Matthews? Why had Titus come?

Amos knocked on the office door as Luke rose. "Mr. Matthews be here to see you."

"Send him in."

Titus smiled broadly as Amos ushered him into the office. "I was hoping to find you home. I decided I'd like to see the pups you mentioned a while ago. Are any of them still unspoken for?"

"Two of them are. They're from two of our best hounds." Titus had excellent dogs of his own. Why was he interested in another pup?

"Do you have time to show them to me today?"

"I can do that." He stepped around the desk, eager to find out why Titus had come with no prior notice. He hadn't acted enthused to hear about the dogs when Luke had told him about them at church a few weeks ago.

"The pups are in a shed by the barn." Luke took his hat from the rack before walking out with his childhood friend. "This brings back pleasant memories of playing with the dogs when we were boys."

"Yes, it does." Titus's grin faded as he halted by the shed door. "I saw Angelique reading in the parlor when I walked toward your office, so I waited until we were well away from the house to tell you why I'm really here."

"I've wondered why you came since the moment you arrived."

"Clarisse and I received a letter from Eugenia with news you should know."

Luke's mouth went dry as he gripped the latch. "What could I possibly need to know about her?"

"It concerns Alton Parker." Titus told him how Parker had intended to kill Paul Stuart and then lied about it to Eugenia's father later. "I realize it's Eugenia's word against his. Even her own father refused to listen to me instead of Parker. But I'd believe her over a man like that any day."

"So would I. After I speak to my father, he'll forbid such a dangerous man from calling on Angelique again."

Titus nodded. "As he should."

Luke's hold on the handle tightened. "Father isn't well enough to deal with such a scoundrel. Pray he'll allow me to tell Parker he's not to see my cousin again."

"Be careful provoking a man like that." Titus clamped his hand on Luke's shoulder.

"I will." Luke took in a deep breath as he held his friend's direct gaze. "Parker challenged me to a duel not long after he returned home."

Titus' eyes widened as his hand slipped back to his side. "I shouldn't be surprised to learn that."

"I didn't want to worry my parents, so I've never told anyone about the incident before."

"I understand. "

"Do you still want to look at puppies?" Perhaps Titus did want to see the dogs.

Titus nodded. "Adding to the bloodline of my dogs wouldn't hurt."

"The runt and one other are not spoken for yet." Luke opened the door.

Titus inspected the dogs. "I'd like the brown-and-black male when he's old enough."

"He'd be a favorite if we kept one." Luke closed the door after they stepped outside. "I dread talking with Angelique. I don't want to crush her." He blew out his breath. "Do you think Clarisse would help me? Angelique might be more willing to listen to your kind-hearted sister than me."

"I doubt my sister would turn down *any* request from you." Titus's eyes twinkled the way they'd done when he teased Luke as a boy.

He ignored his friend's veiled hint about Clarisse. Once they succeeded in their quest to help Angelique, he wouldn't be calling on Clarisse or seeking her out as a dance partner at parties. He'd miss his trusted confidante. No. He couldn't. He wouldn't. Trusting Eugenia had taught him some bitter lessons. But he had more pressing problems to deal with for now.

"The scoundrel will be here to see Angelique Friday. I'll be sure to be home that day. I'll see how my parents want to deal with him after I talk to them. Could Clarisse invent an excuse to come for a surprise visit Saturday afternoon?"

"I'm sure she can. I'll tell her tonight you'd like her to be with you when you talk to Angelique."

"Thank you. I appreciate you telling me about Parker so quickly."

"You're welcome." Titus turned to walk to the barn and get his horse.

Luke watched him leave. He had warned Eugenia about Alton Parker's true reason for wanting to marry her. Now Eugenia was unknowingly protecting another woman from the man. He prayed for God to show him how to keep his cousin safe.

A plan forming in his mind, he marched toward the house. If Father felt up to it, they would have a serious discussion before coming down to the dining room for supper.

Once inside, he peeked into the parlor. Angelique still sat there reading. He tossed her a quick smile before going upstairs. His parents' voices drifted through the door to their room.

He knocked lightly. "May I come in?"

"Of course."

Luke opened the door before his father finished his reply. "Titus was here with information about Alton Parker you both need to hear."

Mother's eyebrows arched up.

He kept his voice low as he relayed to them everything

Titus had told him, then told them about the day Parker had challenged him to a duel. "I regret not telling you about the duel until now, but I assumed the man's words were empty bluster. The sooner Parker is banished from Oakridge, the better."

"I agree." Father took in a shaky breath as he shifted in the side chair beside the bed.

Mother studied him. "Are you all right, dear?"

"I'm fine. Rather I'll be fine once I tell that impudent cad to never call on our Angelique again."

"He's coming to call on her Friday. She told me that after church Sunday." Mother's words were too soft for anyone to hear outside of the room.

Father squared his thin shoulders. "I'll send him on his way as soon as he comes."

Luke sent up a silent prayer that his parents would listen to what he needed to say next. "Given this man's propensity to violence, I should be the one to speak to him. I doubt he has any respect for your age or health."

His father stiffened. "You're leaving tonight for Murfreesboro despite how ill-advised that venture is. How will you talk to him from there?"

Mother gripped the brush in her hand, eyeing him as if waiting for his answer.

"I won't." He sucked in a deep breath. "I'll leave for Mr. Glynne's house this afternoon to tell him why I must return here by tomorrow night. Allow Parker to call on Angelique on Friday to prevent her from suspecting anything. I'll order the man to never return to Oakridge after he's ridden far enough from the house that Angelique won't hear us."

Luke braced himself for Father's response, expecting him to say more about why Luke shouldn't be going to Murfreesboro at all.

Instead, his father shook his head. "Regardless of who sends Parker on his way, we still have to convince Angelique not to do something foolish, such as elope with him."

Father was willing to let Luke speak to Parker. One worrisome weight lifted off Luke's tensed shoulders. "Yes, sir. Clarisse and I will her everything we know about Parker on Saturday afternoon. I told Titus to ask Clarisse to call on Angelique. He assured me his sister will be here."

"I'm sorry things have to come to this." Mother sighed. "Luke, your plan sounds good. I agree you should be the one to send Mr. Parker away."

"With the understanding you're following my orders." Father rose to look Luke in the eyes.

"Of course. I'll be sure he knows I'm speaking on your behalf."

Father's countenance softened. "Next, we pray. Our sweet girl will be heartbroken once we succeed in doing what's best for her."

"Yes, she will." Mother's voice cracked as she reached for Father's hand.

The three of them prayed before Luke walked across the hall to his room. He'd leave for Murfreesboro as soon as he could pack his saddle bag.

He knocked on Mr. Glynne's door a little after six o'clock, thankful he could arrive earlier than usual with no notice. God had blessed him with more than a mentor. The butler ushered Luke in as soon as he answered the door. "Come right in, Mr. Luke. The master and mistress is always happy to see you."

"Thank you, Joshua."

"Is that you, Luke?" Mr. Glynne slid open the pocket door to his library.

"Yes, sir. I came early. I'll explain why as soon as I put my things in your spare room."

"I'll wait for you in my library."

Luke wasted no time joining Mr. Glynne. He took the dark green upholstered chair next to his friend. "I can only work tomorrow and must leave here in time to be back at Oakridge before dark."

Mr. Glynne placed his book on the small table in front of him. "Judging from your solemn expression and clipped tones, your clarification may not be good."

"It isn't." Luke did his best to explain the situation with Angelique and how Luke intended to confront Parker on Friday afternoon. During this telling, he didn't omit to mention Parker had challenged him to a duel.

Shaking his head, Mr. Glynne leaned against the back of his chair. "To think I recommended young Parker to Gerald Hampton as a possible suitor for Eugenia."

"You didn't know. None of us could have guessed the kind of man he is."

"No. We couldn't. But since his father is a good client, I needed to know the son is not the same caliber of a man."

"I agree. I'd appreciate your prayers as we deal with all of this. Especially for me when I confront Parker."

"How can you be sure Alton will never return after you challenge him?"

"I could ruin him if I care to do so. I pray I can convince him it would be in his best interest to never see Angelique again."

"I hope you're right." Mr. Glynne steepled his hands as he continued to study Luke. "You'll be in my prayers. May I tell my wife so she can pray for your family too?"

"Of course. I know Mrs. Glynne would never tell anyone else what we've discussed."

* * *

CLARISSE'S HANDS shook as she rested them on her saddle horn. She peered through the trees for a glimpse of Angelique ahead on the trail. Only God knew how she'd ride today without letting Angelique guess the secrets Clarisse now harbored. Two more days and the ordeal would be over. She'd help Luke tell Angelique the entire sordid truth about Alton Parker on Saturday. How she prayed her friend would listen.

In the meantime, she must pretend this day was as normal as any other day they'd ridden together. Angelique rounded the bend a few feet ahead of her and waved. Clarisse returned her greeting and waited for her friend.

"I hope you're doing well." Angelique rode up next to Clarisse.

"I am. How are you? Especially since I left you with so much to contemplate the last time we were together."

Angelique twisted to look directly at Clarisse. "I'm still thinking about what you said."

"Good. I assume you'll ask Mr. Parker for his side?"

"Of course. Your friend Eugenia must be the one who told you such a thing, so you didn't hear him say it to anyone. Alton should be able to defend himself."

Clarisse shook her head before she could check herself. "Someone I'd trust with my life was present when Mr. Parker said it in front of other people. But I'm not at liberty to divulge the person's name."

Angelique's mouth dropped open. She clamped it shut. Her eyes narrowed. "Why have you waited so long to tell me this?"

"I don't recall you asking for more information before. You wouldn't hear of me saying anything against Mr. Parker."

"I still don't want to hear it. So many people misjudge him."

Clarisse looked Angelique in the eyes. "What would you do if you found out everything I've said is true?"

"I-I don't know." She ducked her head. "Believe you, I suppose."

"I'm glad to hear that."

The most wonderful words she'd heard Angelique utter in so long. Despite having to strain to hear them since she spoke so softly. Rather than ruin the moment, Clarisse kept quiet. Perhaps Angelique was beginning to doubt Mr. Parker's word. If so, she and Luke might be able to help her better on Saturday than they hoped.

"I would believe you because I've never had a friend like you before." Angelique looked up again.

Clarisse's eyes misted. "Thank you. You are the friend I prayed for after Eugenia eloped."

The glowing smile Angelique gave her warmed Clarisse down to her toes. "Could we talk of something more pleasant now?"

"Of course."

"Good." Angelique squared her shoulders and grinned. "Luke's birthday is next month. Aunt Evelyn and I want to have a proper party for him, similar to the one I had. He won't hear of it. You are the only one who can change his mind."

No words of protest would leave Clarisse's dry throat. She shook her head as she stared at her friend. "He doesn't listen to me the way you think."

Angelique's laughter echoed through the woods.

"Hello, ladies," Luke called from somewhere on the trail behind them.

"He's not supposed to be here today." Angelique reined in her horse.

Clarisse did the same. "No, he's not." How much had he caught of their conversation, considering how sounds carried in the quiet woods?

"I'd say you ladies must be having a fine time." Luke chuckled as he rode up to them.

"We are. I've been telling Clarisse about the upcoming birthday supper and ball for your birthday." Angelique tossed him an impish grin.

Luke gazed directly at Clarisse. "There is no party planned of any kind."

"I've been informed otherwise, from a very good authority." Clarisse smiled. "I've already been invited to supper and the ball." She'd explain to him later why she was siding with Angelique. As the honoree and host, Luke would be obligated to dance with other women there. What better way to begin squelching suppositions about the two of them?

Luke shook his head.

"She accepted on behalf of her entire family." Angelique giggled.

"Is this what you do behind my back while I'm gone?"

"Aunt Evelyn and I tried while you were here. And speaking of being gone, why are you not in Murfreesboro?" Angelique smirked as if daring him not to go along with her quick change of subject.

Clarisse held her breath as she waited for Luke's answer, since Angelique had no idea the real reason Luke was here. Or what everyone planned for her the next two days.

"Mr. Glynne didn't have as much work for me, so I came home."

Angelique nodded. "Then you're welcome to join us on our ride."

"I'll gladly accept your invitation."

"You'd never turn down an opportunity to spend time with Clarisse. Plus, you can tell us who else to invite to your supper and the ball afterward."

"Lead the way, dear cousin." Luke looked as if he swallowed a groan.

"I shall." Angelique flicked her reins.

Luke and Clarisse followed her down the trail. This might be the last pleasant time the three of them had together for a while. Everything depended on what Angelique might do or say after Luke and Clarisse told her the entire truth about Mr. Parker and why he was to never call on her again.

Chapter Nineteen

Luke paced in the library with the door closed while straining to hear a knock on the front door. While Angelique made sure her hair and dress were perfect for Parker's arrival, he and his parents had prayed again for what must be done. Most of all, for Angelique. No one wanted her to hurt her, but her sweet-natured naivety left them no choice with her safety at risk. A man willing to murder someone was capable of things none of them wanted to consider. Parker must be banished to never return.

The scoundrel arrived a few minutes past two o'clock. The first time Luke had ever been glad to hear the butler ask the man to come in. Angelique soon joined her caller in the parlor. Law book in hand, Luke slid open the pocket door. He halted in the parlor doorway. "In case Mother or Father needs me, I'll be reading in the flower garden."

"Thank you for telling me." Angelique beamed at him, obviously happy he wouldn't be across the hall from her.

Luke went to tell the groom to saddle his horse. He'd follow Parker when he left for home, then confront him too far away from the house for Angelique to hear his words or suspect what he was doing. He prayed while he sat in his saddle, waiting and watching a short distance from the barn. He thanked God his parents agreed Luke should be the one to send Parker away.

By the time Parker sauntered toward his horse, Luke had checked his pocket watch more than once. Three-thirty. Past time the man should be leaving. He carefully shadowed the scoundrel after he rode away from the barn. He urged his horse into a canter to catch up when the man reached the edge of Oakridge.

"Hold up, Parker. I'd like a word with you." He reined his horse in next to his unwanted neighbor's mount.

"I don't owe you one cent now. What could we possibly have to talk about?"

"Angelique."

Parker halted his horse as he tossed Luke a disdainful glare. "We have nothing to discuss concerning her either."

"Correct." Luke stared, unflinchingly into the man's cold eyes. If only Angelique could see the real Parker displayed in front of him now. "My father says you are not to call on her again. His edict is not up for discussion."

An evil-looking grin inched across Parker's face. "If turning your father against me and hoping to do the same with Angelique is your idea of revenge, your plan will fail, but *mine* will not."

"Revenge? I have no need to avenge myself with you. I lost Eugenia to a wheelwright. As did you. Our rivalry ended the day the lady scorned you and eloped with Paul Stuart."

Parker flinched. Luke's words must have hit their intended target. "*Au contraire*, my friend. Everyone in the county knows how jealous you were and still are. So jealous you spread the false rumors about my inability to pay my obligations."

"Except you bragged in front of me and several other men how Eugenia's father had given you his blessing to marry her. I told Eugenia of your scheme for her own protection, but no one else. Any of the other men there could have talked to someone about your slowness to recompense them."

Parker swallowed hard. "Or Eugenia."

"Yes, Eugenia. I have no idea who she might have told after I warned her about you." He stared into the man's steely eyes, willing the words to sink into his barren soul.

The man squirmed in his saddle. "That wench could well have told half the county."

"Never speak of Eugenia or any other lady like that again. Knowing her as I do, I doubt she told anyone."

Parker's jaw tightened. His scowl intensified to a murderous glare. If the man had a pistol with him, Luke had no doubt the weapon would be pointed at his heart. "Malicious gossip is truly your *mode du operendi* for revenge. You disparaged me to Angelique before we even met."

"I wish that were true, but as I've said, I have no desire for revenge. My parents did tell her you aren't as upstanding as you pretend. But after you took advantage of her and twisted the facts to suit yourself, she refused to heed their warnings or allow me to tell her the truth about you."

Parker pointed his finger toward Luke's chest. "How dare you sound so sanctimonious about what you have or haven't said? You're the one who would most like to see me ruined."

Luke shook his head. "A man with your stellar reputation has many people to suspect of disparaging you. Only Angelique believes your lies."

"Which is why she'll defy your father's wishes and continue to see me any way she can devise. Elope with me, if I suggest it." His lip curled as he hurled his words at Luke.

"Marrying Angelique will be the perfect revenge for the way you've wronged me."

"She won't have you after I tell her how you intended to murder a man then kidnap his grieving widow and force her to come with you."

Parker's maniacal laugh sent chills through Luke's entire body. "You're sadly mistaken if you think dredging up that rumor will turn Angelique against me. Everyone but your esteemed friend Titus Matthews took my word over John Stuart's about what happened that day. Which is why Stuart had to leave for parts unknown to find another job."

"True." Luke fought to keep his voice calm, not sure what the raging man might say or do next. "Except now we have written testimony from two eyewitnesses who have not been in this area since early February. They have no idea you've been lying to and deceiving a lady neither of them knows exists."

Parker stiffened. "What do you mean?"

"Titus picked up letters from Paul and Eugenia on Tuesday."

The rascal's face lost all color.

"So, Angelique will soon know the entire truth about you. Perhaps if you agree to never call on her again, my family and the Matthews family will be kind enough not to dispute your version of what happened when you found Eugenia and Paul."

Parker clamped his open mouth shut as he glared in silence.

Luke stared straight into the man's eyes. "You'll also agree to never socialize with my cousin again. The minute you dare speak to her, I won't be spreading malicious gossip. I'll be telling the truth about you."

The man slumped in his saddle, limp as a flag on a windless day.

"I'll not say a word about this conversation as long as you leave my cousin alone. Also, if anyone asks why you're no longer seeing Angelique, you're to tell them the reasons are between the two of you, and a true gentleman would never gossip about a lady."

"How magnanimous of you." Sarcasm dripped from every syllable Parker uttered.

"Noble is a more apt description for not completely destroying your dubious reputation, don't you think?" Luke rested his hands on his saddle horn.

Parker scowled at him for one long moment, then spurred his horse into a gallop.

Luke sucked in more than one shuddering breath. He hoped he'd never have such an encounter with anyone again. But thank God, the man had left to be seen by his family no more.

How he prayed he was right.

CLARISSE'S HAND shook as she lifted the knocker on the Williams' front door. She hadn't slept well the last few nights out of concern for Angelique. How sad her gentle friend's trusting nature could well have been her undoing if her family and Clarisse weren't here to protect her.

"Miss Clarisse. Please come in." Amos greeted her as soon as he opened the door.

"I came to see Angelique. Is she home?" Clarisse hung her bonnet on the hall tree as she added her question in case Angelique were to hear her. For now, her visit must look to be a pleasant surprise. The truth would be forthcoming soon enough.

"I think she's in her room. I go tell her you're here right away." The butler showed her to the parlor.

Angelique's bubbling laugh preceded her down the stairs, reminding Clarisse that her ultimate goal was to see her friend continue to be so happy. "What a wonderful surprise to see you here." Angelique enveloped her in a hug when she stepped into the parlor.

"Mama didn't require the carriage today, so I assumed you'd like more help planning Luke's party since he was less than enthusiastic about it." Clarisse hoped her words sounded plausible. "My family says they'll be honored to help Luke celebrate."

"His birthday is two weeks from yesterday, so Aunt Evelyn and I will be busy." Angelique took her usual place on the couch next to Clarisse. "Of course, I didn't need to tell you when Luke's birthday is."

Yes, you did. Clarisse replied with only a smile. She remembered the month Luke was born, not the day. But explaining that to Angelique was more than she cared to do. Especially with her nerves already on edge as she watched for Luke to appear as he'd told Titus he would.

A pocket door slid open across the hall.

"Good afternoon. May I join you ladies since I heard my name mentioned?" Luke stepped into the parlor.

"Of course. I sent for refreshments. I'll send a servant to the kitchen and tell Jasmine to add a cup and saucer for you." Angelique grinned at him.

"Thank you, but that won't be necessary." Luke took the chair across from the couch.

Angelique chattered about which guests to include for Luke's supper and the ball until a servant brought in refreshments. "Are you sure you don't want anything, Luke?"

"I'm sure."

Clarisse took the cup of tea her friend offered, wishing she could refuse it. Choking down tea or anything else might prove to be a problem soon.

Luke shifted in his chair as Angelique stirred sugar into her tea "Dear cousin, I'd like to apologize for not keeping my promise to you."

Her eyes widened. "What promise?"

"I told you on our first ride I would continue my insufferable habit of watching out for you just as I did with my sisters. I apologize for not doing that as well as I should have."

Angelique laughed. "No apology needed. You've done quite well at being insufferable. Well enough, Alton and I can't help but notice your *watch care,* as you call it."

Her use of Mr. Parker's given name in front of her and Luke gave this planned conversation more urgency. A quick exchanged glance with Luke signaled he agreed. She handed her teacup to Angelique for her to place on the serving tray. No use trying to fool with something that would soon be in her way.

Luke stared straight into Angelique's eyes. "In that case, I'll be most insufferable this afternoon."

She shook her head. "I don't see how you could manage that."

"I asked Clarisse to come." Luke took a deep breath. "We need to talk about Alton Parker. I supposed you'd like to have your friend with you while we discuss the man."

Angelique turned her regard to Clarisse. "You've been helping Luke with his plan instead of helping me with mine?"

"I've never misled you about my opinion of Mr. Parker. Please listen. You need to hear what Luke wants to say." Clarisse ached for her friend as she reached to pat her arm. Angelique scooted away.

"I love you too much to allow you to continue down the

path you've chosen. After I tell you what you refused to hear earlier, you'll understand." Luke leaned forward.

"I do understand. I'm sorry your jealousy still clouds your judgment of Alton. We have nothing to talk about." Angelique's chin jutted out. Her teacup clattered on the tray as she set it down.

"We do. If Father felt up to it, he and Mother would be the ones having this conversation with you instead of me."

"Everyone in this house loves you. As do I, dear friend." Clarisse fought to keep her voice from cracking.

"Then why won't you all believe what I say about Alton?" She glanced from Clarisse to Luke.

He held her gaze. "I followed Alton yesterday after he left here and confronted him the way I should have done when he first started calling on you."

"He should be the one challenging you over the way you can barely be polite to him in public. You aren't even glad to see him in church." She hurled the words at him.

Luke held up his hand. "Hear me out, please. We had a very interesting discussion. Contrary to what he's hinted to you, his intentions are not honorable."

She gasped. "That's-that's not true." Her faltering tone sounded as if she might doubt her own assumption.

"Clarisse knows some of the things he's done. If you won't believe me, believe what she's tried to tell you."

Angelique glared as she pointed her finger at Clarisse. "How does he know what you've said to me?"

Clarisse flinched at her friend's disdainful tone. "I told him out of concern for you. I wish I could have been even more diligent to protect you too."

"Protect me? From Alton? He's not the evil villain both of you think he is." Angelique jumped to her feet.

"Please be seated and listen to us." Luke rose.

"I will not."

He placed his hand on her shoulder. "You could be in more danger than you know." He gazed into her angry eyes. "We're family. I care deeply about you. Please sit down."

Angelique did as he requested. Her slumping posture resembled a wilting flower almost ready to fall out of its vase. Was she ready to listen or preparing to fight?

"Since you've been wounded and misjudged by too many people, I'm so sorry to have to tell you something else hurtful. But Alton Parker is not who he pretends to be." Luke's tender expression emphasized his words.

"How do you know that?" Her lips trembled.

He sucked in a shuddering breath. "I was present the night he bragged to more than one man he'd pay all his gambling debts as soon as he married Eugenia. As Clarisse tried to tell you, he never loved her. He wanted the money from her generous dowry."

"He quit gambling after someone spread such awful gossip about him. Was that someone you?" She stiffened as she glared at him.

"No. I warned Eugenia about him, but I never said a word to anyone else."

Angelique refocused her scowl at Clarisse. "Since you and Eugenia were so close, she must have confided in you. Are you the one who talked about Alton behind his back?"

"No!" Luke gripped the arms of his chair with such force Clarisse wondered if he'd damage the furniture.

Angelique jumped at his angry words.

Luke relaxed his fingers. "Clarisse has never been one to spread rumors. You know her well enough to be sure of that."

"Then who did?"

"We don't know." Clarisse reached over to pat Angelique's shoulder. She didn't move away this time. "As Luke said, Mr.

Parker bragged about his upcoming marriage to more than one man. He must have angered one of them enough they told someone about him."

"Or somebody felt obligated to warn another woman about Parker for her sake." Luke's now quiet tone matched Clarisse's words. "Didn't you notice you were one of the few ladies who would dance with him?"

"He said he preferred my company to anyone else's."

"He didn't."

Angelique shook her head.

Clarisse ached to hug her distraught friend but doubted she'd accept such a gesture. "There's more you must know."

"And what is that?" Her voice cracked.

"The man is more dangerous than Luke or I believed." Clarisse went on to tell how Mr. Parker had tracked down Paul and Eugenia and might have murdered Paul if Mr. Stuart hadn't ridden up in time to prevent it.

Angelique's eyes widened more with each detail Clarisse added, but she didn't challenge her friend's words.

"You should also know the real reason he's pretended to care for you." Luke shifted in his chair.

"*Pretended?*" Angelique's voice squeaked.

"Yes, pretended." He told her what Parker had said yesterday about using her to distress him and repay him for warning Eugenia and telling others what he'd said about her. "He must still be angry I refused his earlier demand for a duel and decided you were the perfect foil to use against me instead."

Angelique's face blanched. "When did he challenge you to a duel?" Her tone sounded labored, as if she could barely force her words from her mouth.

"The day after he returned from trying to kill Paul. He surmised I had to be the one to tell Eugenia the truth about him. I refused his demand for revenge that day, so he saw you as the perfect way to avenge himself."

"No …" She shook her head once more. "That was months ago. Alton has changed. He told me so." Her voice cracked. She swiped at a tear trickling down her cheek.

"He agreed to leave you alone only because I can ruin him with what Eugenia and Paul wrote. His concern is for his precious reputation. Not for you."

More tears slid from her eyes.

Luke walked over and offered his handkerchief. Then knelt in front of her. "I'm sorry to have to cause you such pain. But I love you and want to protect you."

She sniffed. "I love you."

Luke took the spot on the other side of his cousin. Angelique wrapped her arms around his neck, buried her face against his shoulder, and wept. He enfolded her in his arms.

Mr. and Mrs. Williams walked into the parlor as Luke continued to hold Angelique. Mrs. Williams bent to rub Angelique's shoulder. "I'm sorry, dear. You had such hope after Mr. Parker came to church."

Clarisse rose. "Please take my seat, Mrs. Williams."

She accepted Clarisse's offer. Angelique pulled away from Luke to sit up again. Mrs. Williams squeezed her niece's hand.

"I'll see myself out and allow you all time as a family." Clarisse pivoted toward the door.

"You belong here too." Mr. Williams lightly placed a hand on her sleeve.

"Thank you, sir, but I don't."

"Yes, you do. You've played an important part in helping Angelique." Luke gazed at her as if she were the only one in the room.

"Luke is right. Please stay."

Clarisse took the chair Luke had been sitting in.

Mr. Williams stepped closer to Angelique, stopping just in front of her. "So, dear niece, I'm forbidding you to see Mr. Parker. Luke told him to never associate with you again. I'm sure you understand why."

"Yes, sir." She dabbed her moist eyes with Luke's handkerchief, then got to her feet. She walked over to Clarisse. "Thank you for watching over me too. As I said, I've never had a friend as true as you." She bent to hug Clarisse.

"You're more than welcome." Clarisse sniffed away her own tears.

Angelique returned to her spot between Luke and his mother. Clarisse stood. "I do need to go."

Luke rose. "I'll see you to your carriage." His intense regard unnerved her while she tied her bonnet.

"Did I do something wrong?"

He shook his head. "I'm assuming that bonnet with the red ribbon is your favorite as often as you wear it?"

"Um, yes." How much attention was he paying to her if he noticed what she wore and how often she wore it? Especially after the trying time they'd just experienced.

He opened the door for her to step onto the porch. She definitely needed to go home now.

He closed the door behind them. "Thank you for going well beyond what either of us envisioned when we made our pact."

"You're welcome."

Instead of allowing her driver to assist her, he helped her up into the carriage. Then remained in the yard to watch her leave.

Clarisse closed her eyes as she leaned against the black leather seat. They had accomplished what they'd set out to do. Now what? Thinking about seeing Luke only at church didn't settle right in her mind. She'd see him at his party soon. But dancing with him ... If she danced with him, it wouldn't be the same with no shared purpose or reason to be together.

A long sigh punctuated her musings. She'd be back to the days of dancing with someone only to appease her mother. Back to the way she'd wanted her life to be since she'd lost Garland.

Was that what she wanted now?

Chapter Twenty

After shaking hands with the pastor, Luke followed his family out of the church. Angelique had already fallen in step with Clarisse. Visiting with such a loyal friend would do his cousin good after such a trying day yesterday. But not him. He'd use this time to begin ending the charade he and Clarisse had been playing too well the last few months. He spied Travis Glynne not far from the hitching post and headed toward him.

"Good to see you." Travis smiled as he looked past Luke to where Angelique stood with Clarisse.

"I assume we'll see you Friday at our ball." This man was a much better possibility for a beau for Angelique. He did have a good reason to talk to him instead of Clarisse.

"I'll be there."

"Good. You should have an easier time dancing with my cousin. Parker is no longer calling on her." Luke kept his voice low, rather than risk someone else catching their conversation. Angelique might think he was already interfering with her life again.

"He's not?" Travis turned his full attention to Luke.

Luke nodded. He'd finally found one good reason to talk about the party he still didn't want to attend. "She hasn't said why. But I suspect if you bide your time, she might allow you to call again later."

Travis grinned ear to ear. "I'll keep that in mind."

When a couple of other men joined them, the subject changed to the cotton crop. Luke's gaze wandered toward Clarisse. He'd much rather listen to her no matter what she was talking about. No. Better to remain where he was. The moment his parents walked toward their carriage, he excused himself.

"Did you have a good visit with Clarisse?" Mother smiled at Angelique from the seat across from him and his cousin.

"I did. Clarisse said she could ride with me on Tuesday." Her tone sounded more subdued than normal.

"I'm sure it will do you good, dear."

"Yes. It will." She sighed. "Riding in the woods will be soothing."

Father focused his gaze directly on her. "Luke should accompany you for a while, with his pistol."

Her eyes widened. She shook her head. "I'd like to think something so drastic isn't necessary. I don't like guns after the way my papa died."

"I understand. But if you want to ride, you will have an armed escort or stay home."

Angelique studied Father as if weighing his words. "I want to see my friend. Luke can come with us."

"With his gun," Father repeated his ultimatum.

"Yes, sir."

* * *

"I don't think your weapon is necessary." From her saddle, Angelique watched Luke's every move Tuesday afternoon while he secured his pistol in his saddle pommel holster.

The holster Mother had insisted he have in case he had to travel alone at night to or from Murfreesboro. "I've only fired my gun at empty glass bottles. I have no plans to change that, if at all possible."

"As Uncle Douglas says, you're riding with me only for a while. I intend this to be a short while."

"I'd like that too." He swung up in his saddle.

He and Angelique rode away from the barn in silence. He'd never supposed he'd be happy to listen to her chattering until she didn't. His talkative cousin had grown on him in ways he'd never dreamed possible.

"As much as I don't like it, thank you for caring enough about me to be an armed escort." Angelique glanced over at him as they neared the end of the long tree-lined driveway.

"You're welcome."

"I'll be your chaperone today. I promise not to be as insufferable as you've been with me." An impish grin spread across her face.

Despite her teasing, he'd welcome any sign her usual happy outlook was returning. And welcome the sight of Clarisse more. "Except Clarisse has no idea I'm with you."

"Watch her face when she first sees you. I'll be so glad when both of you quit pretending you're only friends."

"We aren't pretending." His denial sounded flat to his own ears. But further repudiation would be a waste of his time and breath. Especially when he needed to convince himself of his words more than he did with Angelique. He'd eagerly anticipated seeing Clarisse again since the moment Father had said Luke should accompany her and Angelique.

They soon caught sight of Clarisse rounding the bend ahead.

"Watch her face." Angelique whispered as she waved to her friend.

"I didn't expect to see you today." Clarisse's entire countenance lit up when she saw him.

Angelique tossed him a smug grin. The trail widened enough for them to all ride abreast. She positioned her horse to put Clarisse riding in the middle between her and Luke.

"Father insisted I accompany you ladies as a precaution. I agreed since I don't trust Parker any more than he does."

Clarisse's smile faded. "I'm of the same opinion. Titus cautioned me to be watchful before I left. I had a hard time persuading him not to ride with me and Angelique. He'll be glad when I tell him you came with us."

"All of us are happy Luke is here." Angelique's sparkling eyes signaled she was pleased for more than one reason.

Clarisse replied with a slight nod. A strange, muted reaction compared to her glowing smile moments ago. If their chaperone weren't around, he might ask why. But the days of meeting her alone in the woods to discuss his cousin were done.

Angelique's expression sobered. "I can't thank either of you enough for watching out for me and caring enough to tell me the truth even when I didn't want to hear it."

"You're more than welcome." Clarisse beamed toward Angelique. "We're happy you listened to us Saturday, but sad someone hurt you again."

Clarisse's spontaneous use of we and us sounded like a woman who still considered the two of them as a couple. The way she spoke for him reminded him of how his parents did the same with each other.

"Being insufferable has its good points. Does it not?" Luke

teased his cousin rather than continue puzzling over what Clarisse might or might not be thinking.

"Yes, it does." The mischievous glint in his cousin's eyes made Luke wonder what she might or might not do to repay him for aggravating her the way he'd done.

The trail narrowed. Luke took the lead. Clarisse followed with Angelique in the rear. His cousin stayed back when the trail widened enough for two riders, forcing Clarisse to ride alongside Luke.

Clarisse glanced over at him. "You're still enjoying your work in Murfreesboro?"

"I am."

"He's also looking forward to his birthday celebration next Friday more than he'll admit." Angelique's laugh left little doubt she was enjoying being a chaperone and inserting comments the way he and Clarisse had done while riding with her and Parker. The difference being, she'd do her best to keep them together, not separate them.

Luke shrugged. "I've reconciled myself to the party Angelique and Mother have devoted so many hours to."

"You *are* insufferable. To me but not to everyone." She came up on the other side of Clarisse when the trail allowed, grinning at her friend.

Clarisse's cheeks colored. She stared ahead at some distant object.

Luke forced his gaze away from her. The woman in the maroon riding habit was more alluring every time he saw her. Not the way he should be thinking of someone who was only a friend.

Angelique continued her teasing for the remainder of the ride. Enough so that Luke was trying to think of ways to not accompany her and Clarisse again by the time he walked into his room to change clothes. Which he should be considering no matter how much he enjoyed being with Clarisse. Staying away from her or any other woman was the only way to never risk being hurt or betrayed again.

He yanked open his nightstand drawer to put his pistol and holster away, dislodging a wrinkled page at the back. Eugenia's letter of apology. Instead of burning it, he'd saved it to remind him to never trust another woman with his heart. He should reread it, memorize it after he'd let his guard down with Clarisse so many times lately. He pulled the letter out of the drawer.

Sitting on his bed, he fingered the crumpled, folded page. Eugenia would have never been able to give him false hope if he hadn't put himself in that position. Yet the impetuous, unpredictable woman he'd warned about Parker had inadvertently helped him convince Angelique of the same man's lies in her letter to Clarisse.

Impetuous? Unpredictable? As well as headstrong. A perfect description for Eugenia he could now remember with some fondness since he'd let go of his bitterness toward her. Much like the cousin he so dearly loved. His maddening cousin, who often drove him to distraction.

He jerked upright. The letter fell from his grasp. Hadn't Eugenia written something similar? His hands trembled as he bent to retrieve the page from the floor.

Luke,

My dear friend, I hope and pray you can someday forgive me for the terrible way I hurt you. I'm so sorry for misleading you and giving you false hope by allowing you to continue to call on me.

I never wanted to engage in such a charade with you. I couldn't allow Papa to discover whom I truly loved, so I used you as a way to placate my father plus keep Alton Parker at bay. For that, I am deeply sorry.

I prayed Papa would become a Christian and be so changed he would accept Paul Stuart as the husband God intended for me. Then, I planned to tell you the truth about the man I loved and apologize to you in person. Only God knows why my prayers weren't answered in the fashion I'd hoped. As we both know, Papa chose Alton Parker over you. My father intended to force me to marry Mr. Parker as soon as our time of mourning for my mother ended. I couldn't go against God's will and marry an unbeliever like Alton, so I chose to disobey my father rather than God.

I hope and pray, dear friend, you realize someday how I would have only exasperated you if we had wed. Since you were kind enough to warn me of Mr. Parker's less-than-honorable intentions, might I return the favor and offer you advice from one friend to another? You should give prayerful consideration to calling on Clarisse Matthews. The two of you have such similar personalities that you might be well suited for each other.

Once again, I beg your forgiveness. I will always cherish your friendship.

Sincerely,
Eugenia

The words from her letter slammed into his soul like a fist, knocking the air out of him. His old friend had been so right. Life with Eugenia wouldn't have exasperated him—it would have driven him mad. He might have even come to hate her instead of being able to appreciate or enjoy her impulsive ways. He wouldn't think of marrying a woman like Angelique. How could he have believed he'd be happy with Eugenia?

Taking in a deep breath, he closed his eyes. Then what of Clarisse? Could Eugenia be right about her best friend?

He'd come to admire Clarisse the last few months. Had he come to love her? *Yes.* Thinking about Tuesdays without her hurt his heart and soul. But the alliance they'd formed was based on friendship. She'd never hinted she'd like more. If he asked to court her, she could well refuse his suit. But if he didn't ask, didn't take the risk …

If he'd been this fearful of taking chances, he'd have never gone to college to study for a calling his parents didn't approve of or understand. Accepting Mr. Glynne's offer was the first time he'd taken a small step of faith in so long. Trusting God was so much easier to think about than to do. Thinking came with no risks. Doing something did.

Perhaps the letter he'd saved for the wrong reason, God intended to use to embolden him to pursue Clarisse. To go after love no matter the cost, as Eugenia had done. He smoothed the page and refolded it before placing it in the drawer with his holster and pistol.

* * *

Clarisse trailed behind her mother as Titus lifted the door knocker. Like Luke, she'd reconciled herself to celebrating his birthday tonight. Jenette's condition now prevented her from going out. If only Clarisse had some sort of valid reason to stay home. The early supper with only a few guests would be bearable. Enduring a ball as she'd done before she and Luke had made their pact might be an ordeal. Dancing with other men appealed less to her now than it had before.

The only man who compared to Luke had died two years ago. Had Luke now come close to Garland in her regard? Perhaps. Except that Luke had been clear, he rode with her and Angelique on Tuesdays now as a precaution. Not the right sort of reasoning from a man who might return her affection.

"We're so glad to see all of you." Mrs. Williams ushered them inside, ending Clarisse's reflections.

Mr. Williams made a slight bow to Mama. "Thank you for coming."

"We wouldn't miss celebrating with Luke." A smile wreathed Mama's face.

Angelique hugged Clarisse as she walked into the entry hall. "I'm always happy to see you."

"We'll visit in the parlor until the servants are ready to bring in the meal. Adam Glynne and his wife should be here soon. Travis can't come until tonight." Mrs. Williams led the way.

Luke stepped to Clarisse's side. "Thank you for coming." He smiled into her eyes, ignoring everyone else in the room.

"You're welcome." Which he was.

He seated her not far from the couch his parents and her mother claimed, then took the chair closest to her.

Mr. and Mrs. Glynne arrived a few minutes later. Luke left to greet them and ushered them into the parlor. "Allow me to introduce Angelique, the cousin you haven't met yet. I believe you know everyone else."

"We've heard so much about you." Mrs. Glynne extended her hand to Angelique before taking the chair next to her.

"Luke has told me so many good things about you and your husband." Angelique smiled at the lady.

Since Luke and Titus gave up their chairs, Mr. Glynne sat next to Clarisse. Luke positioned himself by her chair.

"Angelique is not the only young lady Luke tells us about." He spoke too softly for his words to carry across the room due to so much conversation buzzing around.

Luke had talked about her? "We have known each other a while."

"Which is good."

Mrs. Williams soon announced the meal was ready. Supper was uneventful, as Clarisse had supposed it would be. One event done. The ball in the evening left. When the men headed to the library, Titus excused himself to ride home and be with Jenette. Clarisse followed Angelique upstairs to her room. A time to change clothes, perhaps relax a while before steeling herself for another dreaded ball. Mama and Mrs. Glynne went with Mrs. Williams to await the ball.

Angelique sat on her bed and patted the spot next to her. "I've been looking forward to time alone with you."

Clarisse settled beside her friend, twisting to almost face her. "I've missed talking to you too."

"Exactly. And Luke gets a chance to visit with his beloved Mr. Glynne."

"He's been our family attorney ever since I can remember. I'm sure Luke enjoys working with him." Clarisse didn't mind Angelique mentioning Luke without adding a single hint about his and Clarisse's relationship.

"He does. He tells me all about it when we're alone." Angelique sighed. "I'm praying and praying my uncle and aunt realize how much Luke wants to be an attorney. They don't understand why Luke would rather argue in some court than run Oakridge. But I'm not telling you anything you don't know." Her teasing tone indicated how much she assumed Luke confided in her.

Luke didn't want to run the family plantation at all? "He's a very selfless man leaving college to help his father when he'd rather do something else." Stating what she did know would perhaps prevent Angelique from guessing how few details Luke had told her about his desires. Most of their conversations had concerned how to help Angelique.

She'd come to admire Luke lately but still knew so little about the man she claimed as a good friend. Perhaps she should remedy that. Her heart grew more insistent by the day.

But her mind cautioned her that being careful with him or any other man was still best.

"He is. I don't wonder that he might sell Oakridge if it were his, but he stays here out of love for his parents. Selfless is a good description of him."

Clarisse thoroughly enjoyed her uninterrupted time with Angelique, especially after learning Luke would rather practice law than grow cotton part of the time. Did not loving a plantation as much as she'd assumed mean he'd be amenable to her thoughts about slavery?

By the time she followed Angelique down the stairs, Luke and his parents stood in the hall, waiting for the other guests to come. He met her at the last step, extending his hand to her. "You are an absolute vision of loveliness." His shining eyes emphasized his words spoken just above a whisper.

"Thank you." She placed her hand in his.

"Please honor me with the first dance."

"I will." Her heart pounded too hard for her to say more.

He led her to the dining room, where they were met with approving looks from Mama and Mr. and Mrs. Glynne. "Would you like some punch?"

"Yes, please."

He seated her next to Angelique. "Could I bring you punch too?"

"I'd like that." Angelique picked up her fan as Luke walked toward the table. "I was close enough to hear Luke compliment you. I have to agree with his assessment." She spoke from behind her fan as she leaned toward Clarisse. "The garnet jewelry is the perfect accent for your garnet-colored sash and ivory silk gown."

"Thank you. I'll tell you later why I haven't worn this outfit in a while."

Luke delivered their punch then returned to the front hall to help his parents welcome guests.

A while later, when the instruments sounded for the first dance, Luke claimed Clarisse. He danced with other women the next few times, as any good host should. Which left Clarisse to accept other partners she was sure would never be more than friends. Amos Browning openly proclaimed he would one day take over his family's plantation. Travis Glynne was already overseeing his father's property.

Luke asked for the next dance and then stayed by her side when it ended. When the instruments began a waltz, he took her hand. "You're my favorite partner for a waltz."

"Your efforts to convince everyone we're only friends are failing miserably tonight." She couldn't manage to sound the least bit severe if she'd had to.

"As are yours. Not one word of protest from you for my behavior."

She shook her head. "Not one." His look of sheer adoration made it hard to breathe, much less speak.

"Would you like to step onto the porch to catch your breath?" Luke had yet to release her hand after the dance ended.

"I would." No matter that she should, she couldn't refuse him. Catching her breath somewhere alone might be safer. But one glance into his eyes sent her caution skittering away like fallen leaves blown by the wind.

He placed her hand on his sleeve as he led her into the hall and out the door. With no one else on the porch, Luke halted by the rail not far from the door. A swath of moonlight lit up the well-cared-for lawn in front of them.

"I'll not tease you about wearing red again. The dark red sash with your light-colored gown is stunning. As is your dark red necklace and earrings."

"Thank you." She fingered the silver filigree necklace inset with her favorite stones. "I haven't worn this ensemble for a while."

"May I ask why?"

"Yes. Being with you gave me the courage to wear this dress and the jewelry again."

"It has?"

She gazed into his eyes, wishing they could talk where the night shadows didn't partially obscure his features. "Pretending to be more than your friend helped me realize I'm ready to move beyond my grief and consider loving a man again."

"Dare I hope I'm one of the men you're considering?" He brushed her arm with his fingers.

His touch sent shivers up and down her arm despite the warm September night. "You may."

The door opened. The light from inside splashed across the porch as another couple stepped outside.

"Could I call on you Monday afternoon so we can continue this conversation? I'd call sooner but I need to see to business I've neglected here in order to be ready for this party."

"Monday will be good." Waiting a few days would be sensible for both of them.

He extended his arm to her to escort her back inside. "I'd ignore the good manners my parents instilled in me and dance every remaining dance with you if I could."

"Imagine the gossip about us if you did."

"True." He didn't elaborate as he opened the door to let her precede him inside.

By the time Clarisse settled onto her seat in the carriage across from Mama, she wondered if she'd stay awake during the ride home. Luke had danced as much with her as he could. She hadn't danced this much since before Garland died.

"As much time as you spent on the dance floor, you must have enjoyed tonight," Mama spoke as the carriage rolled away.

With only the coach lamps outside for light, Clarisse couldn't see her mother's face well but had no doubt how broad her mother's smile must be. "I did."

"I'm glad to see you taking pleasure in parties again."

Clarisse yawned aloud. Mama could be appalled at her poor manners later. For now she'd like to limit conversation about resuming a more normal life. Unless Luke accepted her unpopular beliefs, there would be no social life to talk about. "I had a wonderful time, but I'm too tired to discuss it now." She leaned her head against the back of the seat.

Her mother said nothing more the rest of the way home, leaving Clarisse to ponder her day in peace. She'd taken some monumental steps tonight. Garland would want her to live again. To love again. Perhaps love Luke? A hazardous possibility unless he truly didn't want to grow cotton. But one her heart was too willing to risk.

Chapter Twenty-One

Luke walked into the library not long after breakfast Monday morning. Mother and Angelique were going over meals with the cook. Father had taken a book to read in the flower garden. Luke would use this time to pray about his visit with Clarisse before delving into one of his law books. Judging from the few men he'd seen her dance with last Thursday, he was the only man she was considering loving again.

A loud knock interrupted his thoughts. No one ever called this time of morning. He stepped into the hall as Amos opened the door to reveal Titus Matthews. Luke rushed to greet him, wondering what sort of calamity brought his neighbor here.

"Do come in."

"Thank you. While we were eating breakfast, one of Mr. Hampton's servants came to tell us they found Mr. Hampton dead in his bed this morning. I rode over to tell you as soon I could."

"I'm sorry. I know your family was close friends with him."

Titus nodded. "We were until Eugenia eloped. I came to you first since Clare says you wrote his last will. Riding here is faster than going to Murfreesboro to talk to Mr. Glynne. With the three oldest children in Nashville, what do we do?"

Luke took a moment to think. "Someone should ride to Nashville today to notify his children. That would be faster than mailing a letter. Mr. Glynne should be told." He paused as a possible plan formed in his mind. "Since Mr. Glynne can't go to Nashville, I should do that. Can you ride to Murfreesboro and tell Mr. Glynne?"

"I can. Mother was already saying we should go over there to see that the servants tend to Mr. Hampton properly and be sure his household is in order for when his children can get there. She and Clare can tend to that without me."

"Good. Go home and tell your family of our plans. Please tell Clarisse I'm terribly sorry I won't see her this afternoon—"

"She didn't mention you calling today." Titus grinned.

Words he wasn't sure he wanted to hear. Yet he hadn't told his family of his afternoon plans because he didn't want them to think his visit to Clarisse meant more than it might. Not when she was only considering him, and he likewise with her. "She probably intended to mention it later. I may not see her until Sunday. Please tell Mr. Glynne I'm going to Nashville. He'll know what else should be done."

"All right. I'll be on my way so you can leave as soon as possible."

Luke opened the door for him. "Thank you for always being such a dependable friend."

"You're welcome."

Luke went to find Father. He'd tell Mother and Angelique later. His father sat in the center of the garden on a wrought iron bench beneath the gazebo. He took the spot next to his father.

"Didn't you intend to read in the library?" Father placed his open book on his lap.

"Yes, but I have disturbing news."

"What is it?"

He told Father of Titus's brief visit. "As I told Titus, I'll leave for Nashville as soon as possible. I'd like to arrive as close to dark as I can."

"You'll be gone two days if you go there and manage to come straight back. Do you still plan to go to Murfreesboro on Thursday?" Father turned to look Luke in the eyes.

"Yes. Mr. Glynne postponed some work last week due to my birthday celebration."

Father slammed his book shut. "Which means you'll be here Wednesday and Saturday at best. We're well into early harvest. You can't be gone that long."

"Mr. Glynne is not able to go to Nashville. You know that after seeing him last week. I won't desert a dear friend at such a dire time."

"But you'll desert Oakridge and me at one of the most crucial times of our year?" His eyes snapped as he hurled the words at Luke.

"No, sir." Luke took a deep breath. He had to remain calm despite his father's agitation. "We have a capable overseer. He can ride to the house to speak to you while I'm gone."

He pointed a shaking, slender finger at Luke. "And leave the field hands unsupervised?"

"The overseer shouldn't have to talk with you during the day unless there's an emergency. Otherwise, he can discuss the harvest with you before you retire for the night."

"No. Someone else can go to Nashville."

"Who? It's not the sheriff or deputy's job. A family friend or attorney should tell them. I'm both of those. I'll tell Mother and Angelique of my plans, then pack my saddle bag." Luke rose. "We can talk after I'm home."

Luke marched toward the kitchen. Telling his mother in

front of the servants would prevent her from ranting at him as his father had done. He'd face their rage when he came home.

Mother and Angelique were still in the kitchen when Luke walked in. He told them the news about Mr. Hampton then about his trip to Nashville and why he had to go. "As I told Father, I should be home late tomorrow."

"This is not acceptable." Mother's terse tone contradicted her soft voice.

"I've already talked to Father. I'll see everyone late tomorrow if I can." He placed a kiss on his mother's cheek and walked out the door.

"Luke, wait." Angelique called from behind him.

He paused to let her catch up to him.

"I assume Uncle Douglas isn't happy with your decision."

"He's furious. May we talk as we walk to the house?"

"Of course. You need to be on your way soon. I'm praying for you." She fell into step with him.

He slowed his pace for her. "Thank you."

"I wish I could help you."

"Your prayers are a welcome help. Pray for Father and Mother as well."

"I will. For now, I'll go back to the kitchen. I'll bundle up the leftover biscuits and ham from breakfast so you have something to eat on the way."

"No need to make Mother angry at you too."

"I probably already have. You stood with me. I'll stand with you. Don't leave before I bring your food." Angelique grinned and turned toward the kitchen.

Luke hurried to his room. He hadn't intended to drag Angelique into his disagreement with his parents. But since she'd stepped in of her own accord, he welcomed having her on his side.

A short time later, Angelique walked with him to the barn.

"I put some dried peaches in with the biscuits and ham. Aunt Evelyn didn't object in front of the servants."

"Thank you. I hope she doesn't scold you later." He added the bundle to his saddle bag then swung up into his saddle. "I hope to see be home late tomorrow, but sometime Wednesday is also a possibility."

"Either way, Godspeed, cousin."

He waved to her as he rode away. His parents' conspicuous absence spoke volumes. If they didn't have a capable overseer, Luke would have chosen to stay and help his father instead of Mr. Glynne. But his mentor was the person with no one to help. He couldn't and wouldn't desert the man who'd supported him better than his own family. He prayed for the day his parents understood.

By the time he rode into Nashville, the businesses were closed with only a few people still walking the streets, which meant he couldn't locate either of the Hampton brothers or their sister Grace's husband at their places of work. He'd seen Grace occasionally at her parents' home the last few years. Mr. Glynne had mentioned she and her banker husband lived not far from town. Such a prominent family shouldn't be difficult to locate. Since he'd seen Grace at her parents' home more than her brothers, he'd rather try to find her first.

The second gentleman Luke stopped knew the Stockton family and gave him directions to their house after Luke told him enough details about the Hampton brothers and Grace to satisfy the man Luke's errand was genuine. Details he wouldn't have known if he hadn't listened to Mr. Glynne talking about the family. Like Eugenia, he didn't know her older siblings well.

Darkness had settled in by the time Luke rode up to the Stocktons' two-story brick house. He prayed as he lifted the door knocker. A servant opened the door. Lighted candle in hand, the man looked Luke up and down.

"I'm sorry to call at this late hour. I'm Luke Williams from Murfreesboro. Mrs. Stockton knows who I am. I have important news for her."

"I go see what the mastah say."

The man closed the door, leaving Luke standing on the porch. He would have done the same thing to a stranger knocking on his door this time of night.

A man with thinning brown hair opened the door. "I'm David Stockton. You have news for my wife?"

"Yes, sir. I apologize for the time. But I live near Mr. Hampton and left this morning to tell her about her father rather than wait the several days a letter would take to come."

"All right. Come into my office. Grace is telling the boys goodnight. I'll hear you out before I call her downstairs."

"Thank you, sir." Luke followed the man down the hall, waiting until the servant lit the lamp in Mr. Stockton's office to step into the room.

Mr. Stockton took the chair behind the desk. "Please be seated."

Luke did as told. "Gerald Hampton's servants found him dead this morning." He went on to tell him the few details he had and that Titus had ridden to tell Mr. Glynne. "I'm sorry to bring you such bad news. Since I work for Mr. Glynne now, I took it upon myself to tell you as soon as possible."

"I appreciate that. My wife will too." Mr. Stockton steepled his fingers. "Grace has been concerned about her father for a while. She won't be surprised." He rose. "I'll go get her so you can tell her."

The man soon returned with Grace. Luke rose. "I assume you remember me?"

"Of course. Your family has been friends with my family for

a long time. David says you have something to tell me about Papa." Her voice quivered as she reached for her husband's hand.

"I do. Your father died sometime after he went to bed last night. The servants found him this morning. His passing appeared to be peaceful, from what they told Titus."

"Oh." Grace moaned and slumped against her husband.

Mr. Stockton slipped his arm around her waist. "Sit down before you collapse." He guided her to a chair by his desk, then took the one next to her.

Wiping her tears with her handkerchief, Grace gripped her husband's hand. "This is all Eugenia's fault. He was in perfect health until ..."

Luke could finish the sentence for her as he stood watching. He wasn't surprised she blamed her father's death on what Eugenia had done. But after dealing with his parents, he was beginning to understand why Eugenia had defied her father and married Paul Stuart. He prayed his and his parents' differences didn't result in a permanent estrangement like the one in the Hampton family.

Grace sniffed away her tears as she looked up at Luke. "Thank you for coming to tell me." She stood. "You must be worn out from such a long ride. Please, stay the night with us."

Luke rose. "Thank you. I'd appreciate that."

A short time later, Luke stretched out on the bed in the guest room. Grace had served him what was left from their supper. Angelique would be quite happy to know the Stocktons had received him so well. But would his parents be glad for him? They had been protesting less about his time in Murfreesboro lately. Until today. He'd never displeased them the way he'd done by coming to Nashville.

While enjoying a sumptuous breakfast the next morning, Luke and Grace discussed what should be done next. Grace wanted to be the one to tell her two brothers about their father. She and her siblings would be at their father's house late Wednesday. She wanted the funeral on Thursday afternoon at two, certain Nathan and James would approve of that. He'd agreed to tell Mr. Glynne of their plans. Which meant he'd ride to Murfreesboro instead of home today.

He bid the Stocktons goodbye around eight o'clock. Mr. and Mrs. Glynne wouldn't mind the late hour Luke would be knocking on their door. He feared he would receive a warmer reception from them than he would at home.

Chapter Twenty-Two

Luke awoke Wednesday morning in the Glynnes' guest room and had to remember where he was. Sleeping in his own room tonight would be good. Perhaps. He intended to be home before noon. He'd speak with and try to reason with his parents. Only God knew how that would end.

After shaving and putting on clean clothes, he made his way downstairs. Mr. and Mrs. Glynne greeted him as he walked toward the dining room.

"You must be famished after only a supper of left over chicken and carrots. I had our cook fix a good breakfast for you."

"Thank you." He took his customary chair at the table after Mr. Glynne seated his wife.

The cook set platters with eggs, bacon, and biscuits on the table. Mr. Glynne thanked God for the food and Luke's safe trip to and from Nashville. The conversation about the weather and the latest news in *The Courier* was as pleasant as the company he enjoyed.

Mr. Glynne placed his napkin on the table. "I assume you'd like to leave for Oakridge soon."

"Yes, sir."

"Come with me to my office first. I'd like to talk over a few details concerning the Hamilton family." He stood with the aid of his cane.

Luke followed Mr. Glynne to his office at the other end of the house, careful to match his mentor's slower pace. Mr. Glynne no longer motioned for Luke to be seated in the chair on the other side of the desk from him. "I assume you and your family will be at Gerald's funeral Thursday."

"Yes."

"As will Miriam and I. Travis, too, since Titus told me he would see that the Hampton servants tell the other neighbors." Mr. Glynne shuffled the papers on his desk. "I'll read Gerald's will to his children after the funeral. I want you there with me when I do. I don't know if they want to sell the plantation or hire a manager and keep it. I'll tell them you will take care of whatever they'd like to do."

"I'm honored, sir."

"I have full confidence in you. You'll spare me from trips to and from Gerald's plantation. Possibly from going to Nashville for signatures later." He took in a ragged breath. "You're a Godsend, my boy."

"Thank you." Luke choked out the words. If only his father thought so much of him.

"Your parents still don't approve of you working with me, do they?"

"No." He told Mr. Glynne what Father had said Monday morning about deserting Oakridge and him since he'd arrived too late last night for any such discussion. "But the more I pray about it, the more certain I am this is God's way to answer my prayers one small step at a time."

"I agree. Let's pray before you leave for home."

* * *

ABOUT TEN O'CLOCK, Luke left his horse with the groom. He'd go to his room, empty his clothes from his saddle bag, put away his pistol, and then find his parents. When he walked in the back door, Angelique and Mother's voices drifted from the front of the house. Judging from what he could hear, Mother must be helping her niece with her embroidery. Since Angelique's instruction on needlework had been lacking, Mother had been working to remedy that not long after Angelique had come to them.

"You have a natural ability as quickly as you've caught on." Mother praised Angelique as Luke stepped into the entry hall.

"I have a good teacher."

Luke halted in the doorway. "Yes, you do."

"You're home!" Angelique dumped her embroidery on the couch and rushed to hug him.

With his saddle bag and holster draped over one shoulder, he almost lost his balance. He wrapped his arms around her as best he could. "I'm happy to see you too."

"Did you have a good trip to and from Nashville?" She stepped back to look up at him.

"I did. Mr. Hampton's family appreciated learning about his death in person. I spent last night and this morning in Murfreesboro with Mr. Glynne. So, I'll be home the remainder of the week."

"Wonderful." She clasped her hands in front of her like a delighted child.

Luke glanced past his cousin to Mother. Her solemn expression signaled she must still be upset with him. "I'll put my things away and be down to tell you more."

"We'll be waiting to hear what you have to say." Mother went back to her needlework.

"Where's Father? I'd like to talk to him too."

"He rode to the field to talk to the overseer. He said he wouldn't go too far and should be back soon."

Luke nodded then headed toward the stairs. If he took his time putting everything away, his father might return in time for him to talk to his parents together. He preferred that to having two stressful conversations in one day. Father riding to the field meant one of two things—he was either making a stubborn attempt to prove Luke should have been here to do that, or an unintended testimony to how his health had improved since Luke had left college. Luke welcomed the latter possibility but suspected the first was closer to the truth.

Not long after Luke emptied his saddle bag, he heard his father greet Angelique and Mother in the parlor. He'd put his pistol in the nightstand drawer before going downstairs. This time, he'd be careful of Eugenia's letter lying at the bottom of the drawer. Perhaps her troubling suggestion about Clarisse would turn out to be wise counsel instead. Luke now had the courage to venture out and see what might happen between him and Clarisse.

He closed the drawer. Facing his parents now took courage he'd never known he'd need. As their only surviving son, they'd often indulged his whims. Until they realized he was serious about becoming an attorney. He closed the door to his room, praying as he walked toward the stairs.

"Good to see you home." Father greeted Luke from his chair near the couch the moment Luke stepped into the parlor.

"I'm glad to be back." Luke seated himself in the chair on the other side of the coffee table where he could see both parents.

"Your mother says you had news for us?"

"Yes, sir. Grace, James, and Nathan should arrive at their father's house this evening. Grace wants to hold Mr.

Hampton's funeral at two tomorrow. We should send servants around to the neighbors this afternoon to tell everyone." He'd mention something they'd be interested to hear first.

"Good idea." Father shifted. "Nelson says the harvest is going well."

"Then your confidence in him when you hired him isn't misplaced." Luke worked to keep his voice and expression pleasant despite his subtle reminder to Father about being so pleased with the new overseer in February that he hadn't talked to anyone else.

"We shall see."

"You returned so quickly from talking to the overseer. Do I need to ride out to the farther fields after lunch?" Since his father hadn't taken umbrage at Luke's indirect reminder about who hired Nelson, perhaps this conversation could remain civil.

"Why do you ask a question you know the answer to? Of course, you should be riding the farther fields as well as the one close to home that I'm barely capable of seeing to."

"I'll stitch in the flower garden and allow you to have your family discussion alone." Angelique gathered up her thread and embroidery hoop, ready to stand and make her escape.

Mother placed her hand on Angelique's arm. "Please stay, dear. This concerns you, since you're family now too."

Shaking her head, Angelique turned her questioning eyes to Luke.

"Stay if you'd like." Luke would appreciate an ally but understood if she'd rather not involve herself in the dispute that didn't pertain to her. Perhaps Mother assumed Angelique would side with Father and her instead of Luke since she so adored her aunt and uncle.

"I'll ask a question I don't know the answer to, Father." Luke paused to see what, if any, reaction he'd get.

Father nodded.

"Since you're barely capable of the ride you took, why did you do it? Do you not trust the overseer you chose? Or—"

"We chose."

"No, sir. *You* chose. I wanted to speak to one more man to be absolutely sure Nelson would be the best for the job. Your mind is sharp. I know you remember our discussion." He'd never backed his father down in front of anyone before. Perhaps he'd been wrong not to talk to him in private.

Father sucked in his breath. "I trust Nelson."

"Then why did you put yourself at risk to ride to the field? Was it to make me feel guilty for not being here to do it?"

His father's jaw dropped. He clamped it shut. Luke suspected he'd voiced Father's real reason for riding to talk to the overseer. "You should be more loyal to your family than a friend."

"I agree. Which is why I've seen to you and this land first since I came home from college. I didn't leave you as a man in poor health, floundering for himself these past three days. We have a trustworthy overseer. I keep the ledgers up to date. I write our factor to keep him abreast of the crop and our finances."

The clock on the fireplace mantle chimed twelve times. His parents didn't move. Amos should have already come to announce lunch would be ready soon, but probably hadn't after hearing the strident discussion taking place.

He'd best take advantage of the time he had while he could. "Now that our plantation is doing so well, I see nothing wrong with doing the job that is the desire of my heart for a few days per week. Plus, helping a dear family friend in his time of need."

"Quibbling with someone over mere words or arguing some trivial point in court is not the same as carrying on our family's legacy. This land, our livelihood, feeds us and our servants while helping clothe the nation."

Luke sighed. Father had finally explained why he didn't want Luke to be an attorney. He probably considered the profession beneath Luke. "Practicing law is an honorable and necessary profession. I'm sorry you disagree."

Amos stepped into the room, into the silent void. "We got lunch ready to serve."

"We should eat." Mother rose.

Father stood and took Mother's arm. He escorted her from the room without saying a word.

Luke waited for Angelique. She took her time getting to her feet. Perhaps because of the shock of her uncle's sharp words? "I'm sorry you witnessed all this." He whispered as she stared toward her aunt and uncle's backs.

"I'm not. I'll defend you as soon as possible. I can't imagine what I'd do without *Monsieur* Chirac's help with the chaos my father left. You're now doing the same thing for the Hampton family." She kept her voice low.

"Exactly. We do a lot more than bicker over fine points of law."

She grinned as he extended his arm to escort her to the dining room.

After a meal almost devoid of conversation, Luke placed his napkin by his plate. "I'll write a note to send with the servants about the Hampton funeral tomorrow. Then, I'll deliver the news to the Matthews family in person.

Mother's eyebrows quirked. Angelique's eyes glittered. Let them all see through his façade of a reason for going to the Matthews' house. He'd postponed for too long seeing the woman who now occupied so many of his thoughts. Sitting near her, soaking in her calming presence, would be a comforting balm he desperately needed.

Judging from their conversation at his birthday celebration, he had good reason to think he was the only man she was considering loving again. His heart wouldn't allow him to wait longer to explore that possibility. People who loved each other bared their souls to one another. How he hoped she was home this afternoon and wanted to see him as badly as he wanted to see her.

* * *

A SHADOW CROSSED over the book of sonnets Clarisse was reading. She glanced up from her spot on the iron bench in the gazebo.

"Mr. Luke be here to see you. Does you want me to send him out here or tell him to stay in the parlor and wait for you?" Rose grinned as she waited for Clarisse's instructions.

"Tell him we can visit here. I'd rather enjoy the breeze and cooler weather today."

"Yes, miss." Ruth left to do Clarisse's bidding.

Clarisse closed her book. She hadn't expected to see Luke until Sunday. That he'd come this afternoon meant what? Her heart sped up when he stopped in front of her.

"May I sit with you?" He settled himself on the other end of the bench without waiting for her reply.

She turned toward him. "Titus said you were riding to Nashville and back. I assumed you'd be too tired to call on me today."

"I stayed in Murfreesboro last night and rested well. I've been home since about eleven o'clock." His warm smile faded as he shifted to look into her eyes. "Talking with my parents was disappointing. You listen so well to Angelique. I came to see someone who would listen to me too." His listless tone of voice signaled more anguish than his simple words conveyed.

"I'd be happy to do that. What happened with your parents?"

"My father finally told me why he doesn't want me to practice law. He thinks running our plantation is a nobler calling than being an attorney. Mother agrees with him." His shoulders slumped.

Her heart ached for him. How awful to be so misunderstood by his own family. She doubted her family would be any better to her if they realized the ideas she'd never expressed. "When Papa died so suddenly, he didn't have a will. I don't know what we would have done without Mr. Glynne's help when my unscrupulous uncle tried to lay claim to part of Hopeton."

"I didn't know that." He straightened his shoulders.

"Mr. Glynne advised us not to tell anyone. But since you work with him, I should be able to talk about it with you. Especially since I know how trustworthy you are."

"I appreciate your confidence and trust."

Seeing his troubled blue eyes shine again warmed her heart. "Mr. Glynne told us what to do to prevent any sort of public scandal from erupting. As Mama says, we'll always owe him a debt of gratitude."

"Thank you for sharing with me. But I can't use your family's private business as an example to convince my parents that attorneys are as necessary as growing cotton to clothe people." He huffed out his breath. "Unless ..." A slow smile spread across his face. "I could cite general details without revealing enough for anyone to know whom I'm referring to. An attorney never divulges what happens between him and his clients."

"That's an excellent way to show your parents how wrong they are about you."

He laughed. "It is. You've helped me immensely."

She shook her head. "I haven't done anything."

"You have. You believe what I want to do with my life is right. You believe in me, don't you?"

"I see nothing wrong with aspiring to do something more than run a plantation."

"Thank you." He reached for her hands and pressed them to his lips.

Every one of her fingers tingled. He closed his eyes as if savoring the moment.

He lowered her hands, releasing them onto her lap. "I didn't intend to be so forward."

"I have no problems with your intentions." He had no idea how pleased she was that he'd rather be an attorney than a planter. They'd talked so much about Angelique these past few months and too little about themselves for her to be sure he'd welcome her views on slavery. But she'd wait to tell him why until she learned more about him.

"That's good since I, too, am considering loving someone again." His adoring gaze appeared to say he was doing more than considering love, and she was the one in his thoughts. "Which means we should discuss more than my cousin when we're together."

"Yes, we should. Tell me why you want to be an attorney so badly you're willing to risk your parents' ire." Something she had yet to find the courage to do.

He sobered. "The year before I left for college, a woman whose family has since moved away wrongly accused a friend of indecency with her." He sucked in a ragged breath. "Mr. Glynne quietly cleared his name. Not long after that, the woman's father sold his business and left Murfreesboro."

"How can your parents still think attorneys don't help people after such an awful incident?"

"Because I can't tell them. Mr. Glynne, my friend, and his

parents would be the only ones who know if my friend hadn't confided in me. You are the only person I've ever told."

"Why did you tell me?"

"You've proved your loyalty as a friend to Angelique and to me." He inched closer until their knees touched. "Plus, people thinking about becoming more than friends should share their hearts and secrets with each other."

"I won't divulge your secrets to anyone else. I know so little of happenings in Murfreesboro that I don't know the family you're talking about."

"I assumed that. I've wanted to help people the way Mr. Glynne does since the day he salvaged my friend's reputation."

"A very honorable choice. I'm sorry your parents don't agree."

"I'm praying the more I work with Mr. Glynne, they'll see I can practice law and help Father with Oakridge some too."

His words sent Clarisse's burgeoning hopes skittering to the ground like a china cup dropped on a wooden floor. Helping run his family's plantation even part of the time meant he might not see the wrong of owning the slaves needed to work the land.

"Before I forget. I told my family I'd come here to deliver a message from Grace Stockton. She wanted me to tell the neighbors they'll conduct Mr. Hampton's funeral at two o'clock tomorrow."

His abrupt change of subject jarred her. But perhaps turning her thoughts to other things was good. She must know how committed he was to taking care of Oakridge for his parents before promising her heart to him.

"Thank you for telling me. We'll be there."

"I'll be working with Mr. Glynne after the service. He wants me to help the family sell the land or hire someone to manage it, whichever they decide."

"An excellent way for you to assist longtime family friends."

He nodded. "And into the future with Mr. Glynne, I hope. When he no longer wants to practice law, I'd like to take his place in Murfreesboro."

"You would move to town one day?"

"Yes." He stared off ahead of him. "I recently purchased land in Murfreesboro."

"You did?" He had to be more interested in practicing law than planting cotton.

He licked his lips as he turned to look at her again. "I bought the land on the edge of town that Paul Stuart left behind."

"Oh." She stared at him while trying to collect her thoughts. Until now, she hadn't thought of what Paul had sacrificed for love by walking away from his business and everything he owned in Murfreesboro.

"You are the only person who knows other than Mr. Glynne and the sheriff who sold the property. Have I upset you?"

"No. No, you haven't." She struggled to put her jumbled feelings into words. The ones she could share for now. "Someone would have bought his land eventually. I-I'd rather you have it. I think Paul and Eugenia would agree with me."

"Please keep this confidential for now. I'm praying for the day my parents accept my choice of vocation, and I can tell them about it."

"I wouldn't think of telling anyone. I won't write Eugenia about it until you say it's all right."

"Thank you. Father rode to the field today when he shouldn't, so I'd best go home and be sure he's resting the way he should. I'd rather spend more time with you."

"I'd like you to stay longer, but I understand. I'm glad you came regardless of how long you can stay."

"Then I'll bid you a reluctant goodbye." He lifted her hands to his lips once more.

The wish for him to kiss her lips flooded through her. But as long as they were both only considering love, his way was best for now. He rose, tipped his hat to her and walked away. She stared at his back until the hedge at the edge of the garden blocked him from view.

Only a man in love would bare his soul to a woman the way he'd done. Sharing her secrets with him was only fair. He had no idea how much she'd done to help Eugenia elope. Would that bother him? If so, she wouldn't risk also telling him she'd like to see slavery end one day.

Chapter Twenty-Three

Luke stood near Mr. Hampton's graveside with his parents and Angelique. Clouds roiling in the distance threatened rain later this afternoon. A fitting end for his tumultuous morning. No matter that Luke had ridden a large part of their fields with the overseer not long after breakfast, Father wasn't happy Luke would be helping Mr. Glynne after the funeral.

He glanced toward Clarisse as she gripped Titus's arm. Both of them might be wishing they'd never come, had never tried to do the right thing today by honoring a neighbor and one-time friend. Grace and her brothers blamed Eugenia for their father's untimely death and had voiced their opinion to more than one neighbor who had come to offer their sympathy.

Especially to the Parker family standing on the other side of the open grave from Luke's family. Alton looked their way for a moment. Luke glared at him. Angelique ignored him. The man ducked his head. Luke exchanged glances with his father. They would keep a careful watch on this particular neighbor, who had so far heeded Luke's warning to stay away from Angelique.

He returned his attention to Clarisse. She smiled when she noticed him regarding her. He'd find a way to speak to her before Mr. Glynne assembled the Hampton family for the reading of the will.

James Hampton stepped away from the assembled group of his and his siblings' spouses. "We'd like to thank all of you for coming today and helping us say our farewells to our beloved father." He went on to give a brief history of Mr. Hampton's life and praised him for his hard work to make the plantation so successful. He mentioned Eugenia being the only child born in the mansion Mr. Hampton built, but never said another syllable about her.

After James finished, Nathan extolled Mr. Hampton for being such a great father and example to him and his siblings —without one word about Eugenia. Grace talked about what a fine husband, father and grandfather Mr. Hampton had been without bringing up her sister's name.

A different sort of service with no scripture reading, no prayer, no mention of God. He hoped Mr. Hampton had made peace with God before his death but had no way to know. Luke glanced Clarisse's way whenever he could while the Hampton children talked. She looked terrible in her black dress and bonnet. Enduring the too-long speeches of three people pretending her best friend didn't exist had to torment her tender heart. Her downcast expression signaled his supposition was correct.

After Grace finished droning on about her father, the family members took turns throwing dirt on Mr. Hampton's coffin. Neighbors once again offered their sincere sympathy to them before leaving the family graveyard. After walking out of the fenced area, people stood in small groups, conversing with each other in subdued tones.

Luke took the opportunity to slip away from his family and find Clarisse. She stood alone. Titus had found a couple of men to talk to. Her mother was still visiting with Grace and her brothers. "How are you?"

Her wan smile combined with her sad eyes answered for her. "I've had more pleasant afternoons."

"I'm sure you have." How he longed to drape his arm over her shoulder and comfort her with more than words.

She sighed. "Grace and her boys will be staying a few days to sort through things in the house for her and her brothers. They each want certain mementos from their childhood or other items special to them."

"Of course."

"Mama and I came to see the family yesterday. My mother volunteered her and me to help Grace. I don't know if I can do that." Her eyes welled with tears.

"Oh, Clare. I'm so sorry.

She blinked her tears away. "Why did you call me that?"

"Why? I'm not sure. It slipped out." He paused to think why, at this moment, he'd used the name he'd never spoken before, why it seemed so right. "I've heard Eugenia and Titus call you that as a special nickname only they use. Might I be included in the group who considers you special?"

"You may." She placed her hand on his arm. "Could I ask you to do a favor for me?"

"Anything." He shouldn't have given her such a brash answer when he had no idea what she wanted, but his heart spoke before his mind could think of a more reasonable reply.

"Grace will have to go through Eugenia's things regardless of what they do with the property. Grace says Mr. Hampton insisted on leaving Eugenia's room the way it was the night she ran away. She and her brothers barely speak to me. Since you're their attorney, would you ask if I could have Eugenia's saddle?" Her voice cracked. She grabbed her handkerchief to wipe away fresh tears. "I have so many pleasant memories riding with Eugenia. Please."

"I will do my absolute best to try to fulfill your wish." Or anything else she wanted if he could make her happy again.

She sniffed. "Thank you." Her radiant smile warmed him from head to toe.

"You're welcome. I'll tell you later what they decide, so you don't have to deal with them or perhaps with Grace while you help her."

"I'd appreciate that. The less I have to say to any of them, the better."

They talked until her family went to their carriage. After all the neighbors left, Mr. Glynne motioned him to his side.

"James wants some time here with only family. You and I will wait for them to come to Mr. Hampton's office when they're ready."

"Yes, sir."

Luke soon followed Mr. Glynne into the house. With all the grandchildren playing in various rooms, the usually quiet house reverberated with voices. Since Eugenia was so much younger than her siblings he'd never experienced the place filled with children whenever he'd come here.

Mr. Glynne smiled as they walked into the library. "This house needs the echoes of youngsters' laughter."

"I agree." Luke settled into an upholstered chair not far from the one Mr. Glynne chose behind the desk.

James, Nathan, and Grace came into the office almost an hour later, driven inside by the rain Luke had wondered about before the funeral began. Luke and Mr. Glynne rose. The siblings seated themselves in the chairs around the desk. With no chairs left, Luke intended to station himself behind the Hamptons. But Mr. Glynne motioned him to stand at his side.

The will was short and to the point, leaving all of Mr. Hampton's possessions to James, Nathan, and Grace. After reading Mr. Hampton's instructions, Mr. Glynne studied the three people in front of him. "You don't have to rush to decide what to do with this property. Since my health makes it difficult to serve you as I'd like, Luke will be assisting you with whatever you choose to do."

"He did well, coming to see me so promptly. We'll have no problem working with a longtime family friend." Grace smiled at Luke.

Her brothers nodded their agreement.

"We're still unsure what we'd like to do." Nathan's gaze included Mr. Glynne and Luke. "James, David, and I need to leave tomorrow to return to our businesses. We'll talk more together tonight."

James leaned toward Luke, standing almost in front of him. "Luke, could you come early tomorrow morning before we leave? We should be able to give you our decision by then. You can advise us how to proceed either way."

"Yes, sir. I'll be happy to do that. Would nine o'clock be all right?" To be so accepted by these men perhaps ten years older filled him with pride.

"That would be good." James raised his eyebrows at the others. No one objected.

Mr. Glynne answered a few more questions. Luke followed him from the room. His mentor grinned as they took their hats from the hall tree. Luke opened the door for Mr. Glynne. "Thank you, sir. They all trust me due to your confidence in me."

Leaning on his cane, Mr. Glynne reached to pat Luke's shoulder with his free hand. "My boy, they trust you because of *you.* Because of the way you've conducted yourself since the day you learned of Gerald's death."

Luke rode home, relishing the approval from his new clients. Dodging puddles from the quick downpour a while ago didn't dampen his happiness. The more other people respected his legal guidance, the more his parents had to one day see he was pursuing an honorable profession. If only waiting on the Lord to answer in His time wasn't so difficult.

* * *

When Luke walked toward the barn the next morning, Angelique went with him. "I'm praying for you and with you. Also, for Uncle Douglas and Aunt Evelyn to see how good of an attorney you are. I'm so proud Mr. Glynne has entrusted you to take care of everything for the Hampton family."

"Thank you. Working for them is a trying pleasure. Despite what Eugenia did to me, she doesn't deserve the scorn they're heaping on her."

"Not from what Clarisse has told me about her." She placed her hand on his arm before he mounted his horse. "Should I pray you don't have to bite your tongue in two to keep from telling them what you think of their bitterness?"

"Perhaps you should." He could use her prayers for another reason he couldn't mention.

The more he'd pondered Clarisse's request for Eugenia's saddle, the more he wondered how it would be received. Asking the family to do even a slight favor for Eugenia's best friend might cause problems between him and them.

He prayed for guidance as he rode to the Hampton plantation. He'd taken several small but good strides toward his dream this week. With God's help, he'd continue one step

242

at a time, no matter how small the steps might be. He raised the knocker on the front door as he'd done so many times.

"Mornin', Mr. Luke. Miss Grace say show you to the parlor as soon as you get here." Joseph took Luke's hat as he stepped inside.

Strange to be waiting for the three older siblings instead of Eugenia. But he dared not voice his thoughts to them. How sad to be so vindictive. He'd be walking the same path if he hadn't released his anger to God.

"Good morning," Grace greeted him as she preceded her brothers into the room.

Luke stood. "Good morning."

Grace and Nathan seated themselves on the couch Eugenia had occupied when he'd called on her. James took the chair closest to his brother.

"We want to sell everything. Hiring a good manager and seeing he takes proper care of the house and land is more than any of us wants to deal with."

"All right. I can place a sale notice in *The Courier* whenever you'd like."

They discussed how much the house and land plus the servants were worth and decided on the price they'd like and one they'd settle for if necessary.

"We'd like for all the servants to remain together here. They've been so faithful to Papa that we don't want any of them sold off away from each other." Grace clasped and unclasped her hands in her lap.

"I can make that stipulation in the newspaper notice, plus put it in the deed of sale." The somewhat unusual request pleased him. The South's peculiar institution had unpleasantries he'd disliked for years. One reason he wanted to live in town and perhaps one day not own a plantation.

"Thank you. We appreciate everything you're doing and your willingness to do as we ask." Grace relaxed her posture.

"You're welcome." Luke shifted in his chair. "I've been asked by Clarisse Matthews for a favor from all of you."

Three sets of eyes hardened at the mention of Clarisse's name as they each sat up straight to stare at him.

"Her request is very simple. Please hear me out." His pulse quickened. He'd waited until all their business had been decided in case speaking for Clarisse irritated them enough that they didn't want him working for them any longer. But he couldn't not keep his promise to Clare. She meant more to him than these people's approval.

James nodded.

"She asked if she could have Eugenia's saddle."

"We've been discussing what to do with our sister's personal effects. Grace can tell you later what we decide." Nathan's icy tone sent shivers through Luke.

"I'll wait to hear what you'd like to do. Please don't mention whatever you decide to Clarisse. I'll be happy to be the go between for you and spare you speaking to her." Not to mention sparing Clare from having to speak with people who so disdained her for befriending Eugenia.

CLARISSE SET the last of Mrs. Hampton's china on the kitchen table. Helping a servant wrap dishes, crystal, and silverware to pack into a trunk suited her much better than helping Grace sort through her mother's belongings upstairs. To Clarisse's relief, Mama had taken that task. Clarisse had endured more than enough disparaging remarks about Eugenia at the funeral last week. Spending this entire Monday afternoon listening to the same would have been unbearable.

Pansy, Mrs. Hampton's longtime maid, sighed as she wrapped a platter in a dishcloth. "Ain't never gonna be the same around here."

"No, it won't." Hadn't been since Eugenia left this past February. But Clarisse and every servant in the house dared not say such words aloud.

"I's so happy to see you again, Miss Clarisse."

"Thank you."

They said little as they worked to secure the dishes in the trunk for Grace to take with her. Pansy would have done well without Clarisse's help, but Grace insisted a servant should be supervised while handling family heirlooms.

The back door burst open. Two little boys ran into the room. They paused when they saw Pansy and Clarisse sitting at the table.

"We must be having lots of company." The younger boy eyed the table laden with dishes and drinking glasses.

"No. We're packing all this for your mother to take home." Clarisse smiled at him. "You're Bradley, correct?"

"Yes, ma'am. How do you know who I am?"

"Your mother talks about you and your brother Gerald a lot." Amazing how her almost fib flowed with such ease from her mouth. But mentioning their Aunt Eugenia had been the one to tell Clarisse so much about them would probably cause problems she didn't want to deal with.

The boys' nurse stepped inside. "Don't you be botherin' a thing in here. You play upstairs or outside."

"Let's go back outside." The older boy took Bradley's hand and pulled him out the door.

Their nurse followed.

Clarisse smiled to herself. When she wrote to Eugenia to tell her of her father's death she'd tell her how well her favorite nephews were doing. Plus, mentioned the boys had a baby brother now six months old. The only good news she could impart since Grace had not hesitated to mention their father had burned the letter Eugenia recently sent him without reading a word of it.

Mama and Grace walked into the dining room at about four o'clock. Grace smiled as she scanned the almost bare table. "You've accomplished a lot."

"We have." Clarisse rose. "The vases in the parlor you wanted fit in here too."

"Thank you so much for all you've done."

A few minutes later, Clarisse and Mama climbed into their enclosed carriage to go home. Grace planned to leave for Nashville on Thursday and didn't think she'd need more help. A welcome announcement. Clarisse could enjoy calling on Angelique on Thursday as they had agreed to after church yesterday.

If she'd known Grace wouldn't require help on Tuesday, she'd have planned a ride instead. Luke still insisted on accompanying them, and she could have seen him before he left for Murfreesboro Wednesday afternoon. Sweet Luke, who had taken it upon himself to protect her as much as possible from the Hampton siblings' ire. She doubted she could have mustered enough courage today to ask Grace for Eugenia's saddle.

* * *

Tuesday afternoon, Clarisse walked in the shady front yard. Soaking in the birds' songs and the fresh air always refreshed her. Mama and Jenette sat in the parlor discussing what else Jenette needed for the child she expected in November. Titus was riding the field with the overseer, talking about the cotton harvest. She'd enjoy some time alone after being with so many people the day before.

A familiar dark red coach rolled down the drive. Must be the Williams family. No one else had a carriage that color. But Angelique usually rode over here. As did Luke. She shaded her eyes with her hand as the carriage continued toward the circular drive in front of the house..

Luke waved to her from the window as the coach halted almost in front of her. He opened the door before the driver could jump down from the seat. "How nice to find you outside." His beaming smile lit up his face.

"I do like to walk in the yard." Her inane comment was all she could manage as she wondered why he hadn't ridden to see her instead.

"I have something for you." He walked to the back of the coach as the driver started unbuckling the straps securing the luggage compartment.

Clarisse gasped when he lifted a saddle from the box. "Is it ..." Unable to finish her sentence, she stared at him as he nodded.

He set the saddle on the ground in front of her. "It was Eugenia's."

"Thank you. Thank you." She wrapped her arms around his neck and gave him a peck on the cheek. "Oh, dear." Stepping back, she gazed up at him. "I've never been so forward with a man in my life."

"I won't tell anyone. *And* I won't complain." He bent to pick up the saddle. "Shall I carry this to the barn for you?"

"Would you set it on the porch? I'd like to enjoy looking at it a while first."

"Whatever you wish."

She followed him up the steps. He placed the saddle near the wooden chairs. "Can you stay? I'll send for refreshments to enjoy here on the porch. Mama and Jenette are using the parlor now." She'd never prattled so in her life. But his welcome surprise still had her thoughts as scattered as a jar of spilled buttons.

"Enjoying your company is my treat. I don't need refreshments."

"I can't thank you enough." She took the chair closest to the saddle. Her saddle.

He seated himself in the chair beside her. "I'm glad I can make you so happy."

"I'll always cherish this precious memento of my dear friend." She bent to run her hands over the leather.

"I'm glad her family gave it to you." He shifted to look straight at her when she sat up. "Grace sent a servant with a note to our house Monday evening saying I could pick up the saddle this morning. She told me she appreciated your help."

"I'm amazed she complimented me at all."

"So am I. But I doubt you'll ever have to worry about being invited to her house if you're in Nashville." He grinned.

"I won't. She wouldn't have allowed me in the door Monday if she had any inkling of everything I did to help Eugenia and Paul."

Did his raised eyebrows signal his curiosity or shock? He'd once been as angry with her for being Eugenia's friend as the Hampton siblings were. If he loved her, what she'd done for Eugenia in the past shouldn't matter to him now. If it did, she needed to know.

"I relayed messages from one to the other. I prayed for them and encouraged their love. And ..." She sucked in a deep breath as she gazed into his eyes. "She and Paul were married in our barn the night they ran away. Titus, Jenette, and I were their joyful witnesses."

He clamped his open mouth shut as he stared at her.

She waited for some kind of response. "Do you wish you hadn't done such a tremendous favor for me now?"

"No. I shouldn't be surprised at such a revelation since you were, and are her best friend." His smile returned. "I don't mind Eugenia anymore, thanks to my tempestuous, aggravating cousin."

"Really?" He'd now shocked her.

He leaned closer to her chair. "Does Angelique ever remind you of Eugenia?"

"Often."

"Exactly. She's as headstrong and impulsive as Eugenia. As tempestuous and more. But as much as I love Angelique, I couldn't think of marrying a woman like her." He reached into his waistcoat pocket and drew out a creased, crumpled letter. "Eugenia said it better than I can."

"What do you mean?"

He thrust the paper toward her. "This is the note you delivered for Eugenia. The one I was once so sure you'd read."

"You didn't burn it?" Her hand shook as she took the note from him.

"No. I kept it to remind me not to ever entrust my heart to a woman again."

"You want me to read this?" She turned it over in her hand.

He nodded. "You should. Pay close attention to the last paragraph."

She unfolded the letter she'd delivered in April. So much had happened in the past six months. She gasped when she read Eugenia's suggestion that she and Luke might be well-suited for each other. "No wonder you were so angry with me that day."

"I'm not now and haven't been for a while now. So, should we continue to see if Eugenia's suggestion is true?"

"Yes. We should." Clarisse resisted the urge to jump to her

feet and hug him again. One such demonstration was enough. More than enough until she was completely sure of his love.

They talked and laughed together until Luke decided he should leave for home. He rose and helped her to her feet.

"I must swear you to secrecy about Eugenia and Paul's wedding. My mother would be appalled."

"I won't tell a soul." He raised his right hand.

"Would you like me to carry your saddle to the barn before I go?" He paused by the porch steps.

"I'll have a servant do that later." She walked with him to his carriage.

"Could I call on you next Tuesday?"

"I'd like that. Very much."

"As would I." He tipped his hat before stepping up into the coach.

He waved at her. She waved back and watched the carriage roll down the long driveway until it was out of sight. *Until Tuesday*. Her heart whispered the words to her mind.

The day she must find the courage to tell Luke the other secret she harbored.

Chapter Twenty-Four

The next Tuesday afternoon, Clarisse tried in vain to read in the parlor while waiting for Luke to come. She rose and peered out the window for the second or third time, glad Mama was out making a call, and Jenette rested upstairs. No one needed to see or guess her anxiety over this visit. When Luke finally arrived, she'd talk with him in the flower garden rather than risk Jenette hearing them or Titus returning from Murfreesboro with the mail while they talked.

The door knocker thudded. She forced herself to remain in her chair and allow the butler to answer the door. Before Luke handed his hat to Moses, she stepped into the hall. "Good afternoon. Could we walk in the flower garden?"

"Wherever you wish."

As they neared the gazebo, she stooped to smell a red rose. She wanted to postpone what she needed to tell him as long as possible. "Since we could have frost in a few weeks, I like to enjoy the flowers while I can."

"A good idea. We could soon have days too cool to sit comfortably out here." He seated himself next to her on the bench in the gazebo.

"Thank you again for helping me to get Eugenia's saddle. I intend to use it soon." She had more important things to discuss than a saddle. She'd rehearsed so many ways to broach the subject of slavery with him but still wasn't sure what she'd say.

"You're welcome. I suspect it's not a cherished keepsake to my clients. Their father wrote them how Eugenia deceived him by secretly meeting Paul in the woods."

"Another one of her confidences I didn't divulge."

"Your trustworthiness is why I've told you so many things lately. I still haven't told my parents about the land I bought."

A responsible person didn't keep secrets from the man who might and probably did love her. "I'll keep praying they see attorneys are as honorable as planters."

"I'd appreciate that." His eyes clouded. "Yesterday Father accused me of turning my back on our family legacy handed down from his father to him."

"I'm sorry someone you love misunderstands you so badly."

He nodded. "I'm not giving up. Mr. Glynne says Nathan Hampton boasted about how much I've helped them in front of my father while I was talking to you after Mr. Hampton's funeral. Father didn't dispute Nathan."

"That's wonderful."

"It's a glimmer of hope. I wrote a letter to an architect asking about house plans." His eyes shone. "I'll let you know what the man says when he replies."

"Do you plan on having servants in town?" Changing the subject in such an abrupt manner wasn't the best way to bring up what she needed to say, but she'd delayed telling him too long already. If he didn't agree with her ideas, they had no future to consider. Allowing him to think otherwise was not fair to him.

"Servants? He stared at her as if she'd inquired about owning chickens on the moon. "I hadn't planned that far ahead yet."

She ducked her head, clasping and unclasping her hands in her lap. "Well, uh, what would you think of someone who doesn't want servants?"

"Why are you asking such a thing?"

"Because ..." She forced herself to look at him. "Because I think servants should be free and paid, not owned like cows."

His breath *whooshed* out as if she'd pounded him in the chest. "You're serious?"

"Of course, I am."

"You realize our entire way of life, yours included, depends on maintaining the system we have, no matter how flawed it may be."

She nodded. "I want some sort of gradual, peaceful resolution to slavery that wouldn't dismantle every planter's life."

"Why haven't you mentioned this before?" His gentle tone gave her some hope he'd listen to her explanation, especially when he called their present way flawed.

"From what you've told me, I suspected you might sell Oakridge, if you could. So, I assumed you aren't attached to a plantation lifestyle and all that involves. That you might not want to deal with servants in town."

"You're hoping I might agree with you?"

"Do you?"

He stared at her as if he'd never seen her before. She forced herself not to look away. He got to his feet with the slow deliberate motion of a man three times his age, as if every movement pained him. His sad expression tore at her heart. "No. Choosing a different profession than my father doesn't mean I want to completely rip to pieces his or any other planter's way of life."

Tears stung her eyes as she gazed up at him. His stance and clenched jaw signaled he wouldn't listen to any further explanation she tried to offer.

"I'm sorry, but we have nothing more between us to consider." His voice cracked. He turned to walk away. "Goodbye, Clarisse."

Staring at his back, Clarisse allowed the tears to cascade down her cheeks. How could she have been so foolish? Daring to think she could find love again. She should have told Luke her thoughts long ago. Every bit of her heartache was her fault. Fisting her handkerchief, she pressed it against her lips, stifling the choking sob welling up from deep within.

* * *

Luke took one last look at Hopeton before he rode down the drive toward the main trail. Should he turn back? Talk to Clarisse. No. They had nothing to discuss. Her drastic ideas would not only cause problems between them but possibly serious trouble with him and most of his clients.

The dull ache in his chest made breathing hard. He hoped not to have to manage Oakridge one day, but he couldn't wish total financial devastation on his father and so many other friends or acquaintances.

He loved Clarisse. She acted as if she loved him. But not enough to give up a belief she realized could cause an irreparable chasm between them. Not could—*had*. He couldn't live with a woman who'd turn her back on his and her family's way of life, their entire livelihood.

She'd led him to think they had a future together when

they didn't. How could he trust a woman who hid her true thoughts from him and everyone else and did it so well?

He should not have broken the vow he'd made to never risk loving a woman again. Neither Clarisse nor any other lady would ever mislead him for a third time.

Twigs snapped behind him. Twisting in his saddle, he turned to see what had made the noise, but the bend he'd just traversed blocked his view. A rabbit scurried across the trail. Perhaps a fox had just lost his intended meal.

With his plans for a pleasant afternoon ruined, he didn't rush home. His family knew he'd gone to call on Clarisse. He'd have to think what to tell them to explain why they wouldn't be seeing each other again. Something other than the truth. Nothing that would sully her reputation or hint at what she'd told him. If the wrong people found out about her unpopular beliefs, she might be in danger. He loved the woman he had no future with too much to cause her harm.

The barn came into sight sooner than he wished. After leaving his horse with the groom, he walked in through the back door. His parents' muffled voices came from upstairs. He'd slip into his room and not have to talk to anyone until supper. Mother and Father's door was still closed. Angelique's was open. Since he hadn't seen her in the parlor, she must be outside. Enjoying flowers while she could like Clare?

He groaned as he slumped into the chair by his window. Not Clare. She'd never be his. How to stop thinking about the woman who had dominated his thoughts lately? Closing his eyes, he tried to pray. What to say when his pain was too raw to think clearly? God understood his heart with or without words. If only he could stay in his room and not have to talk to anyone but God for a while.

But he couldn't. He trudged into the dining room after the others were seated. "You must have stayed a while at

Hopeton." Angelique grinned as he took his place across the table from her.

"I'll tell you about it later."

Father bowed his head to bless the food. Luke did likewise.

"How did your visit with Clarisse go?" Mother passed him the platter of chicken.

Later had come. "Not as expected. We have a major difference of opinion on some things. I won't be calling on her again."

"What?" Angelique almost dropped the piece of bread she was buttering.

"A gentleman doesn't talk about a lady behind her back. I'll keep our problems between us."

"I'm so sorry. Lovers do quarrel at times." Mother cut up a piece of chicken.

To keep from having to reply, Luke picked up his water goblet.

"I'll pray you can settle your differences." Angelique's solemn expression matched her serious tone.

Luke shook his head. "We're beyond reconciliation. I'll say no more."

The conversation was subdued for the remainder of the meal. He appreciated no one pressed him for more details than he cared to give. Thinking about not calling on Clarisse again was too painful to talk about if he'd wanted.

With the late harvest progressing well, he intended to ride the fields with the overseer most of the day tomorrow. He'd look over the ledgers and make notes on the yield while Father rested in the afternoon. then ride to Murfreesboro after supper. He'd arrive too late at Mr. Glynne's house to allow much time for conversation.

* * *

ON THURSDAY MORNING, Luke waited in his borrowed room for the Glynnes to enter the dining room for breakfast. His plan for avoiding people as much as possible on Wednesday had worked well.

"I'm glad you came in last night." After saying grace, Mr. Glynne passed the biscuits to Luke.

"I hope I can do that every week now that harvest is almost done."

Mr. Glynne nodded. "Good. I had one man inquire about the Hampton plantation. We'll discuss that and a few other things after we get to our office later."

"Yes, sir." He liked hearing the words *our office*.

"How is your family?" Mrs. Glynne put a fork full of eggs in her mouth while waiting for his answer.

"They're all doing well. Father hasn't had any problems for a while now."

"And your cousin? I still find it hard to believe all the things you told us about young Parker." Mrs. Glynne shook her head as she buttered a biscuit.

"Angelique is laughing again and acting more like herself. Parker has left her alone as Father and I ordered him to do. Since he has, I've kept my word not to tell anyone else what kind of man he is. Except for the two of you, since you should know."

The talk soon turned to more mundane topics about the cotton harvest and happenings Luke had missed in Murfreesboro. His hosts supplied most of the conversation. Neither mentioned his problems with his parents.

A few minutes before nine, Luke walked with Mr. Glynne to his office near the town square. "I'm not imagining your step is more firm." Luke unlocked the door and allowed his mentor to precede him inside.

"Some days are better than others. I can't predict the good

or the bad ones. I told the prospective buyer you were taking care of the sale for me and to come by today if he's interested."

"I'll be happy to meet with him."

Mr. Glynne took his chair behind the desk. Luke seated himself in his usual one across from his friend. "We need to talk about the buyer before he gets here." Instead of reaching for paperwork on his desk as usual, he stared straight into Luke's eyes.

"All right." Something about Mr. Glynne's serious tone and expression set Luke on edge.

"You may not want to assist me with this client. Walter Parker is giving serious consideration to expanding his holdings in the area. He doesn't always come alone."

Alton Parker's father. Luke gripped the armrest of his too-hard wooden chair. "I can be civil to them if they'll do the same with me."

"Walter complimented my choice of assistants when I mentioned you. I suspect his son has not told him or anyone else the real reason he's no longer seeing your cousin."

"I don't doubt that. Alton holds his reputation in high regard. I'll help you as usual unless one of them objects. I don't want to cost you a good client."

"Exactly. Walter's coins pay my bills as well as anyone else's does." Mr. Glynne reached for the top piece of paper on the pile on his desk. "We'll need to file a judgment on land near Stones River to satisfy a debt. Perhaps we can deal with that before our client or clients arrive."

Luke forced himself to concentrate on the work in front of him instead of what might be coming. Maybe Alton didn't want to be in the same room with Luke any more than Luke wanted to be with him and would stay home.

Just before eleven, both Parker men strode into the office. Mr. Glynne rose to greet them. Luke did likewise.

"Good to see you, Walter. I assume you'd like to buy Gerald's plantation." Mr. Glynne shook hands with his client then the son.

"Yes. I'd—we would be foolish to turn down the opportunity to buy such a profitable, well-run property. Despite the unfortunate circumstances."

Luke shook hands with Mr. Parker. When Luke extended his hand to Alton, the man stiffened and merely glared.

Mr. Glynne motioned to two chairs in front of his desk as if the silent standoff between Luke and Alton hadn't happened. "Please, be seated. Last time we talked, you were amenable to the family's price."

"We are. The price is very fair."

Luke took what was becoming his usual spot, standing beside Mr. Glynne's chair. As the conversation progressed, he handed the necessary papers to Mr. Parker and his son to read and sign.

"Luke will take the contract to the Hampton children soon to get their signatures. I'd rather not mail them."

"When?" Walter looked to Luke for an answer.

"I have family obligations, too, so I'll leave for Nashville early next Thursday. I should be back here by Saturday, if that's all right with you." He and Father had decided Angelique and Clarisse should be safe now riding without Luke. But the way Alton scowled at him every time he took a paper from Luke's hand had changed his mind. The ladies he so dearly loved might be safe on the ride they'd planned today only because Alton was in Murfreesboro.

"No need to rush. We'll be fine with that."

The two men left not long after signing the contract, Alton acting as a silent witness the entire time. Knowing what the man was capable of, Luke would be content to never see him again for business purposes or otherwise.

Chapter Twenty-Five

By Thursday morning, Clarisse was ready to count the minutes until she could don her riding habit and meet Angelique in the woods in the afternoon. No one in her family had been happy to hear she and Luke had parted ways. Everyone pressed her for reasons why. She'd received enough advice about how to resolve a lover's spat to last her two lifetimes, if not more.

She dressed and left early enough to sit in her saddle, waiting for Angelique to come into sight on the trail. If Angelique hadn't told her for sure on Sunday that Luke would be in Murfreesboro today and not riding with them, she'd have insisted on calling on Angelique instead of riding with her.

If only she could stop her traitorous heart from wishing Luke was with his cousin. She'd prayed long and hard, trying to decide if Garland was right to have changed his mind about slavery. Once she decided how abhorrent slavery was, she couldn't deny her convictions. Especially after Garland had told her how some people mistreated and abused their slaves.

What she'd do if the day came she had to tell her family what she'd decided, she had no idea. She now had two friends living in Illinois, but hoped the time never came she would have to ask Eugenia and Paul if they would take her in. Angelique rounded the bend and waved, interrupting Clarisse's dire musings. She returned her friend's salute.

"I'm so happy to visit with you alone." Angelique's expression sobered. "I'm sorry. I should have chosen my words more carefully."

Clarisse forced a pretend smile. "I'm glad we can talk alone too."

"Would you like to ride to the meadow? We haven't done that in a while." Angelique's grin returned.

"I'd like that." Clarisse took the lead down the trail.

When they reached the meadow, Angelique halted and let her reins go slack in her hand. "This has become one of my favorite places. No matter how spectacular everyone says fall is here, I'll miss the dancing flowers waving in the grass."

"You should paint or write poetry." Clarisse paused next to her friend.

Angelique laughed. "I tried both while attending a young ladies' academy. I have no talent for either one."

"Nor do I." Clarisse continued gazing across the field. The tranquil beauty of God's creation soothed her. So much better to listen to singing birds than her family's incessant questions and recommendations.

"Are you all right? I hope you feel better than you look or sound. I don't mind listening if you'd like to talk to someone." Angelique glanced at her.

"I'm fine." Or she would be someday. She hoped.

"But you don't want to talk."

Clarisse shook her head.

"Some hurts cut too deep to talk about. Shall we ride along the creek?" Angelique tightened her hold on her reins.

"Thank you. I'm sorry you've been through so much

yourself, but I appreciate you understanding." Clarisse urged her horse toward the tree-lined creek.

* * *

LUKE SAT in the library the next Tuesday afternoon, watching for Angelique to go upstairs and change into her riding clothes. He slipped out to the barn to wait for her. If she'd known ahead of time he planned to ride with her, she'd have gone to see Clarisse in the carriage instead. The groom saddled Angelique's horse, then Luke's. Angelique walked up to them as Luke put his pistol in his pommel holster.

"What are you doing here?" She pointed to the pommel of his saddle. "And why do you have a weapon?"

"For the same reason I carried my pistol and rode with you before." He told her of his meeting with Parker and his father in Murfreesboro, minus the reason they were there. He'd wait until later to tell Father he'd be making another trip to Nashville on Thursday. "Father, Mother, and I all think I should accompany you and Clarisse again."

Her chin jutted out. "I don't."

"All right. You can stay home. I'll ride to meet Clarisse and tell her of your decision and escort her back to Hopeton."

"No. I'm not trying to be difficult, but you're too dear to me to risk losing you in a duel." Her voice quivered.

He appreciated her concern but couldn't allow her to win this argument. Her safety might depend on him carrying the pistol she so detested. "I doubt I'd have to draw my gun. Just the sight of it would probably deter him." How true his blustering words were, he didn't know. Convincing Angelique he'd ride with her was all that mattered.

"Then your presence and an empty holster should be enough. Stuff it with some hay to make it look like the gun is in it." Squaring her shoulders, she stared him down. "Leave the pistol, or I'll stay here and force you to ride alone with Clarisse." She smiled. "Which I think would be wonderful enough, I may let you see her home anyway."

He dreaded seeing Clarisse, even with Angelique. Enduring time alone with her would be like ripping open the still-raw wound in his heart. "Against my better judement, I'll leave my gun here and pray I don't need it."

"I'll pray for the same thing." She allowed the groom to help her up in her saddle only after Luke did as she demanded. "You told him to leave me alone over a month ago, and he's done nothing threatening. Why should today be any different?"

They rode away from the barn in silence. Despite Parker's lack of threats, Luke prayed he wasn't making the worst mistake of his life by giving Angelique her way. The man's menacing scowls still unnerved him several days later. They reached the end of the long drive. He should turn back, get his gun, and insist his cousin stay home. But thoughts of the last time he'd seen Clarisse alone overruled what little common sense he possessed at the moment.

Angelique sighed as they turned onto the trail to meet Clarisse. "I'm praying you and Clarisse can settle whatever differences you have. You're both miserable without each other."

He opened his mouth to deny her words but clamped it shut instead. Misery was an apt description of his present situation. Seeing the woman he loved and knowing her intractable ideas would always stand between them pained him beyond words. Not being with her since last Tuesday had been the worst week of his life.

Angelique waved when she spotted Clarisse riding toward them. Clarisse didn't wave back. Angelique urged her horse alongside Clarisse, leaving Luke to trail behind them. "I know you weren't expecting Luke. Please don't turn back toward home. He says he has good reason to accompany us today."

The familiar dull ache settled into his chest with Clarisse nearby. He should have kept his vow to never allow a woman to hurt him again. Staring at the ladies' backs, he sucked in more than one ragged breath, then told Clarisse why he was riding with them and how Angelique insisted he leave his pistol at home.

She stared at Angelique. "Considering the circumstances, I'll accept an escort. But understand you're the only one I'll speak with."

"I'm praying you'll one day change your mind, but I won't waste an opportunity to see my best friend. Shall we make our ride as pleasant as possible?"

"We should." Clarisse's stiff-sounding words contrasted with Angelique's effort to sound cheerful.

The trail narrowed. Angelique ducked a low-hanging branch. "I'm glad for cooler weather today."

Clarisse followed Angelique until they could ride side by side again. "So am I. As I keep saying, wait until you see our fall leaves. The colors are spectacular."

Unbidden recollections of a similar conversation he'd been a part of while riding with Eugenia and Alicia and Alton Parker forced their way into his mind. More memories he'd shoved into the dark recesses of his mind.

"Stop where you are." Parker's cold words broke through his reverie. "Luke, throw down your weapon. My pistol is pointed at your back."

The trio halted as the villain ordered. Luke's heart pounded in his chest as he prayed for safety and deliverance, sure his companions were doing the same. How foolish to assume a man like Parker would be deterred from thinking Luke was armed Why had he let Angelique convince him to leave his pistol behind?

Parker rode up next to Luke, weapon in hand.

"I'm unarmed." Luke raised his hands and slowly turned his horse to meet Parker's gaze. "Since I'm the one you so despise, let the ladies go."

An evil grin lit up Parker's face. "I do despise you. Enough to wish you the worst you can imagine and more." He aimed his pistol at Clarisse's back. "Miss Matthews stays with me. Go home and return with your pistol. I will not be denied a duel with you any longer. Angelique, go with your cousin."

Staring into Parker's hard eyes, Luke's fingers itched to try and knock the gun from the man's hand. But the fiend would shoot Clarisse at the slightest movement from Luke. "Why wait for a duel? Let the ladies go. You can easily shoot me and ride away before either of them could bring help."

Parker shook his head. "Do as I say, or Miss Matthews' blood will be my ultimate revenge for your wrongs to me."

"Alton, no!" Angelique twisted enough to see his face.

"Angelique, yes. If you value your best friend's life, do as I say before what little patience I have wears out." Parker placed his finger on the trigger.

"What guarantee do I have that your patience won't vanish in the time it would take me to retrieve my gun?" Luke stared, unflinching into the man's devilish, gleaming eyes.

"Shooting you in a duel will be the sweet revenge I so richly deserve from the two people most responsible for turning Eugenia against me. Can you think of anything worse than you dying and your Clarisse being forced to watch your demise?"

Luke didn't dare give Parker any satisfaction by admitting such a thing. The man would soon co-own the land he'd hoped to receive by marrying Eugenia. Why he still craved revenge made no sense. But pointing out facts to a man who'd lost all sense of reason would do no good.

"Do as he says, Luke. The sooner you return, the sooner you can dispatch this madman." Clarisse's calm tone had to belie the terror in her heart.

"All right. Angelique, come with me." He turned his horse toward home. Tears spilling onto her cheeks, Angelique followed.

He rode until well out of Parker's sight, then motioned for his cousin to rein her horse in. "We'll circle around and ride to Hopeton for help. Titus can loan me a pistol, but I'm leaving you there. No arguing." His whispered words barely carried to Angelique's ears.

She nodded.

* * *

Clarisse continued praying for strength and protection as Mr. Parker urged his horse alongside hers. She must not panic and give this glaring monster the gratification of knowing how he terrified her.

"Off your horse. Now. I won't have you trying to gallop away." He aimed the gun at her heart.

Just as Eugenia said he'd done to Paul. Shivers coursed through her. He kept the weapon pointed at her as she dismounted. Her heart pounded so hard, she marveled he couldn't hear it.

He yelled an obscenity as he slapped Merry on the rump and sent her running down the trail. A foolish move on his part. But his thirst for revenge now blinded his sense of reasoning. Her riderless mare returning home would cause an uproar. Titus, his hounds, and more than one servant would soon be scouring the trail to find her.

"Now, we wait." He rubbed his other hand over the barrel of his pistol as if he were caressing a loved one.

Clarisse stared back at him, schooling her features to look as expressionless as possible. No answer would be best.

"I had no idea you're such an unfeeling creature. What does Luke or Angelique see in you?" He leaned against a tree, the gun still aimed at her.

"You'd have to ask them."

His maniacal laugh echoed through the woods. "After today, no one will be asking your beloved Luke anything."

Her heart thudded harder. She struggled to breathe while fighting to maintain her composure. *Lord, please protect Luke.* Watching another man she loved die would be more than she could bear. But she dare not let Parker know how her knees were trembling beneath her skirt.

How long the crazed man taunted her, Clarisse couldn't guess. Every chirping bird or chattering squirrel magnified the silence between her and her captor as she strained to hear hoofbeats coming from the direction of Oakridge.

When Luke rode in much faster than he should on the wooded trail, Mr. Parker jerked Clarisse in front of him. Luke reined in his horse and jumped to the ground.

"Let her go. No real gentleman uses a lady as a shield unless he's afraid of the man challenging him to a duel." Luke's dark scowl would be enough to terrify any sensible person.

Mr. Parker shoved Clarisse to the ground, sending her careening into a tree. As he leveled his gun at Luke, a shot from Luke's weapon reverberated through the woods. Clutching his hand to his chest, the fiend cried out and crumpled to the ground.

Tossing the pistol into the dirt, Luke ran to Clarisse's side. He knelt, cradling her in his arms. "Are you all right?"

"I am now." The tears she'd held inside flooded down her

face as she pressed her head against his chest, relishing the safety of his embrace.

"My precious Clare. I'm so sorry you had to witness this." He laid his head on hers and pressed his lips against her hair.

"Thank God you're both safe." Titus, flintlock in hand, stood over them. Where he'd come from, Clarisse didn't know. "You shot him just before I did."

Luke nodded.

"I'll check on Parker." Titus walked the few feet to where the man lay. He knelt over the still body. "He's no longer with us."

Looking her up and down, Luke gently wiped her tears from her cheek with his thumb. "Did he hurt you?"

"No, the tree did more damage. But I'm fine now." She pressed closer against him, savoring his nearness, his gentle voice. Cherishing *him*.

"Yes, you are." His eyes shone as he gazed at her. "We'll talk later."

"I'd like that."

"Sorry to interrupt. We need to get this man to Murfreesboro and let Sheriff Crockett know what happened. He or his deputy can ride out to the Parker plantation and tell them about their loved one's demise."

"You're right." Luke unwrapped his arms from around Clarisse before getting to his feet. He helped her up.

"Will the sheriff want to hear from the ladies about what they saw?" Titus glanced at Luke while Clarisse dusted leaves and twigs from her riding habit.

"Perhaps not if they write out statements for us to take to him."

Titus looked his sister up and down, concern on his face. "We'll try that. Clarisse especially has been through enough. Help me take care of the body so we can get my sister home."

Together, Luke and Titus hoisted Mr. Parker's lifeless form over his saddle. Luke turned to Clarisse. "Where's your horse?"

"He spooked her. I'm sure she's home by now."

"You can ride double with me if you'd like." His hopeful expression warmed her soul. He still wanted her. Perhaps they could settle their differences as Angelique had been telling her.

"Or with me if you're worried about propriety and appearance." Despite his serious expression, the mischievous gleam in Titus's eyes signaled he wasn't worried about the concerns he'd voiced.

"I'll ride with Luke. Mama will be so glad to see I'm not hurt, she'll forget to be aghast at how I get home."

"That she will." Titus picked her up and set her in Luke's saddle. She tucked her skirt around her dangling limbs as Luke swung up behind her.

Clarisse reveled in the comfort of Luke's strong arms around her as they rode to Hopeton. Titus led Mr. Parker's horse behind his. The men didn't speak. Clarisse didn't interrupt the silence.

Mama, Jenette, and Angelique rushed onto the porch before Luke halted his horse by the steps. He dismounted, then spanned Clarisse's waist with his hands to lift her down. He released her the moment she touched the ground.

Tears running down her face, Mama trotted down the stairs to smother Clarisse in a hug. "Oh, my darling girl." Jenette and Angelique soon enveloped her in hugs too.

"Angelique, I'll escort you home then come back here to help Titus take Mr. Parker's remains to the sheriff."

Angelique's face lost all color. "I feared it would end that way." A tear trickled down her cheek. She squeezed her eyes shut as if to prevent more tears from escaping.

Mama kept one arm around Clarisse's shoulders. "Tell us what happened."

"Yes, please do. Where is Titus?" Jenette scanned the area.

"He went to the barn. He'll probably be in soon to wait for Luke's return. I'd rather tell you about our ordeal after Titus is with us." Clarisse's voice cracked.

"Of course, you poor dear. Let's sit in the parlor until he comes in." Mama cupped Clarisse's elbow in her hand, ready to propel her toward the porch.

Luke stepped up to Clarisse's side. "May I have a word with you first?"

She nodded then turned to her mother. "I'll be in soon."

Mama and Jenette exchanged smiles as they walked toward the porch.

"I know my way to the barn to get my horse." Angelique winked at them before walking away.

Luke took Clarisse's gloved hands in his. "As I said, we'll talk later. Are you up to seeing me tomorrow since I'll need to go back to Murfreesboro on Thursday?"

"Tomorrow will be fine." More than fine, perhaps.

He smiled. "Tomorrow."

Chapter Twenty-Six

Sitting at the table, Clarisse pushed the eggs on her plate from one side to the other with her fork. "I'll try to eat later." She placed her napkin beside her water goblet.

"Can I do anything to help you, dear?" Mama's eyes misted as Clarisse got to her feet.

"No. I may walk in the flower garden for a while. Perhaps get my Bible and sit in the gazebo. I'm not sure." Her listless tone likely did nothing to ease her mother's concern. But her numbed soul and aching body made making decisions difficult.

Titus stood. "We're all praying for you. Let your maid bring your Bible to you since going up and down stairs can't feel good right now."

Clarisse shook her head. "I didn't leave my Bible where she'd know where to look for it." Her sore ribs and shoulder would protest the trip up to her room, but Rose, who was carrying her unborn child, was busy straightening Clarisse's room and shouldn't be making extra trips up and down stairs.

After taking her time retrieving her Bible, making her way

to the bench in the gazebo took considerable effort. She set her Bible beside her while catching her breath. She wouldn't be going on a long walk anywhere until her sore left side healed. Leaning against the back of the iron bench, she closed her eyes and inhaled the fragrance of the roses nearby. For now, she'd sit and enjoy her favorite flowers without stooping to smell them better. She soaked in the soothing quiet around her, interrupted only by the sweet song of a mockingbird.

Despite her efforts, images of yesterday afternoon intruded into her mind. She squeezed her eyes shut, banishing the sound of a gunshot and the sight of Mr. Parker falling to the ground to concentrate on leaning her head against Luke's chest as he held her close. He'd kissed her hair beneath her dislodged hat. Called her his precious Clare.

Her eyes flew open. She jerked up straight. Yes, her memory served her right. He'd called her his. She hadn't noticed it then. But the recollection now was so vivid she could hear his gentle voice, feel his arms enfolding her.

Did he want her despite her beliefs about slavery? Convictions she wouldn't give up. If she were as precious as he'd said, perhaps he was willing to love her despite their differences. Only God knew if such a life were possible. She'd pray a while before opening her Bible.

"May I interrupt?" Jenette paused at the edge of the gazebo. "Mama and Titus insisted someone should come see about you. I volunteered."

Clarisse patted the spot next to her on the bench. "I appreciate everyone's concern. I'm doing some better." She wouldn't voice her thoughts about Luke to anyone since she wanted to talk to him first.

Jenette accepted her invitation. "You don't look as if you slept any better than the rest of us."

"I didn't. I wish things could have ended differently."

"We all do. But Luke did what he had to do under the circumstances." She patted Clarisse's not-sore right arm.

"Yes. He had no other choice. I thank God that Luke wasn't hurt or worse. When he all but galloped back to help me, I feared Mr. Parker would shoot him on sight. The man was mad with rage from the supposed wrongs Luke had done to him." She paused to stare at Jenette as the words she'd spoken sank into her still-befuddled mind. "Luke risked his life for me."

"He did. He loves you."

Jenette's words were an appreciated confirmation. A most welcome balm for her tattered emotions. If Luke loved her enough to die for her, surely he loved her enough to accept her and her unpopular beliefs, whether he ever came to agree with her or not.

But the way he walked away the day she shared her innermost thoughts still haunted her. "I hope and pray you're right."

"Titus agrees with me." Jenette got to her feet. "I'm going inside to rest. Titus and Mama are talking about naps after lunch, but I may not wait that long."

"I'll relax out here a while longer. Luke intends to call on me sometime after two o'clock."

"You'll see then how right Titus and I are about Luke." Jenette grinned before walking away.

After once wishing in vain that Luke would love her despite her views, Clarisse couldn't muster the necessary strength to hope like that again.

* * *

LUKE TOOK care to make as little noise as possible as he walked downstairs. He'd retrieve his hat from the hall tree and be on his way to Hopeton. He'd told everyone of his visit and asked them to pray. His parents were resting upstairs. He assumed Angelique's closed door signaled she was napping too. He hadn't slept any better than the remainder of his family, but rest wouldn't come until after he talked to Clare. The groom should have his horse saddled by now.

"There you are. I'd hoped to see you before you leave." Angelique stepped out of the parlor as Luke reached for his hat.

"I do have somewhere to be soon."

Her eyes sparkled. "And someone to see. I'll walk with you to the barn."

He'd rather she didn't but doubted he could think of a way to dissuade her today any better than he usually did once she made up her mind about something. He opened the door for her to precede him onto the porch.

"I'm praying more fervently than I've ever prayed for you and Clarisse. "

"I appreciate that." He assisted her down the steps.

"I still don't know what happened between the two of you. I'm certain my dearest friend would forgive you of anything. But don't you dare not forgive her if she did or said something wrong." She paused and pointed her finger at him. "If you rob me of claiming Clarisse as my dear cousin, I'll never forgive you. Aunt Evelyn and Uncle Douglas agree."

Her words had a teasing tone to them, but her solemn eyes testified to the seriousness of her threat. "I'll see what happens."

"And I'll pray. Godspeed to you." She patted his arm. "We'll talk when you come home. I'm expecting good news." She headed back toward the steps, leaving him to walk to the barn alone.

Angelique's words about forgiveness haunted him as he rode toward Hopeton. Clarisse had done nothing wrong. He had nothing to forgive her for. If so, why had he been so sure her strange ideas about slavery would be a wall between them he couldn't climb over or go around. Couldn't or wouldn't? She said she didn't want a violent end to slavery. He hadn't given her the opportunity to tell him the kind of solution she'd offer. But if Angelique was right, Clarisse would forgive him for anything. He prayed the rest of the way there that his cousin was right.

The Matthews' butler answered the door moments after he knocked.

Clarisse stepped from the parlor to greet him as he walked inside. "Could we talk in the flower garden since everyone else is upstairs resting?"

"I'd like that."

She reached for her bonnet with a pink ribbon.

"No red today?"

"The flowers embroidered all over the light pink don't go with red." Her smile signaled she wasn't aggravated by his teasing.

"You're beautiful in any color." He matched her slow steps as they walked outside. "Do you feel up to walking at all?" The bruise on her cheek made him wonder how many other bruises she must have from Parker's rough treatment.

"I plan to sit on the gazebo bench in the flower garden and not move from there."

"A good idea."

She paused by the rose bushes she'd stopped to smell the last time they'd talked here. "I'll have to wait to bend and enjoy them better."

"I'm so sorry you're in pain." He seated her on the bench in the gazebo before taking the spot next to her and turning to be able to look at her. Their knees touched. She didn't move away. "How are you?"

"I'll be better in time. The shock of it all is wearing away a little." She placed her hand on his arm. "Thank you for watching over me. You could have been killed."

"I was thinking only of you, not me." He placed his hand over hers. "I'd do the same thing again for you."

"You'd die for me?"

"Yes. Without hesitation." Without having to think of his reply. "Facing the possibility of losing you forever showed me what—who—is most important to me. I love you. Enough that I will find a way to love you if we never come to an agreement about owning slaves."

Her eyes misted. "You do?"

"I do." He stood and slipped his Barlow knife from his pocket. He squatted beside the rosebushes. Her favorite red rose bush sat between bushes with yellow and white blooms. He fingered a red rose. Knife on a stem, he gazed up at her. "May I?"

She nodded.

He cut several roses off the bush, enough for a nice bouquet. Before sitting beside her again, he stripped the thorns from each stem. He held out the roses to her. "Red roses for love."

"You love me?"

"I do." Enough he didn't mind repeating himself to reassure her. He rose then knelt in front of her. "Everything I hand you in life will not be free of thorns. But I love you. Do you love me? Would you marry me, thorns and all?"

"Yes, I love you. Yes, I'll marry you."

He jumped up to take his seat beside her. Taking her in his arms, he kissed her the way he'd only allowed himself to dream about.

She pulled away. "I need to breathe."

"I'm sure you do. Did I hold you too tightly considering how sore you must be?"

"No." Her radiant smile emphasized her denial.

He took her hands in his. "Perhaps I should have talked to your mother or brother before asking for your hand. But after yesterday, I'll toss propriety out the window and not wait to declare my love to you."

"I don't mind."

"I'm happy to hear that. I've contemplated little else since yesterday other than telling you of my love. So little else that I have no house to offer you. I have little of my inheritance left after purchasing the land. I'm not making enough money practicing law to hire the architect I wrote to, and—"

"Hush." She slipped one hand from his and placed a finger on his lips. "I have a dowry and can't think of anything I'd rather use the money for than a house for the two of us."

"So, when the architect replies, I can tell him we'd like to meet with him and discuss plans to build our house?" The words *we* and *our* flowed from his lips without a thought. The way it should be. *Would be* for the rest of their lives.

"Yes, you should."

He kissed her again, this time more mindful of his embrace and her bruises.

She pulled away enough to trace his cheek with her finger, smiling into his eyes. "We should tell my family. I'm sure they're rested by now. They've all been praying we could resolve our problems."

"My family too." He told her of Angelique's threat to never forgive him if Clarisse didn't become her cousin one day.

Her expression sobered. "I'm glad they all want me, especially your parents. But do they still dislike your wish to be an attorney?"

"Unlike waiting to build our house, we'll have to be patient with my parents. They are not as quarrelsome as they were. I'm willing to wait on the Lord for His solution and timing concerning Mother and Father." He captured her hands in his again. "But I couldn't wait to tell you how much I love you and ask if you'd accept me, thorns and all."

"I will and I do. For the rest of our lives."

Betty Woods has been a storyteller since childhood. She still has the notebooks of her handwritten tales, plus the first "book" she wrote in fourth grade. An incurable history buff, she was mistaken for the tour guide at an historical site while answering her grandchildren's questions. Touring museums or old houses to do research for her books is fun instead of work.

She and her husband walked through Dr. Maney's house in Murfreesboro, Tenn., and hiked some of the wooded trails her characters could have ridden along. She can tell you more interesting tidbits about our past than you might want to know.

She and her husband enjoy their grown children and spoiling grandchildren and great grands. They share their

Texas home with a spoiled Chihuahua. Spending time with family, especially going on multi-generational vacations is one of her favorite things to do.

When life hands you lemons, don't just settle for lemonade. Taste and see that the Lord is good! (Psalm 34:8).

Get your copy here:

https://scrivenings.link/treasureandtrouble

* * *

Love's Twisting Trail

Trails of the Heart—Book One

Stampedes, wild animals, and renegade Comanches make a cattle drive dangerous for any man. The risks multiply when Charlotte Grimes goes up the trail disguised as Charlie, a fourteen-year-old boy. She promised her dying father she'd save their ranch after her brother, Tobias, mismanages their money. To keep her vow, she rides the trail with the brother she can't trust.

David Shepherd needs one more successful drive to finish buying the ranch he's prayed for. He partners with Tobias to travel safely through Indian Territory. David detests the hateful way Tobias treats his younger brother, Charlie. He could easily love the boy like the brother he's always wanted. But what does he do when he discovers Charlie's secret? What kind of woman would do what she's done?

The trail takes an unexpected twist when Charlotte falls in love with David. She's afraid to tell him of her deception. Such a God-fearing, honest gentleman is bound to despise the kind of woman who dares to wear a man's trousers and venture on a cattle drive. Since her father left her half the ranch, she intends to continue working the land like any other man after she returns to Texas. David would never accept her as she is.

Choosing between keeping her promise to her father or being with the man she loves may put Charlotte's heart in more danger than any of the hazards on the trail can.

Get your copy here:

https://scrivenings.link/lovestwistingtrail

* * *

Redemption's Trail

Trails of the Heart—Book Two

Newly widowed with her second child due in a few months, Lily Johnson has nowhere to go until Toby Grimes, her late husband's boss, asks her to stay on as housekeeper at his ranch. Remaining in the house Mr. Grimes built for her and her husband is an answered prayer. But malicious gossips see her godsend job as a ruse for a sinful dalliance since her employer is a nice-looking, single man.

God and a lot of others turned their backs on Toby during the war, so he returns the favor by keeping to himself. Yet the need to care for and protect Lily overwhelms him. The way she tugs at his heart scares him more than going into a losing battle.

Unwilling to allow anyone to destroy a fine woman's reputation, he proposes a marriage of convenience. After much prayer, Lily accepts. Her first marriage was a love match made in heaven. The second leads down a trail only God knows. The peace she has concerning a marriage to a troubled man she doesn't love begins a walk of faith to a destination neither she, nor Toby, can guess.

Get your copy here:

https://scrivenings.link/redemptionstrail

* * *

Independence Trail

Trails of the Heart—Book Three

To escape an arranged marriage to benefit her father's business, Heidi Schultz runs to the ranch owned by her sister, Lily, and brother-in-law, Toby. No one will ever run or ruin her life again. She'll find a job in nearby San Antonio and fulfill her dream of living on her own. She'll never surrender her independence to anyone, especially not to a man. But when her father finds her, Heidi agrees to Toby's idea to postpone her plans for a new life and stay at the ranch a while longer just to be safe.

Jethro Bannister likes his life as foreman for Toby Grimes. Memories of the way his Georgia family turned on him don't plague him while living on a secluded Texas ranch. With God's help, he's made peace with his painful past. Until Heidi interrupts his carefully arranged, placid world of quiet. The too talkative woman could worry the horns off an entire herd of longhorns. Plus her family problems remind him too much of what he left behind.

Watching Lily and Toby love and depend on each other chisels away at the wall of independence Heidi has built to protect herself from being betrayed again. Despite their misgivings, Heidi and Jethro form a tenuous friendship based on their common wish to be left alone. They understand each other better than anyone else around them does. Confiding in one another deepens their friendship more than either intends. Will Heidi and Jethro's past wounds bond them together in an unexpected love or push them apart?

Get your copy here:

https://scrivenings.link/independencetrail

Stay up-to-date on your favorite books and authors with our free e-newsletters.

ScriveningsPress.com